D0232729

The Southie Pact

By Kevin Devlin

"...In the midst of darkness you can always create light."
(Elie Wiesel)

This book is dedicated to Patrick Devlin, my godson,
who died before his time.

Acknowledgements

I would like to take this opportunity to thank my wife, Mary, for her patience and input regarding this book. I would also like to thank Joseph Bianculli and Grace McMann for their contributions.

Most importantly, I would like to applaud my daughter, Deirdre, for her inspiration, devotion to writing, and the time, energy, and expertise she contributed unselfishly over time to help make this endeavor not a dream but reality.

KD

April 2017

ONE

I sat in the back seat of my dad's car but didn't say a word. Nobody did. It was a time for reflection, a time for tears. My parents shot glances back and forth to each other and I could see sadness etched across their faces. I could feel sorrow clawing at mine. I couldn't erase the image of Mr. O'Toole standing at the gravesite. He was lost, desperate to understand why he was burying his son, searching for answers which would never be revealed. It seemed he was thinking it would be easier to die than be left behind. His eyes portrayed his pain and his words *before your time* echoed repeatedly in my mind. Echoing and echoing in an unsettling manner that made me shiver with unhappiness and uncertainty. It seemed like my world, along with Mr. O'Toole's, was out of whack, seemingly crumbling without any hope of salvaging the future.

When we arrived in "Southie" as it is affectionately called, my mom, Catherine, stopped by our house to grab her purse, which she forgot to take to the funeral. When she went inside, my dad, Marc, turned around and looked at me momentarily before speaking. He knew I was hurting bigtime. I was hurting inside, outside, everywhere my thoughts took me.

"Are you okay Johnny Mac?"

He loved calling me Johnny Mac, or Mac which was short for MacCallum. I felt like I was getting too old for that nickname, but today I didn't mind. Today I welcomed the shelter it brought with it.

I looked at him and thought I was going to implode with grief. "I don't know dad. Don't know what to think or feel. My whole body hurts. My head feels like it's gonna explode."

He shot me a sympathetic glance. "Losing a friend is never easy. We all experience losses sooner or later. Sad to say but true. Every time I lost a friend it changed me. Life is never the same. It can't be-because of the loss-it just can't."

"Why did this have to happen?" I asked.

I wasn't sure if he'd have an answer for that. Who really does?

"Sometimes people do things they shouldn't do," he said, his voice trailing away.

I looked out the car window and saw two kids walk past the car laughing and bouncing their basketballs. Enjoying life as it should be enjoyed. I wanted to jump out of the car and go with them; escape this pain and pretend it never happened. Pretend Tools was still alive.

Tomorrow would come and everything would be back to the way it should be. I'd call Tools and tell him I had the weirdest dream. We'd have a good laugh.

"Sometimes the grief is so bad you think you won't ever recover," he said. "But, we grieve, we cry, we adapt, and then we move forward. That's how we manage to survive, to live and laugh again. We bury the pain and sadness deep within us, that's how we cope."

Death was something I wasn't familiar with. He understood that all this was new to me and I sensed that he was thinking back to his own youthful days when tragedy struck and how he reacted. How he dealt with it. Now his words swirled around inside me as I tried to make sense out of Tool's death.

He lit a cigarette and took a long haul. He smoked a bit too much as far as my mom was concerned yet that never deterred him from lighting up in her absence. I guess he was right in saying people do stupid things. Everything after all is relative. I put my head down. I felt like I'd never be happy ever again. My dad read my mind.

"Living in the past will rip you apart," he said. "You must realize the past cannot be altered. Never changes no matter how many times you toss it around inside of you hoping for another outcome."

That's how Southie was. Tough love. Had to grow up fast.

Tears scurried down my face. I didn't want to hold them back. I didn't understand at the time that tragedies weren't insurmountable and if they took over control it would destroy you.

Was that what life entailed? Was that what friends now gone would want? It was obvious I needed reassurance so he softened his approach.

"Remember the good times you had with Tools and he'll live in your heart forever. I know it's hard, but just take it easy and keep busy. You'll be okay in time. Time will be your friend."

Right...time...all I need is time? I looked at him hoping to appear at ease. More tears were knocking but I didn't answer. I looked out the car window again hoping for a diversion. I counted to ten.

"Johnny Mac."

I looked at my dad.

"Let me say this before your mom comes back out. Death is inescapable. But that's why life is so precious. Gotta take the good with the bad. Life is like a giant, drawn out jig-saw puzzle. All the parts eventually create the whole picture in the end."

My dad was a longshoreman, muscular and manly, but he

had his philosophical moments. It wouldn't be until later in life that I finally understood what he was trying to tell me. The dualistic essence of life is ever-present. We can't appreciate one without the other and the balance of opposites naturally keeps order in the universe. Good versus evil, truth versus deception, light versus darkness, love versus hate, life versus death, each inextricably complementing each other and forming the core of our earthly existence.

As my dad drove us to the hall, I couldn't stop thinking about the funeral Mass, which was worse than the wake. Older people warned me that it would be. They were right. It was the first one I went to which involved a close friend. The church was packed. The air, heavy.

Seventeen, eighteen, nineteen, twenty. I counted things. I counted anything to get my mind off of what was happening. Anything to stop me from crying. I was counting the groove marks in the pew in front of mine. They seemed to continue to infinity. Good. The music really got to me. The songs were simultaneously sad and beautiful so I shifted from counting to going through baseball stats in my head. More numbers to neutralize the moment. I was successful in distracting myself until the casket and family came down the aisle at the end of Mass. Then I lost it. I looked around at my friends – TK, Sully, Al, Pete, and Sal – we were all crying. It was the first time I saw any of them cry before. We didn't even try to hide it.

Then I envisioned Tools standing in front of the Francis L. Murphy Rink that time, the only time, I confronted him about his problem. I knew he was getting hooked by how haggard he looked. I told him we'd be dead for a long time and there was no reason to rush it. I told him with death there was only oblivion –

12

nothingness – devoid of any consciousness, essence, or being. He laughed and called me an atheist. He said he was going to tell my parents I was a sinner, and inform Father "Joe" I was a non-believer. He said he believed in the afterlife, one filled with plenty of things to do, beers to drink and so on, so he was all set one way or the other.

I reminded Tools about Jay McDonough. Jay liked showing off, trying to impress the girls and his friends, but was always a follower. If someone hooked school, he would hook school. If someone threw snowballs at bus windows he would throw snowballs at bus windows. If someone did drugs…he eventually joined them. One day, Jay was with Matt Callahan and Louie Cappola and they were hanging up behind the Perry Elementary School. Matt and Louie were two of the older guys, both about nineteen years old, who hung around with younger kids. They were two scrubs who partied all the time. Louie had a homeless guy buy a case of Bud Light in exchange for two dollars and five cigarettes. Jay had a few beers and then Louie gave him some Amphetamines, uppers. Jay had quite a buzz on, so as he was leaving Callahan gave him a few downers "to take the edge off" before going to bed. Jay never woke up. His older sister Janice found him dead in bed the next morning. He was only sixteen years old.

I begged Tools to think about Jay. I asked him how he thought his parents and sister felt when they buried him. He didn't answer. I asked what went through his mind when he heard about Jay's death and he responded that that wasn't going to happen to him. I told him there were no second chances when it came to life and death. I said he'd be destroying the lives of those who loved him. I asked him to imagine the pain and suffering his family would feel if he ever overdosed and died. He looked away, then looked me square in the eyes and said he would stop.

I wanted to believe him but he obviously wanted me off of his back so he told me what I wanted to hear. And I took the bait.

Was this simply part of growing up in a world filled with temptation? Did it have to be this way? Were drugs always going to haunt us? Destroy the willing? I didn't have the answers. I looked away from the casket, down to the floor, feeling guilty. I thought Tools was going through an ugly phase in his life that he'd outgrow. But he didn't. He never got the chance.

At the cemetery Father "Joe" Graham spoke briefly then recited the final prayers. Everyone loved Father Joe. Godliness was within him and it seemed to gush out of him as well. He was a people's priest and always a text away when you needed him.

I hugged and kissed Tool's mom. She held my hand and cried, "Why is my baby gone? Why?"

I didn't have an answer. "I'm so sorry," is all I could say. She held rosary beads to her heart and started praying to herself while looking at me. It was haunting.

When people began dropping roses on the casket, I saw Mr. O'Toole with a handkerchief, masking his overdue tears. It was the first time during the wake and funeral I saw him cry. I thought I could console him but looked at the casket and couldn't speak. He put his hand on my shoulder and said, "You don't want to end up with my boy *before your time*. Do you understand me?" I looked up and shook my head acknowledging what he had said.

The wind picked up, sending an unwelcomed chill

throughout my body. Father Joe crossed himself and said, "May he rest in peace," and then, they lowered the casket into the ground. I looked around. The solemnity of the moment was etched across everyone's face. Everyone was crying, some hiding behind the façade of their sunglasses.

Sadness encircled the gathering.

Heads were bent in agony.

Then a silence arose around us and birds could be heard chirping in the distance.

Suddenly I was awakened to the unsettling balance between life and finality. I felt sapped of my youth; and cheated. Once the door is opened, it can never be closed again. Innocence flees incapable of being recaptured.

I always felt like I would be a young boy forever. I thought time would stand still. I would remain firmly entrenched in my own, happy world with protective parents comforting me and keeping me out of harm's way, shielded from and unaware of the vicissitudes of life. I realized now change can't be averted and life transforms like the seasons. No matter how hard we fight it, human life is not exempt from earth's seemingly endless changing systems and cycles.

It's irrefutable.

Life is also about choices.

And some people don't make the right ones at the right times.

I was only fourteen years old and so was Tools.

And he was dead.

TWO

After the funeral collation, and without mentioning it to anyone else, I decided to walk up behind the Murphy Rink to the spot where my friend, Kevin "Tools" O'Toole, had died. It wasn't that far from the hall and I felt it was where I should be at the time. The dog days of August had arrived but an immense cloud cover suddenly transformed the blue sky into an eerie darkness uncommon for any summer afternoon. Like the uninviting sky, my thoughts were dark.

So this was it. It finally hit me. He was *really* gone and we'd never see him laugh or smile again. Never hear his sarcastic responses that made some laugh and others recoil. He did that to people. But it was over for him in this world. Now his story had been written and the book shelved for future generations to read and ponder what might have been. For Tools, it was all she wrote.

One by one members of the crew arrived. I guess they had the same idea. Salvatore "Sal" LaMattina, Michael "Sully" Sullivan, Pete Winkowski, Tommy "TK" Kane, and Al Sawyer walked up from different directions. We stood in silence for a while. Pete, a big, boxlike type of a guy, was the first to break the silence. "I still think it's a bad dream and I'm going to wake up and see him standing right in front of me."

Sal, now over six feet tall and lanky, nodded in agreement. "Yeah, I'm with you. Feel like I'm in a fog waiting for him to walk out of the mist. Still can't believe he's dead." Then he blessed himself and looked up to the sky as if God was going to spare us from grief and Tools was suddenly going to descend

16

from Heaven. He bowed his head respecting his faith yet knowing deep inside that such hope was only hope. Not real.

"Can't change shit now," said Al, our resident wannabe wise guy.

Sully, an awkward kid, who was our jokester on many occasions, but not this time, was nervously moving his fingers back and forth through his long hair. He said, "Once you start using it ain't good that's for sure." He sat down and with uncertainty looked to us for support.

"And I bet you I know who supplied him with the poison," TK said, now taking his turn at the invisible podium. His short, compact frame matched his explosive personality. "It was probably those fuckin' project rats. Drug-dealin' pieces of shit. Maybe Bobby Adams from Old Colony? Not the first one he's hooked on the shit."

"Who knows who gave it to him? Isn't hard to find drugs in Southie," Sal said. "Anywhere else for that matter."

"Guys, give it a rest will ya?" I didn't want to listen to that crap. All I could think about was Tools overdosing, over and over again, once, twice, one thousand times. Needing a moment alone to clear my head, I walked away from the guys and up the slight, grassy hill and opened the gate to the outdoor rink. Not knowing what else to do, I sat down in the middle of the rink. I began to feel as if Tools' spirit was hovering above me. He was, after all, found dead just a few yards away from me on the benches surrounding the outside rink. I'm not sure how long I sat there for – the minutes seemed to pass by like seconds. All I know is I suddenly turned around and saw a five-year old Tools skating next to me. We were back in "Arnie's Army." Arnie taught all the local kids how to skate, preparing us for Southie youth hockey. Naturally, Tools was the first to skate on his own without a milk crate to help him balance. He was looking back at me as I struggled on with my own milk crate until I inevitably fell. He jumped on me, laughing as we wrestled on the ice. Tools got up and skated down the ice. He was now fourteen. He swirled in front of the goalie and guided the puck into the upper left-hand corner of the net. It was his calling card. Then his ghost-like image faded and I found myself lying down alone in the middle of the rink. I just laid there for a while. Then I walked back down to where the guys were and sat down on a rock next to Sully but didn't say a word.

"Where the fuck were you?" Al asked. I just shrugged.

Suddenly, Pat O'Malley, Mark "Jaws" Jaworski, Pam Winkowski, Dianne "Dee" Modica and Kaleigh McDonough appeared out of the darkness.

Our whole gang was now present, except, of course, Tools.

But was he there?

Soon, we all started talking about our favorite memories of Tools. Like the time he jumped into Sully's pool with his clothes on, or that time he ate seven hot dogs on a bet and threw up all over Dee, or the time he dressed up as a sexy bunny on Halloween and all the guys were hitting on him, not realizing who it really was. What I liked best about him was he never backed down from anyone and always did what was right. More importantly, Tools had a mind of his own.

The thing about Southie is this; everyone may be tough, but very few have a mind of their own.

Tools didn't care what people thought. One evening he was walking on West Broadway when he saw two white teenagers, about his age, beating up a younger Hispanic kid. They kept

18

kicking him in the face and calling him a spic. Tools jumped in and hit one of the teenagers smack in the jaw and knocked him off his feet. Within seconds both cowards ran away. Tools helped the young kid up off of the ground, and walked with him to his apartment in the housing project.

In most cases, the projects were off-limits to us. We could play in the hoop league held at the outdoor courts on summer days and check things out but walking through at night wasn't a smart idea. We were from "The Point" and the projects were in "The Lower End" and the tensions were high between the two. We never challenged that unwritten rule, except for Tools. He wasn't afraid. Nothing fazed him.

Stories about Tools were popping up one after the other. We laughed about how he repeatedly told us he was going to strike it rich and own the biggest boat imaginable. We were going to live forever and be rich and famous. Every weekend during the summertime, he was going to take his friends and family on rides throughout Boston Harbor and the islands. It was going to be fun and we'd always be together. Funny thing, he never liked to swim, but he was going to be the captain of his ship and entertain everyone. That wasn't going to happen now unless he rose from his grave at Cedar Grove.

The realization made me sick. There were so many things Tools wanted to do, and now he never could. I listened as the guys told stories until we had no more to tell. And then we sat in silence. We didn't say a word for what felt like a long time.

Although not cold I shivered.

Pete looked in my direction. "Hey, you okay?"

I was far from okay but was able to say what I was thinking. "It's too late for Tools. But it's not too late for us. I say we make a pact never to get fucked up on drugs, and if we do, we'll help each other until our dyin' days. You guys with me?"

At first no one said anything. We all just exchanged glances.

"Yeah, let's do it," Sal said.

Pam said, "Yeah, I'm in."

One by one everyone affirmed their allegiance to the pact.

"C'mon," Al said. "Let's do this right."

We held hands and stood in a circle as we looked around at each other, forming a singular desire to safeguard our future. We pledged we wouldn't prematurely join the ranks of the dead if they did indeed exist. Sully joked. "What's next? We gonna exchange blood vials? Jesus Christ, I feel like this is the beginning of a horror movie."

"Shut up Sully!" TK yelled to him.

"No you--"

"Everybody shut up. We need to remember this," I said. "We're forming this Pact-our word...that we'll never let each other down."

"Yeah, never forget," Al added. "Our Pact forever."

We silently nodded in agreement.

We continued to reminisce.

We continued to laugh.

Tears intermittently found the surface of our faces but were dismissed without acknowledgement.

Several more times we reminded each other about our promise that we wouldn't die *before our time*.

Then there was silence. And suddenly only sadness.

It was time to leave.

THREE

When I arrived home I sat down on the front stairs. The light was on in the living room but I found myself not wanting to go inside. I noticed my neighbor's cat scamper by and disappear into the darkness. Her name was Misty because of her light gray coat. I always hated that cat, but tonight I felt an odd sense of affection for her. I glanced across the boulevard to the bay. *I live in the best place in the world* I thought. M Street Beach was literally across the street. I headed over and sat on a lone bench. The wind was picking up and the sand swirling about. The moon seemed to be peaking at me from behind the clouds trying to read my mind. I wouldn't let it.

M Street Beach was always my favorite place for reflection. Always felt like home. Something about looking at water puts my mind at ease. When the water at M Street is wavy, it's a soothing, incessant stream of motion rippling across the bay from one end to the other. When the winds are absent, it is calm and looks like one huge mirror, appearing as if you could walk upon it without sinking from sight.

On the right end of the beach is a wooden enclosure sealing off the Curley Community Center, historically known as the L Street Bathhouse. Looking to the left, you can see the beach end and a string of yacht clubs begin, where small moored sailboats and motorboats bob back and forth not too far from the shoreline. Countless planes destined for Logan Airport soar past, oblivious to those watching underneath. They appear so close one would think you could reach up and pluck them out of the sky. One night I counted one hundred. They appeared seemingly

21

out of nowhere and vanished just as fast.

When the sun rests and the moon says hello, the reflected lights from buildings across the bay appear in the water as columns of light stretching from their base to the shoreline. The bright white beams of light emanate from the white exterior face of the JFK Library into the water. The red lights from the UMass building and the blue lights from the Marina Bay condos also dance in the mirror of the bay, reminding me of the American flag. Every time I get upset, I look toward it and remind myself I live in the greatest country in the world and there is still hope.

As I sat on the bench, my thoughts flashed back to one Saturday at the beach in early June. It was like watching a movie without the popcorn. It was unusually hot. We were totally psyched. Everyone was geared up for a carefree day at the beach.

"Hey guys," Dee yelled. "Let's play horseshoes."

"You should just lay there and work on your tans," Al shouted.

"You're sad ya know that," Pam said.

"Let them play the next game," Pete interjected. "You afraid they might win?"

"No way," Al said. "Girls can't beat guys in sports."

"Yeah right," Sully said. "They're probably betta than us."

"I doubt it," TK added.

I stood there soaking in the sun and my friend's typical exchanges. Life was good. All was fine in the universe; it was summertime of course.

"I can beat you guys by myself," Kaleigh said. "Been playing with my uncle in his backyard since I was six."

"I say let them play," Sal said. "Kaleigh, Dee, and Pam against Al, TK, and Johnny."

"Sal and I will be the judges if there's any disputes," Pete interjected. Nobody messes with the girls he thought. He loved playing the hero-the big brother-with the girls, especially Pam.

"Yeah, and I'll keep an eye on them," Tools blurted out, after drinking his water. His honest approach to life, indeed a refreshing quality, would unfortunately abandon him sooner than we'd ever imagine. He would be dead within months.

"What about me?" Sully asked. Tools said, "We'll both watch the judges. Me on one end you on the other. No cheating."

"Okay," Dee said. "Now we'll see whose best."

We played and we lost. Al and TK were pissed. I laughed. Sal grinned. Pete smirked. "Looks like you guys are the losers," Tools roared. "Beginner's luck," Al said. "Let's play again." We played again. We lost again. I laughed again. "Horseshoe's is for losers anyway," Al yelled.

"Not even a real sport," TK said. "Told ya they might win," Sully mumbled, under his breath. The girls laughed and gave each other high fives. The sun was relentless and the baked sand was unkind to our feet. TK and Al were burning up inside; their egos deflated. They walked down to the welcoming ocean and dove in. They needed to cool off.

Pam walked towards me with a big smile on her face. "How come you're not mad at us?" she asked. "Why should I be? You won. We lost. You were better than us. What can I say?" She smiled again and I felt like an ice cream melting under the summer sun. She moved closer to me, put her hand on my shoulder and kissed me softly on the right cheek. "That's for being a good sport. I like that."

So did I…but didn't realize it at the time how it would affect my life.

23

My thoughts returned to the present and it started to rain. I continued to sit there. I couldn't stop thinking about Tools and the swift progression of his addiction. Tools drank his first beer in late May prior to his sophomore year. We were at Evans Field one night watching a Little League game when an older kid named Joey O'Brien, a senior, came over with some beers. I think they were buds. Tools wanted to find out what beer tasted like and had a few. And then soon we all started drinking on the weekends. It was fun. Got our first buzzes on. But Tools really liked to get hammered. He didn't know when to stop. Then, unbeknownst to us, he started drinking on the weeknights. Although nobody realized it at the time it was the beginning of the end for him. It didn't take him long to ratchet it up into hyper-drive, taking Percocet, OxyContin, then Klonopin, and who knows what else. His journey into the world of drugs seemingly happened overnight.

A few months later, Tools was found dead by a state maintenance worker behind the Murphy Rink, no more than one hundred yards away from Evans Field. The police notified his parents who later identified him at the Boston Medical Center's Coroner's Office.

The cause of death was determined as an opioid overdose.

He was three months shy of his fifteenth birthday.

FOUR

After Tools died walking became my salvation. I had a few designated routes, like a lot of people in Southie. Walking along the boulevard to the Sugar Bowl and around Castle Island was one. Castle Island is home to a large fort, not really a castle. It was built by the English in the 1600's and was renamed Fort Independence after the American Revolutionary War. Another route I'd take was up to Dorchester Heights, the exact location where the American rebels drove the British out of Boston. With all the problems Southie has, it's easy to forget all the history that's here too. I try to remember, keeps me distracted from the present. I decided to walk up M Street that night to M Street Park. The park consists of a playground, the Medal of Honor Park, thought to be the first Vietnam memorial in the nation, three baseball fields, and the Michael Pano basketball courts. I walked down the crumbling cement stairs and reached the courts. Sometimes there are old balls left behind and I'd take a few shots. Sometimes I'd even see some old friends hanging around.

Even though it was late September, it was still hot as hell. No one was around. Most people had already fled inside to the comfort of their air conditioners. As I looked around for a ball, I noticed out of the corner of my eye a solitary figure sitting on a bench. I jumped a little. A normal response I guess when you think you're alone and discover you're not. I thought it was a homeless person. I soon realized it was actually my friend Charles "Chico" DiManno. I knew him from Little League. I hadn't seen him since we were ten. He only played Little League for one season. He was an awful player but well-liked. He was funny and

25

always pulling pranks on us during practices. We loved it. The coaches, not so much.

"Hi Chico, long time no pranks."

He smiled faintly acknowledging my reference to his Little League exploits. But the closer I got to him, the more I realized he wasn't the Little Leaguer I once knew. He was whiter than hell and looked malnourished. His face was littered with pockmarks. His left eye was out of whack, drooping. I stopped three feet away from him.

"How ya doin?" I asked.

"I'm doin' great." He smiled small, attempting to hide the fact that he was missing several teeth. I heard that he was using. Now I witnessed his plight first hand. I sat down on the bench beside him and saw drug paraphernalia on his lap which he surprisingly didn't attempt to hide. I shifted back and forth. Last thing I wanted was to get busted with a junkie.

"Gonna get high huh?"

He laughed. "You should join the FBI." At first I didn't respond hoping to refrain from another inept statement. He scratched his arm several times in typical junkie-fashion. "Sorry, it was a stupid question."

"It's my way to numb the pain."

What pain? What happened that was so horrible he had to stick a needle in his arm to forget? I couldn't grasp it. "So that's why you get high…to get numb?" I asked. He scratched his irritated, red left cheek. It made my skin crawl. He noticed. "I know. I know I'm disgusting. I still kinda have my boyish good looks though." He laughed and then got quiet.

I hardly knew Chico yet I knew his story. Most junkie stories in Southie are about the same. He started by getting drunk with

26

his friends. Then he added some Percocet to his regimen, upping the ante. Next stop was OxyContin. The problem with Oxy is this; they can cost as much as eighty bucks on the street. It doesn't take a mathematician to realize that if you're taking them every single day you're going to run out of money pretty quickly. And you'll inevitably graduate to heroin, which is far cheaper and can fuck you up more. At least Tools didn't get to that point, then again, what does it matter? He was dead.

A sense of calm emanated across Chico's face. He started to laugh like it was all a cruel joke but then got serious again as he explained himself. "Once you start fuckin' around with a needle there's really nothin' else good enough to satisfy you. There isn't any substitute for *that* high. You just have to have it. You hate to love this shit but you fall in love with it."

I couldn't help but see Tools as I looked at Chico.

"Can I ask you something?"

"You just did." He laughed again. "Sure, go 'head, I got all night."

"Ever wonder if you might end up in jail for a long time or a nuthouse? Or overdose and die."

"That's like four questions dude. Are you tryin' to confuse me?" Even in his bad state, he still had his sense of humor. "But yeah, every time I shoot up."

He looked down again towards his shit with an eerie look of simultaneous love and hate, anticipation and dread. "I've been in detox twice. It works for a while, but when I get back out, I return to my old haunts and start using again."

The saying "Once a junkie always a junkie" popped up in my head. But was that really the fate of everyone in these sinking boats? I wanted to think otherwise, that there's always hope and a clear path to follow for those willing to make the trip. I remained silent. What could I say? I think he wanted me to leave. I could tell he was getting antsy and wanted to get high.

I wanted to tell him he was a smart guy. I wanted to tell him people can take control of their lives if they really desire to do so. That he knew what he needed to do. That he only needed the courage and strength to take that first big step in the right direction. But only he could change and he needed to reach out for help. It wasn't too late. If he didn't want to keep using, he could go to rehab again, start working out and get his life back in order. Go down the L and lift weights. He could get a natural high from working out or taking a dip in the cold ocean waters. I wanted to say all these things but all that came out was, "Take it easy, Chico."

He sat motionless. I didn't want to wear out my welcome so I shook his hand, said good luck and goodbye. His eyes suddenly opened wide as he saw an opportunity for another joke. He said, "Yeah, good luck? Problem is the only luck I have is bad luck. See ya later."

I walked away and then heard him say, "Hey. Got ten bucks? Need to eat." I knew he'd probably use the money for booze or drugs but for some reason I gave it to him. I couldn't say no. I felt bad for my Little League friend. Also, I wondered, "Where were his parents?" then I remembered his mom was a junkie too. She lost her younger son to DSS last year. Department of Social Services. Chico had gone to live with his grandmother but she couldn't control him. He was already spiraling.

As I was leaving, I noticed two hypodermic needles on the ground. They were five feet away from the nearby Tot Lot. I looked around and picked up a paper bag off of the ground. I carefully picked up the discarded needles using the paper bag as a protective barrier and threw them in the nearby barrel. "What ya got there," Chico yelled over to me. "Nothin,'" I said. "Just some litter."

I decided to walk around some more. I visualized Chico sitting, years ago, on the Little League bench, with his mischievous smile, planning his next prank. Again, his situation rekindled memories of Tools.

I tripped on the uneven pavement.

Fuck.

Shit.

There it was again. Guilt, all dressed up and snickering at me, the smug bastard. I kept thinking over and over again what I could have done to help Tools. My mind was like a merry-go-round of misery. Round and around it would go, never with a new answer, always with the same outcome. I reminded myself; *yes, I talked to Tools about his drug problem. Yes, I believed he was going to stop.* Maybe I was too young to deal with it, too gullible? Perhaps I conveniently relied on the easy way out. I guess I was in denial myself. I wanted to believe him. I really did. And Chico? Another friend. I literally just gave drug money to. What if he buys dope with that and overdoses? It will be my fault. *Stop. I've got to get off this merry-go-round.*

As I walked home, I found myself on East Broadway, one of the main streets in Southie, and noticed those around me. I couldn't believe how many people were high. No one seemed immune.

Junkies are easily identifiable with a faraway look in their eyes, always on borrowed time with one foot in the grave. They're alive, barely, yet surely living in Hell. They're nodding off, they're scratching their arms, they're walking down the street looking like they're about to fall down. They don't seem to know where they are, they ramble on incoherently, they tell you they hate their lives. Once the first step is taken on that unforgiving, dark road, the perception of there being any way out fades from consideration. They're like mice caught in a maze unable to find the opening. The chance of finding a safe exit fades more and more with every high. They're aware of their dilemma and hope someday to leave it all behind. When asked why they get hooked they respond because it feels good. The lure of the drug, the "instant euphoria" is impossible to ignore. They're content when the drug kicks in, but when it fades they're back into the abyss, anxiously awaiting their next fix. Some learn from their mistakes, successfully battling their demons and move on, while others are hooked for life, and in many instances, silenced prematurely by death.

There was no pattern to who exactly got affected. No common denominator, well, other, than they all lived here. Athletes, gifted or not, students, smart or lazy, got caught up in the shit. These once handsome guys and beautiful girls completely lost their looks.

I needed to get away from them. I felt like I was in my own horror movie surrounded by zombies. It was at that moment, I realized I wasn't walking anymore.

I was running.

FIVE

I grew apart from some of the members of the Pact in high school since we attended different schools. I went to Boston Latin School while Al went to Boston Latin Academy, both exam schools. Pat and Jaws went to Southie High, Sal went to Boston College High in Dorchester, Pete went to Catholic Memorial, also known as CM, in West Roxbury, TK and Sully went to Archbishop Williams, aka Archies, in Braintree. Dee and Kaleigh went to Fontbonne Academy in Milton and Pam went to Latin School with me but she mostly hung with a different group. Even though the crew hung out on the weekends, it wasn't the same. Or maybe it was for them, but I felt myself getting further and further away from them as time went on. Occasionally, we drank and hung around like teenagers searching for things to do. Some smoked weed. Some didn't. Guys would drink Bud and the girls would have Smirnoff Ice. It was fun. We hung at L and 6th. That was our spot. Everyone knew us individually as an "L and 6th kid". Every weekend it'd just be us. Sometimes there'd be some outsiders, some CM or BC High kids, but mostly it was just us.

In retrospect, the high school years flew by, but during those years, Death never took a vacation in Southie. It was always working overtime. Kids from other corners were dying all the time from overdoses. Mostly heroin. When you'd walk around, you'd see junkies everywhere; a constant reminder of a problem that you couldn't fix.

Chico was an "O and 2nd" kid. I hate to admit it but I hadn't thought of him since that time I saw him in the park. About two years later he was found dead on the same bench we sat on that hot September night. His lifeless body was discovered by a mom and her ten year old daughter as they walked by on the way to school. The girl was just starting her life. Chico's life was over. His cold, blue remains were brought to the city morgue. Chico's obituary didn't mention the cause of death. Like too many others, the funeral notice informed readers that he left this world "suddenly."

One by one more people became like Tools. Like Chico. Young kids were dying "suddenly" or "unexpectedly" which were simply code words for suicide or an overdose. "It's happening again," I heard my mom say to my father one night. Her face filled with anxiety. I knew what they were referring to. Southie in the late nineties was really bad. Drug use had spiked. People were overdosing left and right. Within a nine month period in 1997, an odd thing happened in Southie. Teenagers were committing suicide at record breaking rates. One boy hung himself on the back porch of his triple decker. One girl was found dead in her apartment closet. Another boy hung himself from the lifeguard post down at the Lagoon. They were all addicts. Medical professionals labeled this unnerving epidemic as "suicide contagion" but in my opinion, it was just another type of overdose.

I remembered being ten years old, hearing about this, thinking how sad it was that all these people only a few years older than me would end their lives. What could happen to me in the next five years that would make me want to do that? I couldn't stand the thought. Now, I was a teenager, and the victims were my friends.

Like most families, mine wasn't immune to this deadly scourge. Two of my first cousins overdosed and my uncle on my mom's side committed suicide because he couldn't deal with his drug addiction any longer. He was a veteran who never quite came home. These deaths were also all heroin-related. I didn't even know they were using. It came as a surprise.

I was sick of drugs ruining the lives of young and old people alike. Sick of suicide. Tired of wakes and funerals. I needed to leave. Needed change. It's easier to cope with the present and plan for the future when you bury the past. And we sure did a lot of burying.

So I went away to college, never looking back. My absence from Southie was a Godsend, a reprieve from the unwelcomed drama of personal destructiveness. I decided to study education at St. Bonaventure in upstate New York. Life seemed normal. Stable. I loved the campus atmosphere. I was happy and living life the way it was meant to be lived. People weren't dying all around me. I felt like I finally escaped from the past. The memories of the living dead from Southie faded away. I was free from the pain of feeling helpless around those I loved, those who were struggling within the throes of addiction one way or the other.

For four years, I embraced academia and submerged myself into my studies. I also made new friends. And I only thought about and talked to those friends. My Southie friends called me but one by one I stopped returning their phone calls. It wasn't on purpose. Perhaps it was a subconscious desire to disconnect from the past. It just happened. I lost touch with everyone other than my parents.

Even in the summer, I opted to take internships in New York City, doing anything I could not to go back to Southie. I couldn't confront the town, couldn't confront my guilt and

33

shame. I never even talked about Southie. When people asked me where I was from, I'd say Boston. If I was further questioned about where in Boston, I'd lie and just say, "Oh, just a small suburb outside of the city." I did this because I wanted to avoid the barrage of questioning which would inevitably happen if I said I was from Southie. Like, "You don't seem like you're from Southie?" or "Ever see anyone get killed?" or "Are you racist like everyone else there?" Or they'd mention the latest Hollywood film depicting the place and ask, "Hey is it really like that?" "You ever do heroin?" etc. The list went on. It was a lot of unwanted attention. So, instead, I lied.

Like high school, college was over in a blink of an eye. It was almost as if time had sped up even more than I thought possible. After graduating I moved to Brooklyn and had a sweet deal bartending at a local pub a college friend's dad owned, while I looked for a teaching job. I finally got a job teaching math at the Collegiate School, one of the most prestigious private schools in Manhattan. I felt like I finally made it. I was teaching all different levels of math from Algebra to AP Calculus. I loved math. It made sense. There was only one right answer. Even in high school, I buried myself in numbers when life was too tough to handle. Now, as a teacher, I jumped into my work, taught extra classes, got lost in a world of numbers. When I'd go out in Brooklyn for a beer or a date, if I got nervous, I would go back to my old habits. Counting. I'd look in the corner and count the tiles on the floor. I'd count the glasses on the bar. I'd look for patterns. Anything. Anything to keep the thoughts off myself. I didn't get too close to anyone though. Not sure why. No girl in New York wants to date a teacher, even if he does teach at a nice private school in Manhattan.

I taught at Collegiate for five years. The kids loved me. I totally immersed myself in that school. Knew the kids. Knew the families. Went to all the school events. I really liked the kids. They were hard working albeit privileged. But there was something missing. It didn't seem quite real to me. At first I was happy but soon the pretense of it all eventually got to me. I didn't relate to the other teachers and the faculty was snobby. Soon, every time I went to work, I felt like I was living in a vacuum filled with empty blazers and fake smiles. I was thinking of an excuse to come home. It was the first week of June. My classes had just ended. I was starting to get anxious. What was I going to do this summer? How was I going to stay busy? Could I tutor math in Brooklyn? Maybe teach summer school? Maybe in Brooklyn? Give back to the community? Get more involved in the inner city? Why hadn't I planned this out? Later that day, my mom called and told me my father had a bad fall and broke his hip. She asked if I could come home to help out for the summertime. I was on the next train. I was twenty-eight years old and hadn't been back to Southie, except for Christmas holidays, since I was eighteen. I was returning to a place I loved but feared.

Upon my arrival in Southie I was shocked by how different it had become. There were more condos than ever, parking was a mess, worse than ever before, and there was even a Starbucks on Broadway. An organic grocery story on H and Broadway where the old Hub Video used to be? I couldn't believe it. I went to get a coffee at Dunkin's and heard yuppies referring to Southie as "Sobo." It was annoying. Who were these people? Why were they here? When I walked into my house some kid even yelled "yuppie" out his car window to me. Great, I was a stranger in my own town.

When I walked in the front door of my house on Marine Road my parents were standing in the foyer, smiling and happy as life itself. They took turns hugging me and my mom was busy wiping away her tears. "Here, let me take your suitcases," she said. "Can't have your dad carrying anything heavy." I said, "Ma. I'm a big boy now. I can handle it…but thanks anyway."

We laughed and walked into the front room. I took a few minutes and walked through the house. Everything was about the same. It was like going back in a time machine although everything still seemed brand new. They kept the house spotless and it showed. Literally, nothing in my room had been touched. I guess that goes along with the territory of being an only child.

My mom was all smiles, as beautiful as ever with her large green eyes, pearly-white teeth and short platinum blonde hair. Her diminutive stature belied that fact that she was the truly tough one in the family. My dad had aged yet still looked pretty healthy minus the hip issue. He had broken his hip and the subsequent surgery had unforeseen complications. So he was facing an extensive recovery period and more medication than one could count. My mom refused to feel bad or dwell upon my dad's injury. The reason she didn't let him feel bad about it was because she knew it would be counterproductive to his recovery. He tried to pull the pity-party routine once in a while but one look from her and he changed course. Occasionally he tried to sneak a beer or two on the weekends but she put a stop to that. "You can't be drinking on those meds," she'd tell him. Since my mom was retired, she could be home most of the time being his nurse, but still needed my help.

My first night back home we ordered some Chinese food and sat in the living room, eating and talking. My parents were glad to see me and I couldn't believe I had been gone so long.

"Hey mom. I got you something from New York." I reached for the bag I had taken out of one of my suitcases earlier in the evening and placed it next to the coffee table. I took out a box and gave it to her. She opened the gift and smiled. It was a beautiful pair of Waterford Irish Crystal Lismore coffee glasses. "They're beautiful, John. Thanks so much." She got up and gave me a big kiss. "They are very nice," my dad said. I waited a few minutes before I reached into the bag again. "This is for you dad." "Oh," he said. "I get one too." "Very funny," I said. I handed him a small package wrapped in a recycled paper bag I got from a supermarket in Brooklyn. "Sorry about the lame wrapping," I said. "I was rushing and--" "No problem," he interjected. "Like buying birthday cards...it's a waste of money."

My dad's nieces and nephews got a kick out of him when he went to family parties and simply handed them cash without a card. It was his trademark of sorts I guess. He'd say, "People just throw away the cards anyway. Sometimes they make believe they're reading them while they're sticking the money in their pockets. Why should I make someone else rich by buying those cards?"

He unwrapped the present. It was Jim Bouton's book "Ball Four." It was a first edition and it was in great shape, cover and all. My dad loved baseball but I never watched the games that much unless the Red Sox were winning. I was definitely a fair weather fan. But to me, watching baseball was like watching paint dry. Boring. I liked the action in hoop and football. "Wow. Thanks. Can't wait to read it. His book created a lot of controversy."

"Speaking of famous people," I said. "How you feeling?"

"Yeah right," my dad laughed. "Getting better every day."

"Good."

"The doctor told me that it would be a slow process for me since I had those complications and my age and all. But he's optimistic and so are we," as he lovingly looked over to my mom.

"Well, I'm here for you…but the question is can you afford me." We laughed. "Only kiddin' dad," I said. "I'm all set with that so don't worry about it."

Inevitably the conversation turned to my friends. I had no idea what they were up to. Luckily Southie was a small town and my mom knew a little about a lot of people. She told me Sully was driving for UPS. That made sense. He always liked to drive. Traffic never bothered him. He enjoyed being behind the wheel when he was with us so he could control the radio and tell jokes. TK worked in a service department at a nearby Toyota dealership in Dorchester. He liked it, so he said. Pete was working as a custodian at Southie High's charter school. Pat and Jaws were flaunting the system, evading trouble with the law, selling hot stuff out of their cars. Dee just had a baby with Pat. Kaleigh and Al were mysteries. She hadn't seen them for a while. Pete was up to no good. Sal was working downtown as a banker.

"What about Pam," I asked. "Have you guys seen her at all?" My dad shook his head. He hadn't seen her. "She's doing well," my mom said. "I ran into her last month. She's working a few odd jobs as a waitress. I think she said she's going to school part time. Wants to be a nurse. Help people."

"She'd be good at that," I said.

My parents sat in silence waiting for me to ask something else about Pam but I didn't. "She's still single," my mom said, as she walked into the kitchen to get dessert.

I couldn't sleep so I watched TV until 2 a.m. When I finally put my head on the pillow I was still wide awake. My mind was racing around and around…changing gears from one subject to the next, from one person to another. Would they be happy to see me or just mad that I hadn't stayed in touch? I felt anxious, so I started planning my days in advance. I'd do this, I'd do that. I'd see this person and then I'd call that person. My thoughts raced. Short-lived thoughts zigzagging around my mind like darts, fireworks without the noise.

I turned the TV back on. Hoping it would quiet my mind but inevitably my thoughts reverted to a problem that I preferred to keep tucked away in the deepest recesses of my mind. Moving back home was a reminder that I needed to clean up my act concerning one problem which I kept hidden from everyone I knew. And I meant *everyone*. In New York I needed something to keep me preoccupied. Teaching math, correcting math exams, solving advanced calculations in my apartment for fun, counting numbers, finding patterns everywhere – it wasn't enough. I turned to gambling. I was confident I could find patterns in the lottery as well. Somehow beat the system. Find an algorithm that I could benefit from. To be honest, it wasn't about the money. It was about the rush. Sometimes I'd win. But I lost more. And when I won I usually gave it right back one way or the other. Then came the drought, I couldn't win so I lost and I lost. It wasn't pretty. After a while I wanted to stop but couldn't. I was like a junkie but my nemesis wasn't drugs. I was getting high off the rush but really just wasting my money and stressing myself out to the max. I guess I was trying to fill a void in my life. Whatever that was I really wasn't quite sure. I went to some gambler's anonymous meetings in the Big Apple but it didn't do any good. I'd go to a meeting then bet again promising myself I'd win and then be done. It never quite worked out that way.

Then I heard something from the TV. It was Joel Osteen. I didn't even realize he was on. Up until this moment the TV was just white noise for me. Joel Osteen was talking about Paul the Apostle. How he admitted he was weak and said, "The things I want to do I don't do. Things I don't want to do I end up doing." That described me to the letter and I was hoping the change of scenery would help me do the things I wanted to do. But what did I really want to do? I wanted to be like Paul and change. Eventually, albeit conveniently rationalizing, I figured time would provide me with that answer whatever it might turn out to be.

I grabbed a book but couldn't read. I needed to settle down. I needed to sleep. So I called upon an old friend and started counting once again. I'd count, "one-and-two and, one-and-two and, one-and-two and," and so forth. It kept me focused on nothing, only the counting, and freed my mind of any disconcerting thoughts.

My mind relaxed.

I drifted away.

And finally I slept.

SIX

Several days later, TK and Sal knocked on my front door. They said they were going to Calo's Café for dinner that night and told me to meet them there, have a little reunion. Of course I said yes.

When I walked into Calo's, I assumed it'd be different - renovated, upgraded, modernized - like most stores, bars, and cafes in Southie were, but it still had the same look and feel from years ago. The café was located at the corner of L and East Sixth. It was a donut shop in its previous life then Calo Moretti bought the store and turned it into a café when we were about ten. We ate plenty of honey-dip donuts on that street corner before we started buying pizzas and subs from Calo.

The café's a tiny place with about eight small tables. The décor wouldn't win any awards. The picture of Sicily still hung on the side wall and multi-colored plants sitting comfortably on the window sills gave the place a pleasant look. The clock in the corner was still hanging slightly crooked. The joint could use a fresh coat of paint and enhanced lighting but who needs ambience when you've got great food? The kitchen rests in the rear of the store, and there's one long table in the back where my old "gang" hung their proverbial hats. It would eventually become my table as well.

Calo, in his mid-fifties, was an old school Italian who was proud of his heritage. He had gained a few pounds since I went away to college but he was still in decent shape for an old timer who loved to eat and drink. He was well-liked and fun to talk to. Like many people said over the years, "He was a good guy that guy." Calo was lucky to have Angela Rosetti as his chief cook. Her cooking was the main reason why the café was prosperous and not because Calo loved to hold court and discuss the issues of the day. Admittedly he did that well but was occasionally close-minded.

The old gang was sitting at a table in the rear of the café. Pam and Dee stood up and hugged me. Sully gave me a high five and then guzzled down his Bud Light. Pete stood up and shook my hand. Sal and TK simply nodded, smiling, knowing full well they were the architects of this dinner engagement.

"Johnny Mac…longtime no chicken parmigiana sub," Calo said, as he laughed then hugged me. "I heard you were home. Your boys told me the other night."

"Yeah, I'm back."

"Mac is back!" Sully said.

I grabbed a chair and sat down. Everyone had changed including me I guess. Pam looked beautiful. Wow, I didn't remember her looking so great. When did she become so beautiful? She had long hair, piercing eyes and dark red lips. Dee still looked cute but a little haggard and disheveled, as if she'd allowed indifference to take over her life. Perhaps motherhood was too much to handle. Or perhaps it was something else. And the guys? They all put on a few pounds but ultimately seemed to have their shit together. And they were as obnoxious as ever.

"C'mon let's order," Sal said, smiling, eager to dig in.

Sully piped in. "Some things never change."

As we were eating and drinking, old stories were told, some of them exaggerated to the hilt, some not.

"That story about Al was crazy," I said. "I vaguely remember that. Couldn't believe he'd jump off the yacht club roof into the water. But he did."

Al got the stupid idea of jumping off the yacht club roof from a homeless guy nicknamed Two Times who we met at the park one summer night. He was given that name by his homeless pals because he always said the same thing twice. "How ya doin? How ya doin?" he'd say. "What's up? What's up? Ya got some spare change? Ya got some spare change?" he'd ask. Al's eyes widened the first time he heard this crazy exploit from Two Times who took credit for consummating this dangerous deed.

Al landed in the water no problem. However, it was too shallow and he broke his leg.

"Al was so smart he forgot to factor in the tide," Sal said, laughing inside.

TK said, "Deserves what he got the stupid fuck."

"Al was certainly a piece of work," I said. "What's he up to these days?"

TK got a kick out of this one. "Oh Johnny, you been gone too long," he said. "Al's the biggest dealer around Southie. Talk about going against the Pact. But he's not alone."

"Yeah, Al's quite the whore," Sal said.

Al's the biggest drug dealer in Southie? That was hard to digest. Before I could ask any more questions about Al, the subject was changed and we dove into other memories - us partying down the beach, hanging on the corner, our first kisses.

After eating, Pete went outside for a bit. He said he had to make a few phone calls. Smoke a few butts. When Pete returned he was with Pat O'Malley and Mark "Jaws" Jaworski, but he looked different. Everyone at the table noticed but nobody said anything. Pete was clearly high. Pat and Jaws didn't look any better. They were clearly junkies. I guess that's what TK was talking about a few minutes ago when he indirectly referenced other violators of the Pact.

"Well, well, well," Pat said, happily. "Look who the devil brought in. Can you believe it? Me and Jaws were walking by and Pete said you were in here! I said no ya lying! Johnny Mac isn't in there! He said see for yourself and here you are!"

"I'm here," I said, not sure what else to say. "Missed you guys." I got up and hugged them both. "You look good," Jaws said. Pat agreed. "You guys do too," I said, clearly lying. I wonder if either one of them had mirrors in their houses because I could only wonder what they thought they looked like. Pat bent over and kissed Dee on the cheek and put his hands on her shoulders. "Thanks man…but who wouldn't look good around these guys?" TK threw Pat a nasty look but then a smile crept across his face. "I'll consider the source," TK said.

Dee looked annoyed. "Can't you guys be nice for a change?" she said. TK remained silent. Pat said, "Of course! I'm always nice to you ain't I?" Dee didn't respond. She took a sip of her wine and brushed aside Pat's hands that were still on her shoulders. Pat dismissed her aggravated state as a normal condition that didn't warrant concern. I could only wonder how they treated each other behind closed doors.

"You guys staying out of trouble?" I asked, masking my true feelings between hope and reality.

"Course," Jaws said.

"Yup," Pat said. "We go to church every day."

"Ya do?" Sully said. "Really?"

"Sully, put a lid on it will ya," TK said. "The church would go on fire if they ever walked in."

Pat simply blew TK off with a "yeah whatever you say"

attitude and turned to me. "What brought you back to town?"

"My dad broke his hip. Parents needed my help. So here I am."

"Lucky. All the painkillers he wants…and no one can give him shit about it," Pat said.

"Wouldn't say a broken hip is lucky," TK fired back.

Jaws shot Pat a disapproving look and quickly changed the subject. "How long ya gonna be home?" he asked. "For the summer," I said. Just then Angela refilled our wine glasses. "Plus I needed to come back 'cause I missed Angela's cooking," I said.

"Yeah, who wouldn't," Jaws said. "I could eat her chicken, broccoli, and ziti for breakfast, lunch, and dinner."

"I'm gonna gain some weight if I keep eating dinners like this," I said.

Pete, who was in his own world for a while finally snapped out of it, "Nice accent by the way, see ya pronouncing ya r's now."

"Out of town for a while. It just happened," I replied. "Sure you didn't take one of those accent reduction classes?" Pete said. I laughed and threw a piece of bread at him. "No."

Pat and Jaws seemed to be getting antsy. Pat looked down at his watch. His eyes shifted to Jaws. Jaws nodded. "We'd love to stay and shoot the shit," Pat said. "But we got things to do."

"Great seein' you Johnny," Jaws said. "We'll see you around town."

"Thanks for stopping by," TK said, brimming with sarcasm.

"See you guys in church," Sully said.

They left.

"Those two haven't been in church since their first communion," TK said.

Pete looked at me.

"How about you Johnny?" he said. "Still the resident atheist?"

SEVEN

Pat O'Malley and Mark "Jaws" Jaworski walked into the pro shop at the Wellesley Country Club.

"Good morning to you," Pat said, to the young man behind the counter. "Great day for golf wouldn't you say?" Before the man could speak, Jaws said, "Any day's a great day for golf if you love the game."

The young man, barely sixteen, who was wearing glasses and had braces, smiled. "Gentlemen, good morning."

"Please, no formalities," said Jaws. "My name is Mark Stanford and my colleague is Pat Walsh. Call me Mark but don't call him late for dinner." Jaws laughed at his own joke but nobody else laughed. Pat added, "Don't pay any attention to my friend. He didn't take his morning medicine." Pat gave Jaws a sideways warning glance that said "what the fuck are you doing?"

"And what's your name, young man?" Pat asked.

"Oh, it's Logan…Logan Dwyer."

"Logan, I like that name," Pat said. "Irish hey kid."

"Yup."

"Good. I like the Irish. I'm Irish. People of the earth."

Jaws almost burst out laughing as Logan smiled again and thanked Pat with a handshake. "So what can I do for you?" he said. "We'd like to take a look at your golf clubs," said Pat. "Top of the line only."

"Yes sir. Come right this way."

They walked to the rear of the tiny shop.

"These ones are TaylorMade. You'd love this brand if you golf a lot."

47

"Let's see," Jaws said. He grabbed a putter and looked it up and down. "I like the feel of this."

"Course you do," Pat said. "That's because you got great taste."

Pat took a five iron and playfully took a half swing.

"Listen young man," Jaws said. "We'd like to take these out on the course for a hole or two to see if we really want to buy them. Can we do that?"

"Ahh, against store policy. Can't get them banged up. Plus we'd need money up front anyway."

"Geez, was hoping to check them out," Pat said.

"Sorry gentlemen."

"What if...what if we give you our Rolex Watches, as collateral, you could say. Cost more than these clubs. We'll just take them out onto the practice range and take a few shots. Clubs won't get damaged. We'll treat them with kid gloves. C'mon, chance for a big commission here."

Pat could see that Logan was apprehensive. It was clear he was new at the job, any job for that matter, and didn't want to break any rules. Pat looked at Logan and smiled. "Look," he said. "We're in town just for a few days, visiting the Gately's. We're meeting them at the restaurant after the boys' tennis lessons."

"So you guys know the Gately's?"

"Used to be neighbors," Pat said.

"So what do ya say?" Jaws asked.

"Geez guys, I don't know."

Pat took out his wallet. "Look, here's my Amex gold card. If we're not back in a half hour, charge my card for the two sets of clubs."

Logan checked the card. The name Pat Walsh was on it.

48

"Okay, but just a few shots and then come right back. Okay?"

"You got it Logan," said Pat. "Don't worry about anything."

As they turned to leave, Jaws looked back at Logan. "Hey kid, is this your first job?"

"Yes sir."

"You're doing great, man," he said. "Here's a little something for you." Jaws slipped him a fifty dollar bill.

"I can't take this."

"Take it kid, you earned it."

Pat and Jaws walked out of the pro shop, and in an instant, were driving back to Southie.

"Kid's gonna shit when the card is declined and tells his boss," said Pat.

"At least he made fifty bucks on commission," Jaws said, then laughed loudly.

"Hey, what can I say," Pat answered. "You win some. You lose some. Now let's go make some money for ourselves."

Poor Logan didn't see it coming. He took the bait. He had no idea that they had been casing that pro shop for weeks and knew he'd be working the afternoon shift today. He also didn't notice how they both wore hats and kept their heads just low enough so that they'd be unrecognizable on the security camera tape. Logan was thrown off base when Pat said he knew the Gately family. But what Logan didn't know was, at that moment in the store while they were talking, a family walked by the front of the store. The woman obviously a rich, stay at home mom, dressed to the nines, was with her two boys who were carrying tennis racquets. One of the boys had a backpack on that read "Gately." Pat noticed this and played it to their advantage.

"By the way," Pat said. "What the fuck was with that lame

'late for dinner' joke?"

"I dunno, ya know just wanted to lighten the moment with the kid. Tell a corny joke. Get his guard down," Jaws replied. Then he remembered and said. "And who the fuck are the Gately's?"

"If I told you I'd have to kill you," Pat answered, smiling.

They laughed and kept on driving along the Turnpike.

We first met Pat and Jaws during our youth hockey days but they ditched the sports scene after a few miserable seasons of sitting on the bench. They rebelled, quit the team and formed their own little group with other frustrated kids. They started drinking, drugging, and getting in trouble with their parents and the law. I think that's why parents care so much about youth sports in Southie because as the old saying goes, "A kid in sports stays outta the courts."

Pat and Jaws *were also part of the Pact* that we formed seemingly so long ago. But we drifted away from them soon afterwards and became more like acquaintances as they had carved their own niche in the neighborhood. They became first-rate thieves but it didn't happen overnight. In Southie, someone is going to take you under their wing, you just got to make sure it's the right person. They were mentored by Jimmy "Jumpin" O'Hara, a well-known thief who taught them the intricacies of the trade. He taught them the art of deception. You needed to play the role. Walk into a place dressed in a suit coat and tie. Be convincing, and around here, make sure you pronounced your r's so people think you come from money. It's role-playing worthy of an Oscar. Where's Jumpin now? He disappeared. He probably retired in Florida. He never spent a minute behind bars.

These two characters were inseparable. Like twins, they shared the same mind. They knew what each other were thinking. They made enough cake to survive and get banged-out. They fooled everyone, had nine lives and were always one step ahead.

Pat and Jaws arrived back in Southie still laughing over their productive golf game. They walked into the Mercury Bar on West Broadway. They hardly ever went there but knew a new movie was being shot in Southie and production just wrapped-up. The movie crew was apparently partying at this bar. Pat and Jaws were hoping to sell some leather jackets they'd stolen the other day. They already had a buyer for the clubs. They went to the bar and skipped the drinks. They were there on business.

"God," Jaws said. "I hope they get the Boston accent right in this movie. They never do."

"Who cares? I just want to sell some shit." Pat walked up to the crew, a mixed group, mostly men, some were women. "Hey. You all deserve Oscars for all your hard work."

One of the crew members smiled, used to locals always trying to get in touch with the A list actors that often grace Boston movies. "We only work behind the scenes…no movie stars here…sorry."

"Don't worry, you're just the people we're looking for," Pat said.

"See this leather jacket," Jaws blurted out, as he took it out of a shopping bag. "Gotta get rid of it. Sell it to you for four hundred. Price tags right on it." One woman looked at the price tag which read a thousand. The others looked on, intrigued. "Is this part of a house sale or something," she said, jokingly. "Somethin' like that," Pat said.

"Tell you what," another guy said, reaching into his pocket and pulling out three brand new c-notes. "I'll give you this... for that..."

"It's a deal. I'll take that...for this," Jaws said.

They shook hands. Another crew guy spoke up. "Hey, my man, got any more jackets?"

"Or anything else to sell?" a woman asked. Pat and Jaws smiled. It was their lucky day.

"Yeah, we do. Be right back."

Pat and Jaws went to their car to get the rest of their high end stolen goods.

They brought in a half dozen bags.

And that's how Pat and Jaws made 3,000 dollars in fifteen minutes.

EIGHT

Over the next few weeks, we met Pete several times down at M Street Park. We watched softball and talked about the Red Sox and the upcoming Patriots season. We also hung at Calo's, ate, and drank, the usual. But Pete didn't look good. He looked worse than before. Pale. Skinny. Whitish.

Before we knew it, it was July Fourth. Luckily, TK's dad has a boat at the Southie Yacht Club and he said we could use it to watch the fireworks and listen to the Boston Symphony Orchestra on the Charles River. My favorite part was driving the boat from the harbor into the Charles River. When we got there, we were all having a good time, partying, reminiscing. It was the whole crew, me, TK, Sal, Sully, and Pete. Next thing we knew, Pete was nodding off once the fireworks started and the orchestra started to play the 1812 Overture. He must have taken an Oxy at some point on the boat ride. I couldn't take it anymore. We couldn't take it. We had to do something.

Two days later, Pete heard a knock on the door. He opened it and there we stood, ready to conduct our first intervention.

"C'mon in guys," he said. He looked like he just woke up. It was 4:00 p.m.

Pete directed us into the back room of the house, an old study area where he and his sister, Pam, used to do their homework. It was modestly furnished with a sofa, a few small chairs, a desk, and two lamps. The room seemed stuck in time, but Pete's mom, Mrs. Winkowksi couldn't part with the memories. A few pictures hung on the back wall depicting American Revolutionary soldiers in full uniform holding their long rifles. An old-fashioned dartboard hung precariously on the side wall with three darts protruding from the middle of the board. The many tiny holes on the wall encircling the board revealed to us that we weren't the only bad dart players in Southie.

"What's up?" Pete asked.

"Need to talk to you," Sal said. "We're concerned…"

"About you," TK said, finishing Sal's sentence.

"About me?" Pete said, with a fake voice.

"Look at yourself," Sal said.

TK said, slowly and emphatically, "*You are a mess.*"

Pete never took criticism with an open mind. He was obstinate and remained silent.

"You forget about the Pact?" I asked. "Yeah, the Pact we were going to live by forever."

"The Pact?" he shot back.

"Remember that day we sat in the park where Tools died?" I said. "We promised we'd never end up like him. One by one, we all said we wouldn't die 'before our time'".

The guys looked at Pete. "I haven't forgotten the Pact. I plan on keeping my promise."

Okay, so no one's forgotten the Pact, it's just that it didn't hold much sway over those who had sworn by it.

"Keeping your promise?" TK asked, in exasperation. "You've already broken the Pact."

"Yeah, but I got it under control. I don't plan on dying anytime soon. Not dying before my time."

"If you keep on using, you'll be planning your cemetery plot next to Tools at Cedar Grove," Sal said.

"Yeah, do you like mahogany or silver metal for your

casket?" Sully asked, trying to lighten the mood a little bit but also make a point. Pete shot Sully a sideway glance.

"Everything will be okay. I'm good."

"Pete," TK said. "For starters…you'll only be good if you stay the fuck away from Al and his goons."

"Fuck Al," Sully said.

"Haven't seen them lately."

"It's pretty obvious that you have," Sal said.

"I agree," I said, not sure what else to say.

"How 'bout you get your own fuckin' life. You go off to college forget about Southie then come back and bother me."

"Oh, so, I'm bothering you? I'm just trying to be your friend."

"Friend? First time you've been around in a decade."

Really? This is how it's going to go? I thought. I didn't want what happened to Tools to happen to Pete. I was determined to help. Silence wasn't an option. But how can one person change another person's life if help isn't welcomed? I thought about my own shortcomings and felt like a hypocrite. After all, an addiction is an addiction is an addiction. Who was I to give advice but I needed to try nevertheless.

"Hey!" TK yelled at Pete, interrupting my thoughts. "Stop avoiding the subject. You need help." I was stuck in my thoughts. For a second, I thought TK was yelling at me.

"I…we…only want to help," I said to Pete, who just stared at me. Suddenly the doorknob turned and the door opened. Pam walked into the room. "Oh sorry guys didn't know you were here." She was about to leave but then surveyed the room again, noticing our serious expressions. "Let me take a wild guess why you're here. Never mind. I've asked him over and over again to stop but he doesn't listen. Good luck with that." She walked out of the room. When the door closed Sully, always trying to break the tension, said, "See that guys? She was looking at me."

Everyone laughed.

"Look Pete," Sal said. "Bottom line. You look rough. We're worried about you."

"I've got a cold or something. Nothing to worry about."

We stared at him. Our silence made him protest more. "Look I'm fine. Really I am. I'm just low on dough. Can't do much. I stay home most of the time. And go to meetin's."

"I think you're in de-ni-al," Sully said. "And I don't mean the river in Egypt."

"Sully, you legit tell the worst dad jokes," Sal said.

"Shut up. At least I try."

"You nodded off on the fourth of July!" TK yelled.

"I was tired! Okay? Is it against the law to be tired?"

"You were legless and there was an orchestra 200 feet from us and loud ass fireworks. You were high, dude." TK shot back.

Pete didn't have any answers. He sat there, silent. "Life's not a dress rehearsal. No second chances pal," I said.

Pete didn't say anything. We all sat without speaking for what felt like forever. Uneasiness walked in and sat down with us. Finally Pete spoke again. "Don't worry about me. One day at a time."

"You can't live one day at a time when you're dead," I said.

Pete turned ugly. He fired back. "I'm fuckin' fine! Suddenly you're back and you're mister fuckin' Southie again? Want to help me with your college degree? What are you a doctor now?"

"You can't become a doctor just from doing undergrad," I said.

"I know, I was joking. This is just another example of how you think you're better than me. Better than everyone else."

"We're just trying to fuckin' help you, Pete," TK interjected. "My man, Johnny, included."

Pete looked at me. "What? By telling people that after death there's only a void? Yeah, that really helps! You tried to pull that shit on Tools. He told me."

No one said anything.

"Yeah it didn't work did it?" Pete continued. "He's dead."

I noticed myself getting choked up but had to say something. "It's just the way I feel about it. I can't help it. I think our lives are all we have. Then it's over."

"Yeah yeah…Your worldly philosophy on death and the afterlife, or the lack thereof, is well-known in Southie. They pray for *you* to change."

I was surprised how angry Pete got about this matter. I assume some did pray for me. In Southie people don't look kindly upon self-proclaimed agnostics or fencing-sitting atheists.

Sal zeroed in on Pete. "Listen, I believe in God. You don't have to listen to anything you don't believe in. I believe when we die we'll be reborn in Heaven with God. Life will begin again but will be different. But that ain't gonna help you survive in this life is it Pete?"

"How did this fucking intervention turn into a Confirmation class discussion?" Sully asked. TK gave Sully that look. Pete laughed and said, "Johnny wouldn't know anything about that Sully. He doesn't believe in God, do ya Johnny?"

"I've never actually said that."

"You've never said that huh?"

"I believe there are things in this world we don't understand or believe. Uncertainty and disbelief doesn't negate the fact He may exist."

"See what I mean," Pete said. "Never get a straight answer from the professor."

He laughed but I knew where this was going. I really didn't want to get into it with him. God is tough to understand and sends out mixed messages from where I stand. Perhaps God's greatness and existence as perceived by so many, is too sophisticated, too complicated for my solipsistic view of the universe. Maybe someday I'll realize what others seem to embrace so easily and enthusiastically on a daily basis throughout their entire lives.

Sal interrupted my thoughts. "Just because you can't see Him, it doesn't mean He's not out there, anywhere, somewhere, perhaps, everywhere." Sully threw his hands up, "God-Almighty. Let's stay focused."

TK stood up. "Yeah, nice try Pete…seriously well done, trying to get us off on a tangent, but we're here about you."

"Yeah man, if you don't stop, someday *it* will stop you," Sully added.

Pete sat down in the far corner of the room with his head down and his hands on top of his head. I could hear birds chirping outside, cars whizzing by, and kids playing, but inside the room silence was supreme. No one spoke. We just waited to hear what Pete might say. Finally he lifted his head and looked at us. His eyes were red. He wiped away a few tears that were rolling down his cheeks.

"Listen," he said. "I do need help but it's so hard to stop. So hard to…."

Pete's voice trailed off. Pete's on and off battle with drugs started one fateful day, then turned into weeks, then months, then years. He was right. It wasn't going to be easy. But he needed to change.

"Okay, I will. I'll do it. I'll try. I promise on the Pact."

NINE

My dad's rehab had been slow. He was still in a lot of pain. More unforeseen complications arose. He was rushed to the hospital, had a blood clot in his left leg and was put on Coumadin, a blood thinner. He was also experiencing atypical pain in his other leg that his doctor couldn't explain. More tests were scheduled. So I was staying. I got a job teaching at the Newbury Charter School on Dorchester Street. I was excited.

I guess our visit with Pete worked, hit home. He started in earnest and saw a doctor who prescribed Suboxone to help him fight his heroin addiction. Suboxone, a combination of buprenorphine and naloxone, aka "Bupe" is a prescription medicine for opioid addiction which suppresses withdrawal systems and reduces cravings. He attended counseling sessions to help him with the powerful life changes he'd have to embrace on his road to recovery. Sixty seven days later he was doing great and had as many days of sobriety under his belt. There I was with that counting quirk again.

Pete started volunteering as a youth hockey coach at the Murphy Rink, something he always wanted to do. Talking about it always put a smile on his face. He really loved the kids and they loved him. One day I met him down at the rink. He was in his element. His team was scrimmaging. I watched them skate for a while and then Pete noticed me. He skated over and I stepped into the team bench area.

"Whatdaya think, Johnny, wanna jump on the ice and show the kids a few tricks?"

"Not today, Pete, just gonna watch. These kids are pretty

good. Quick. Smart. I like the way they skate."

"They got a lotta promise for sure," Pete said.

"I tell you what," I said. "When I'm free I'll come and watch your home games."

His eyes lit up. "That would be great."

"Then it's a deal."

"Hey, before you go," he said. "Ya gotta watch this kid." Pete yelled to one of the players on the ice. "Hey Bogacz, take a few shots on net." He nodded and started firing away. "The kid is from the projects. His name's Richie. He's the real deal for a twelve-year old. Gonna be the key to our season."

I concurred, youngster had talent. I know Pete saw a lot of himself in Richie and wanted to steer him right. "Gonna take these kids to tournaments," he said. "So they can get some exposure outside of Southie. I think that's important, teach them there's more to life than this town."

"You're reminding me of Lahey!"

Pete laughed. "I was *just* thinking of him the other day."

"I'm serious."

"Ya know what? I'm gonna be just like him," Pete said. "Dedicate myself for years to come to the kids in this town."

"That would be good."

"Maybe I'm the Lahey for this generation."

Pete smiled.

Then I left and drove home.

"Lahey" was the man when we growing up. For years, he coached us on the ice, even coached CYO basketball and Babe Ruth. He was always officiating, coaching, or organizing some youth athletic leagues. It seemed like the dude never went home.

61

Talk about a guy with 'Southie' written all over his sleeves. But he was more than a coach to us. He took us out for pizza after games. He was always there to listen and give advice. We all wanted to be him, and when I saw the players look at Pete, I knew they felt the same way about him.

I was busy at school teaching, Pete was into coaching bigtime, and naturally it consumed a lot of our time. But I kept my word and saw a bunch of games. TK, Sal, and Sully kept me company in the cold rink. Pete's kids were getting pretty good. They won a lot of games. It was exciting for everyone. As Pete continued coaching he saw their potential and became too hard on them. His own regrets with the sport he loved started haunting him.

Pete's dad had been an overbearing son-of-a-bitch who thought his son was going to be drafted by the Bruins. And for good reason: Pete was one of those kids who actually had a shot.

His dad put a lot of pressure on him and he soon grew wary of his relentless interference and incessant bragging. After leading his school's varsity team to back-to-back state titles, Pete was on top of the hockey world but he burnt out seemingly overnight. In his senior year, a pivotal moment, he gave up on hockey, which was bad, and then on school, which was worse.

One night at the rink in between periods Sal and I took a quick walk outside to get some fresh air. He gave me an update on Pete of which I was unaware. With the passage of time Pete's relationship with his dad had worsened and this was tearing him apart below the surface. When he had a few drinks in him, he'd say to the boys, "Guess I won't be playing in the NHL anytime soon," and would subsequently add, "So what ya think my father thinks of me now?" Then he stopped talking about his dad and lost dreams altogether. They never asked yet knew it still bothered him.

There wasn't any doubt that Pete was either totally inspired or depressed. There was no in between for him. He was pumped when they won and heartbroken when they lost. He was like a little kid. One day he'd be totally jazzed about coaching. The next, he seemed to realize how bad he blew it and couldn't escape his own destiny. His roller coaster ride was ongoing. I didn't realize it at the time but Pete was probably bipolar and his drug use was an inevitable self-medication.

Then Pete decided he'd stop taking the Suboxone and opted to do it on his own. He didn't need the Suboxone or any more counseling sessions to give him the empowerment to live drug free, mend relationships, and realize the necessary life changes he'd need to cleanse his soul, heart, mind and body. He was wrong on all accounts. It wasn't long until he started using again, and as time passed, his erratic behavior got worse. Parents started to notice. They knew he must have been on drugs. The league let him go. They cited something vague about liability issues.

The day after they canned him, Pete came by my house. It was cold but we sat on the front porch and talked. It looked like he lost his best friend. "I'm all done down at the rink," he said. "Fuckin' league commissioner said they were revamping the manager's ranks and thanked me for my time. Fuckin' asshole doesn't even know what a hat trick is. And he's revamping? I should revamp his face."

I could tell he was high. It was really sad to watch. I wasn't sure what to say, but he continued. "I wanted to do the right thing. Help others. But all I got was a *thanks, but no thanks.*" I tried to calm him down but he sank in the chair and stared at the ceiling. Moments later he looked at me as if I could make everything go away.

"I'm a good guy ain't I Johnny?"

"Course you are."

"Don't humor me for Christ sake."

"I mean it. It's their loss. But you can't be coaching kids all fucked up."

"Fuck you Johnny. Coaching is all I had left now that's gone too."

"Look, if you get clean again, you'll have another chance. All isn't lost."

I saw hope flash across Pete's face. He wanted to believe he'd be fine. But hope doesn't change reality. Doesn't change the fact that he was using again and mired in shit.

"I'm tryin' to kick it. But it ain't easy."

"Try harder."

"Remember when we used to have those all day snowball battles in your back yard?" Pete asked.

"Course."

"I miss those days. Miss being young without a worry in the world. Why can't it be like that now?"

What person wouldn't want to transported back to the past and start over? I know I would.

"Hey, we can't go back in a time machine like they do in movies."

"Yeah. That really sucks," he blurted out.

"Can only think about today and tomorrow," I said.

"Yeah, that's great," he said, sarcastically.

"Doesn't mean you can't embrace the past...nothing wrong

with that."

He smiled faintly. "You always loved Pam."

"What? No…" I heard myself say. "That was random? Where'd that come from?"

"Still thinking about the snowball fights. You liked her then!" Pete said, with delight. "I remember seeing you look at her. Never said anything because I didn't want to bust your balls."

"We're just friends."

"Don't try to pull that. What do they call it, a Platonic relationship? That's funny."

"I don't like your sister."

"Dude, relax. We're grown," Pete said, with a face like you can't lie to me. "I think you'd actually be good for her."

I tried to suppress a smile.

"And she'd be good for you. Just don't blow it."

I didn't say anything. Pete continued. "You got nothing to lose and everything to gain. Look at it that way."

"I wish you could look at your own recovery that way, Pete."

"Easier said than done, buddy."

"I know," I said, unfortunately understanding first-hand how hard it was to break an addiction. Pete and I were exactly the same. Only difference was my addiction was a secret. For now.

Surprisingly Pete stood up and hugged me. It was more like a bear hug. It seemed like he didn't want to let go. Finally he backed off, smiled and then said, "Everything will work out and we'll laugh about this when we're old men."

I laughed. "I'd like that."

"Alright, I'm outta here," Pete said. "I'll call you tomorrow."

"Okay."

"I'll see you soon too. Swear to God. Get it…swear to God? You atheist punk."

"Same joke, different day."

We hugged.

He left.

He never called.

TEN

Pam knocked on the door and Al answered. He thought his eyes were deceiving him. Pam? What did she want?

"C'mon in. You look great," he said, hiding his surprise.

"Thanks."

"Grab a seat."

Pam walked in, sat down, and took off her jacket. She looked around his apartment. Everything from the black leather furniture to various oil paintings was top shelf. Impressive. Topping it off was a sixty-inch high-Def TV with surround sound.

"Nice apartment."

"Could be better with a woman's touch."

Pam faked a smile but didn't respond right away. Then she said, "Nice TV."

"Yeah got it cheap if you know what I mean."

"Sure do."

"Can I get you a drink?"

"No thanks."

"So what's new?"

"New York. New Hampshire."

"You must have heard that from your dad."

"Sure did."

Al was trying to unlock her brain and discover why she was there. Pam knew. She was on a mission. She wanted to convince Al to stop selling drugs. To stop selling drugs to her brother. But she needed to be careful. Really careful.

"Hey, heard about a big bust on G Street last week and

67

another one at the Old Colony Development a couple of days ago."

"Yeah, fuckin' guys are stupid. The G should stand for gaffes. And those retarded spics in Old Colony sell to anybody. Gotta be careful in that business."

"You mean your business right?"

Al didn't acknowledge her statement but also couldn't deny he sold drugs. Pam knew he sold drugs to Pete. Al knew she knew. Everyone knew. Denial wasn't an option. He was clever and easily manipulated people, avoiding direct conversations or being forced into a corner he didn't want to be in. He was as tightlipped as possible about his dope deals.

"What are you drinkin'?"

"Pretty persistent hey Al?" she said. "It's been a whole fifteen minutes the last time you asked."

Determined, he walked over to his wine fridge which was filled with an assortment of wines. "I've got red or white?" he said. He stood there thinking about which bottle would best suit the occasion and then opened the fridge door and grabbed a bottle from the top shelf.

"This red wine cost five hundred a bottle," he said. "You'd love it."

"Let me guess. Did you get it from the local wine cartel?"

"I like that. Wine cartel. Very original."

"I try."

"The boys always got the best shit. I actually got five bottles for the price of one. Can't beat that."

"Anyone I know?" Pam asked.

"Maybe."

Pam opted for water and Al drank his precious wine. He put

the R&B music channel on his TV.

"Like I said earlier. Couple of busts in Southie. Gotta be careful sellin' that shit. Heard the snitches are comin' out all over the place after they're busted on the street."

"What are ya tryin' to tell me?"

"Just want ya to be careful. Southie's hot. Cops have eyes and ears everywhere hoping to bring down the big dealers."

"Ya I know. Got nothin' to do with me...I'm no big deal."

"Really?"

Pam could see the engines revving up in Al's mind. He appeared antsy.

"Why the sudden concern for my welfare?" he asked.

"All I'm saying is if I had plenty of money I'd walk away from trouble. That's all."

"C'mon Pam, we go way back. Why are you really here?"

She took a deep breath. Her heart was pounding.

"I want you to stop selling Pete that shit."

Al's eyes widened. 'So that's why she's here' he thought to himself. She couldn't care less for my well-being.

"Hasn't he been clean?"

"Was clean...just don't sell him any...*please*..."

Vague and noncommittal, Al said. "I'll see what I can do."

"That's all you can say?"

"I can't control what happens on the street."

Pam was angry. Angry she even bothered with him. He'd never change. It was always about Al.

Her visit was unexpected, inexplicable. Even though her concern for his well-being was initially confusing, her intent was now evident to Al, so he slyly welcomed her presence, hoping in his mixed-up mind, for more to come. Then they heard a knock on the door. He shook his head. Timing is everything. He opened the door. It was the Murphy brothers. He forgot they were coming over. They saw Pam but hid their surprise.

"C'mon in guys. Just havin' a few cocktails on this beautiful day with this exquisite gal."

"That's beautiful. 'Exquisite' could be the word of the day," Ryan said.

"You're such a sweet talker, Al," Pam said, hating every word. "It's amazing you don't have girls banging on your door all the time."

"Nah only sweet on you," Al responded. The Murphy twins laughed in unison. Al didn't.

"On that note, I've gotta go to the little girls' room," Pam interjected. She walked into the bathroom and left the door slightly ajar as she turned on the water. She stood near the door and listened.

"Did that deadbeat Caccamo pay up?" Al asked.

"Yeah, tracked him down last night. Fuckin' greaser always tryin' to beat us," Joey said.

"He's got more excuses than a deadbeat dad," Ryan said.

"So what do ya got for me?" Al asked. Ryan reached into his pants pocket and pulled out a fistful of money and then took out two envelopes from his jacket pocket. He handed Al all the money.

"Good week hey guys?"

"Always a good week in Southie," Joey said. "Junkies have insatiable appetites."

"Another word for the day. 'Insatiable'," Ryan said. "Fuck the stupid talk," Al interrupted. "When we put together the packages today we'll lace a few with fentanyl to whip up some business. And make sure that fuckin' deadbeat gets the first package."

"Will do boss," Ryan said, enthusiastically. Joey nodded, apprehensively.

Pam was beyond angry but not surprised that Al could be so evil. She knew what Fentanyl was, a synthetic opioid more powerful than morphine. She was aware what it did when mixed with heroin. It gives the user a far greater high and is highly dangerous, resulting in many fatal overdoses. But the druggies take the chance even though they're aware of the dangers. They feel the high is even worth challenging Death. They're so messed up they don't give a fuck. And neither do the despicable dealers who sell them the shit.

Al looked toward the bathroom door and motioned to the guys to change the subject. Pam walked out of the bathroom a few moments later. "I thought you fell in," Al said. "Very funny," she said.

"Anyone want a drink?" Al asked. The twins nodded. Pam declined again. "Time for me to leave," she said. "Leave you boys alone to do whatever you do."

"C'mon," Al said. "I just need a few minutes with them."

"No...all set. Got what I came for."

Al took out a roll of money and pulled out a few c-notes and looked at Pam. "All set with that too," she said. Not to be totally shot down, especially in front of his boys, Al tried to kiss her on the left cheek. She abruptly moved away. Then he opened the door. "Goodbye," Pam said, as she walked out.

"What was that all about?" Joey asked.

"Nothing to worry about but one of these days I'm gonna tap that," Al said, his twisted mind always at work. "Just a matter of time."

"Yeah, that would be interesting," Ryan said.

"C'mon boys," Al said. "Time to make the donuts. And don't forget we're gonna add some fentanyl to some new packages."

"Hey Al," Joey said. "Really think we should do that?"

Joey's reluctance was ostensible.

Ryan was puzzled.

Al wasn't thrilled.

"You got a problem with that there's the door," Al said, looking at Joey.

"No, I'm good," Joey said, now trying to shield his innermost feelings.

"Good, I'm glad," Al said. "I'm gonna show you right now how to do it."

"Sounds good," Ryan said.

"Now see this little ole' package," Al asked, rhetorically. "This is fentanyl that I will add to the heroin."

"Did you make that shit," Ryan asked.

"No. What do think I'm a chemist? I just add it in and mix it. I got this from a reliable source who knows how to process this. It can get complicated. All I know and want to know is that one gram of pure fentanyl is equal to 100 grams of good street heroin. So…when it's mixed up…bang…junkies love it.

"Junkies are whacked," Joey said. "I'd rather get punched by a heavyweight than get punched by that shit."

"Good analogy," Al said. "But who really gives a flying fuck about those idiotic junkies anyway?"

"Yeah," Ryan said. "They'd stick anythin' and I mean anythin' in their veins to catch a buzz. Fuckin' crazy."

"Don't make no sense," Joey said, as he walked over to get a drink from the table.

Joey was a scoundrel of sorts but feeding druggies he knew a dangerous cocktail didn't fit well with him. If those poor souls had any sense they would have stopped using drugs which poisoned their mind, body, and soul. But common sense had long been thrown aside, thoroughly abandoned in search of that next high.

"And I sure don't have qualms keeping them happy as long as I can make a buck," Al said.

"Are junkies really happy?" Joey said. "Happy to overdose on that shit?"

"I don't care how many overdose, or how many say goodbye to this world because I'm not holding them prisoner. I'm just a businessman cashing in. Somebody's gotta do it. Might as well be me."

The Murphy brothers left and Al sat on his favorite leather chair drinking the last of the red wine. He was amused at Pam's visit. She wanted him to cut and run, leave while the going was good. Why bother? Did he deserve notice that he'd be better off cashing in his chips and enjoy life before it was too late? She wanted him to help Pete. How could he save Pete from himself? If he wanted the shit, he'd get it somewhere else if not from him. It was as if the only ones who needed him were the junkies and others just wanted him to leave.

Al sat there wondering if he had any real friends. He was wondering if all this was worth it, sitting here by himself, talking to himself, and wondering if he was as happy as he thought he was. He questioned if all the fancy furniture, jewelry, clothes, new car, and a six-figure checking account was worth sitting here talking to himself and trying to convince himself he was actually a good guy worthy of consideration. He wondered if the one night stands really made him happy.

Al wasn't sure if any of this was worth selling his soul for.

Doubt entered the room and said hello.

Despair followed.

He threw his wine glass against the wall.

Then he got up, shut out the lights, and went to bed.

ELEVEN

It was nighttime and I was sitting by myself in Jake's Groceries on the corner of P and Fourth having a cup of decaf coffee and playing Keno. There was plenty of action with each game going off on the lottery TV every three minutes. Pick your numbers. Hand off your money. And watch as your numbers didn't come out. Then do it again. Play your numbers. Bet more money. Watch the screen and shake your head. Tough game to walk away winning but why should that deter me or anyone else?

The door opened and in walked Steve Cutler. He walked over to my table and pulled up a chair. "How you hittin' em, my friend," he asked, with that big shit-eating grin that was known throughout Southie.

"How do you think?" I said.

"Betta off just playing Liar's Poker," he said. "Guys got a chance at that game if he's got balls."

"Great advice," I said. "Let me write that down. I'll ask my dad how to play."

"How are the boys doing?" he asked.

"Good," I said.

"TK still bustin' everyone's balls?"

"No way," I said, laughing. "Since when does TK bust balls?"

"Since he was born…"

"You could have a point."

"Tell them I said hello."

"Of course," I said. But that wasn't the truth. I wasn't even going to mention I saw Steve. I'd be better off sending a red flare up in the sky rather than tell my friends I was talking with him. Too many questions I wouldn't want to answer for too many obvious reasons.

"Hey those guys gamble?" he asked.

"No not really. Maybe the daily number once in a while but that's about it."

"That's too bad," he said, under his breath.

Steve was hoping for more fish to reel in. He's been taking bets independently for a long time. He hung in a dingy bar on Boston Street up a mile or so from Andrew Square. He was a loner and liked it that way. TK introduced me to him one day when we were teenagers at the skating rink. TK's cousin and Steve were best friends. Steve was eating a slice of pizza and watching his nephew play in a Bantam game. Pretty sure Southie was hammering Charlestown, an arch foe.

I took an envelope out of my left front shirt pocket and placed it on the table next to me. Steve grabbed a few Keno slips and filled them out. "I'll play these on my way out," he said. "Check them on my laptop when I get home." Then he picked up the envelope and stuffed it into his right coat pocket. "Do I have to count it?" he murmured. "Nope...it's all there." *All fifteen hundred* I reminded myself, wondering if I'd ever learn from the stupidity of my behavior.

"Lots of football and hockey action coming up this weekend," he said, smiling like a car salesman. "You can call me on this number. I got a new cell phone for my preferred customers." He handed me a piece of paper with a number on it. "Don't pass it out to anyone. I'll take care of that. Don't want any deadbeats...who can't pay up when they lose."

He left and a few minutes later I did too. As I was walking

home, I couldn't help but think that I was the deadbeat…a loser wasting time and wasting money. It would have been easier if I simply burnt my money. Or ripped into little pieces and thrown to the wind. Essentially that was what I was doing. Would I ever learn? Could or would I ever change?

I looked at the piece of paper my friendly bookie gave me with his telephone number on it and instead of throwing it away, stuck it in my pants pocket.

TWELVE

It was a Sunday morning. 11 a.m. to be exact. I was making coffee for my dad when the guys showed up at the front door. I grabbed my jacket and gym bag and headed out. "Hey Dad, gonna get a quick workout, see you in a few." As I walked out to meet Sal, Sully, and TK, I got a call from a number I didn't recognize. I let it ring a few times.

"You gonna answer that or what?" TK asked.

"I don't know who this is."

Sully looked at my phone. "It's 617. It's local." Sal said, "I never answer numbers I don't know. Let it go to voicemail." But something in me told me to answer so I did.

"Hey Johnny, it's Okie."

David "Okie" O'Connor worked as a Boston Police Department community liaison officer. We used to play hoop together back in the day. We were on a team named the 'Good Guys' because we thought we were good but really, we sucked.

"Hey man, haven't heard your voice in a while," I said. "I've been meaning to catch up with you."

"Look, I have some really bad news."

My heart sank.

"Lay it on me," I said.

"BPD got a call this morning. Pete's mother found him in the bathroom, needle sticking out of his left arm."

"What?"

"He's gone."

He could've hit me over the head with a sledge hammer. I didn't answer. My anxiety skyrocketed. My thoughts caught in a whirlwind of disbelief. My mouth was dry. Then my world stopped. I closed my eyes. Everything was black. It was a nothingness that allowed me to escape from my worst fears. I was afraid to open them. It was easier not to think of anything while hiding from everything. As I opened my eyes, the words escaped me. "Are you fucking serious?"

The guys looked on with dreaded uncertainty.

"Yeah man, sorry…"

Stunned, I hung up the phone. My legs betrayed me as I collapsed on the front stairs. The guys exchanged glances. Fear was digging a hole in my stomach. TK asked, "What the fuck Johnny, what did Okie say?"

I burst into uncontrollable tears. The same gut-wrenching uneasiness I felt in the pit of my stomach when Tools died began to inflame my insides. The nightmare was repeating itself like a bad rerun on cable TV. I stood up to go, not sure where, but then sat down, at a loss. I started counting silently, five, ten, fifteen, twenty; in an attempt to deflect reality and soften the blow.

I looked at my friends.

"It's Pete."

"He's dead."

THIRTEEN

My mind flashed back to the day Tools was buried. We were entering the Cedar Grove cemetery. I got out of my dad's car and started counting the vehicles in the procession. One, two, three, four, small cars, big cars, SUV's, Toyotas, BMW's, Hyundai's, black, red, white, and gray, a total of 52. I don't know why I do that...count things when I'm upset. But I do and I don't think I'm ever going to stop. Now, Pete was dead. How many cars would I count in that procession?

Feeling guilty about not doing enough can be devastating. Omission eats away at one's inner being. It's relentless. Unforgiving. I don't think any of us really understood where we stood or how we felt at this moment. Now there was another funeral to attend. More tears. More grief accompanied with doubt as to what one could have possibly done to prevent this tragedy, if anything at all. Why didn't Pete and Tools listen and stop playing Russian roulette with their lives? Clearly they just couldn't stop, but I still felt like I failed to help a friend.

Sully's voice startled me. My friends were all looking at me. We were still on the porch, the phone in my hand. They knew I was notorious for zoning out at times so they merely waited for me to dial back into the present.

"We tried at his house," Sully said, still looking directly at me and as if reading my mind. "We tried. We can't blame ourselves."

"Yeah, maybe we can," I said. "Maybe we didn't do as much as we could have. As much as we should have done to help."

"Can't you see," TK interjected. "Pete didn't listen. *They* don't want anyone's help."

"So Pete is a 'they' now hey TK?" I said. "Just a piece of shit junkie not worth saving?"

"You know I didn't mean that," TK answered. "But it was his choice."

"It was his choice at first," I said. "I agree with that. But after a while when you're hooked, it's really no longer a choice. It's a sickness."

My thoughts overtook me. There's little doubt that you lose that freedom of choice when you enter that world because those drugs control your every thought and hardly ever allow you to slip through their deadly grasp. That's what people need to understand. As bystanders we need to feel empathy and not look upon those who use as worthless human beings unworthy of consideration, love, and assistance. Concerned friends and family members need to wonder why and offer solutions for them to travel a different pathway. Need to help not judge. Otherwise the stigma only worsens and no one benefits in the end; only Death.

Then I was awakened by my own voice.

"We need to go to Pete's house," I said. "See the family."

"Maybe we should wait," Sal blurted out. "Give them some time."

"I'm with you. See them at the wake," TK said.

"No way. We'd look like shitheads if we didn't stop by the house," I said. "I think they'd like to see us. Let's go."

We walked to Pete's house and hardly said a word. It was a nasty, depressing day with gray skies. The chill in the air went right through me. It looked like it was going to rain. I knew the guys were as distraught as I was and knew they weren't looking forward to seeing his parents. They didn't need to see us weak and slobbering. We needed to be strong.

Mr. Winkowski answered the door and invited us into the living room where his wife was sitting. We shook his hand, kissed her on the cheek and sat down. They thanked us for stopping by. We told them how sorry we were. They looked awful. A family torn to shreds by despair, desperately searching for answers to questions they knew could never be answered. The silence was suffocating. Mr. Winkowski excused himself and walked into his TV room down the hall. TK picked up a magazine which was on the coffee table. He made believe he was reading but I knew he wasn't. Sully, with tearful eyes, remained silent. Sal looked at each of us over and over again. He seemed to be searching for answers he thought he would discover etched upon our faces. He didn't discover anything, only emptiness. Mrs. Winkowski went into the kitchen and brought back coffee. Several picture albums lay open on the brown leather couch. She started rummaging through them, showing us pictures of Pete playing sports, involved in school activities, and clowning around at family cookouts. We were in some of the pictures. It seemed so long ago, like a different life entirely. Life seemed so fleeting. There was nothing to grasp onto.

Mr. Winkowski returned and sat down beside his wife. She showed him a picture of Pete in his high school hockey uniform. Everyone continued looking at pictures, reminiscing, telling stories about Pete. Mr. Winkowski sat there motionless; his anger building. When Mrs. Winkowski took another picture out, he let out an ungodly scream without warning and grabbed the picture out of her hand and tore it into tiny pieces. "I don't want to see any pictures. I want to see him here...in this room...in front of us."

In one swift motion, he pushed all of Pete's pictures off the table. They went flying everywhere. Coffee spilled on rug. His wife tried to console him but he ignored her, pushing her away. He left the room with his head lowered talking to himself. It was heartbreaking to see Mr. Winkowski break like that. His wife just sat there, embarrassed. She avoided eye contact with all of us. "I'm sorry boys." Before we could tell her not to apologize for anything, we heard a knock on the front door. It was neighbors with trays of food. Mrs. Winkowski let them in and several minutes later, more friends rapped on the door. The house was getting crowded. We were invited to eat but we left, letting others spend time with Pete's family. We walked outside and contemplated what to do next.

And I contemplated life. My thoughts entrapped me. What's the purpose of living? Grief? Disappointment? Shattered lives? Shattered dreams? We exist. We struggle. We suffer and die. Is that all there is for us? I didn't have an answer.

"Hey guys," TK said. "Where was Pam?"

I was wondering where Pam was too. I wanted to ask. I wanted to see her. Tell her how sorry I was and would be there for her every step of the way. Considering Mr. Winkowski's outburst of grief it was best we didn't ask.

"Maybe she was lying down," I said. "Didn't want to talk to anyone."

"I know it sounds selfish," Sal abruptly said, in a barely audible tone. "We shouldn't even be thinking about food, but we hafta eat."

"Yeah whatever he said," TK said. "We do need to eat. It's gonna be a long day."

Sully blurted, "Why didn't we just eat at Pete's then?! There was a ton of food back there? It's free."

"Always classy, you cheap bastard," TK said.

"Let's go to Calo's. I love their meatballs," Sal said.

"Course you do," Sully shot back. "You are a meatball, you meatball!"

"Fuck you, you big, fat corned-beef!" Sal responded, jokingly. "Fuckin potato-head, go drink a million beers, ya muck face Irish-drunk."

"I'm a drunk? Look in the mirror and go drink a gallon of wine, you fucking greaser."

"Greaser?" Sal said, as he gave Sully the finger and they both began to laugh.

With my guys, talking shit was an escape mechanism from anxiety and sorrow. Like me counting. And they were good at it. I knew they were trying to bury their hurt but they needed to bring it down a notch. "Hate to see how you'd treat each other if you were enemies," I said.

We continued walking down L Street towards the café. As I stepped onto East Fourth, I was interrupted from my inner thoughts when Sal grabbed my left arm. "Fuckin' Johnny" Sal said, as I heard tires screech. "Watch it! Wake up for Christ sake! It's a green light!"

I was in the middle of the street, inches from a car that abruptly stopped.

The driver gave me a dirty look and sped off.

TK snickered.

"Ya almost got introduced to the Toyota family…ouch."

FOURTEEN

As usual the café was busy. The tables were filled with families, friends, and kids, most we knew, some we didn't, eating or eagerly waiting for their meals to arrive. They all seemed engaged in carefree conversations they'd forget the moment they left. One young couple was sitting in the front right corner of the café with fixed gazes upon each other, fearful if they blinked all else might be lost. We walked up to the rear of the café and sat down at our table.

Calo turned to us. "Sorry about the bad news." I said, "Thanks." The phone rang. Calo put his finger up to me, saying "one moment." He took the order and yelled to Angela to make three cheese pizzas. He then grabbed a roll from the tray and it disappeared in two bites. He said, "It's such a waste of a young life." Calo looked at us and we nodded. "I'll tell Angela to whip up something good for you guys. You should eat. It's on me."

"Thanks Calo," TK said.

"We just left Pete's house," Sal said. "What have ya heard?"

"He was found dead this morning. It was definitely a heroin overdose. An officer from the new Boston Police Drug OD Unit was there taking an initial report. Pete's mother went outside as the coroner took the body out. She wouldn't leave his side. She was crying. Then she started screaming. Poor woman. Nothing worse than seeing your child die before you do. It's not right. Not what God intended."

Sal blessed himself. I wish I had his faith in the existence of God. Doubt is never easy. Sometimes I feel like I'm walking around blindfolded in a dark room trying to find the door and a way out towards the light. And I'm always hoping to find a way out; to find God.

Unwilling to initiate a controversy about God's intentions I concurred. I had to agree that of all the tragedies in this world, the universal belief, and rightly so, is that nothing compares to a parent losing a child. Mother Nature, or The Universe, or God, or whatever you want to call it doesn't prevent such occurrences. As far as I'm concerned, they could go to Hell. Not a lick of humanity between them.

Calo interrupted my thoughts. "We all have our own lives and our own problems. Sometimes people can't be saved."

Deep down, I knew he was right but couldn't accept it as truth. He took a sip on wine. He asked if I wanted some but I declined. "There's nothing you and your friends can do now except say a few prayers for him and his family," he said. I nodded. Calo said, "I remember my brother, Octavio, lost his son, my godson, Guy, to fucking drugs. Found him dead in a run-down motel off of Route 128. He was with friends but they took off and didn't even call for help. The maid found his body. Octavio and his wife, Maria, went to the grave every single day for three years."

There's nothing sadder than losing a child no matter how it happens. But when it's drugs, there's always that gut-wrenching pain in your mind and heart and those unanswered questions endlessly lingering and tormenting your soul every waking moment. Questions like what could I have done to prevent this? Could those who were with him have saved him? What could they have done? What could anyone have done to save this soul, these souls, from an unnecessary, premature exit from life?

"If I found out someone was with Pete when he OD'd and

86

they left him," TK said. "I'd fuckin' lose it."

"Doubt we'll ever know," I said.

"Maybe Pam knows something," TK said.

"Don't know," I said. "It would help if we could talk to her."

As we continued talking the door opened and six kids walked into the cafe. Calo got up and walked towards the counter to take their order. "Your food will be out in a moment," he said to us.

Sal's patience abandoned him as his stomach growled. "I'm starvin' guys."

Sully couldn't resist. "It's always about the food hey Sal?"

Sal and Sully enjoyed an intense love-hate relationship but Sal wasn't in the mood to take any shit today. "Fuck you." He grumbled and gave Sully a look that would kill an elephant. The mood was set. Now it was time for TK and I to sit there listening to them battling back and forth about food and the Italians versus the Irish. They'd been inseparable since kindergarten but were constantly on each other's cases. They even got in a couple of fistfights in middle school but were best friends the next day.

Minutes later we were given a reprieve when the waitress came out with our food. We knew from experience when food was on the table, Sal never talked. He just ate.

"Watch this," Sully said, in a low-pitched voice as he looked towards Sal. In an instant Sal was nearly finished with his meal. "Need a drink," he said. "Burnt my tongue."

"Course you did," TK said. "You almost started eating it while Angela was putting it on the table." Sully said, "I thought you were gonna take a bite out of her arm." TK said, "You got a problem with food you know that?" Laughter engulfed us and Sal almost choked on his food. He took another sip of wine to clear his throat. Sal always devoured his food while it was still steaming-hot. He didn't let his food cool off even for a second. He always said it was an "Italian thing" and didn't care if he burnt his tongue. As far as he was concerned, it was worth the pain.

I could barely taste what I was eating. My mind was racing along the tracks at full speed searching for order in a disorderly world.

"I'd like to talk to Pam," I said.

I stood up.

"I think I know where she is."

FIFTEEN

We tipped the waitress and left the café. We walked down L Street, along M Street Beach, past the yacht clubs, and up to the entrance of the Lagoon. I never got tired of seeing Castle Island sitting contently across the water.

"Jesus Christ, why are we here? I already jogged the Island earlier today," TK said.

"Just trust me."

We took a right and approached the man-made strip of land that encircles the Lagoon from the rest of Boston Harbor and stretches around to Castle Island. In the middle of the strip is a small patch of land with an open-air enclosure to partially protect people from the elements. It's called *The Sugar Bowl*. People go here to fish or just relax on the benches while enjoying the scenery. Right next to the entrance to the strip leading up to the Sugar Bowl sits a World War II Memorial with far too many names engraved on it. Sal stopped us. "Oh, hold on." TK knew what he was doing, "Seriously? Today you're doing this?"

Today was different. Today we lost a friend. Angst was all around us yet Sal responded differently. He wasn't in a rush, wasn't going to deviate from custom, from his faith. He kneeled in front of the memorial, and as usual, said a prayer in remembrance of his uncles and others who made the ultimate sacrifice. I could only assume he added Pete in his thoughts. We waited. We knew the drill. He seemed to find solace in God, in prayer. "Geez, you finished yet Sal...we'll be fightin' another world war before you get off your knees," TK said. Still kneeling, he looked at TK. "The vets sacrificed their tomorrows so we could continue to enjoy our freedom and way of life today," he said. "Southie never forgets our heroes."

"I know. I know. My uncle served in Nam. Let's just speed it up, will ya?" TK said. Sal blessed himself and got up. "And FYI....God don't like comedians," he said. "He thinks they're classless...rude."

"He told you that?" Sully asked.

"Sure did...I got a pipeline to His office. Talk to Him every week, sometimes several times a week." Sully gave him a look. TK shook his head, laughing on the inside, and then turned to me. "Okay, Sherlock, now that we're here. Can ya tell us what we're doing here?" I looked out to the Bowl, hoping I was right. "I think Pam is out there. It was her favorite place to go when we were kids. I dunno. I just have a feeling she's there." "Good call," Sal murmured.

When we were younger we loved hanging out at the Sugar Bowl. We'd jump over the small wired-fence onto the huge rock walls and throw stones into the water. Fisherman would grumble, saying we were disturbing the fish. They would yell at us to stop. We usually did but then we'd throw seaweed at each other. Other times, we'd sit on the huge rocks that lined the slanted seawall and look up, basking under the inviting sun, appreciating the richness of the beautiful blue sky. We were learning about the different clouds at the time in school and would point out the cirrus clouds and the cumulus nimbus clouds, thinking we were smart. We watched sailboats and motorboats glide along and planes descend towards Logan Airport. We'd look at the tree-filled islands across the bay and wonder what it was like over there. They were mysterious, beautiful to us.

As we inched closer to the Sugar Bowl, random thoughts

about Pam were swirling around in my head. I can still remember her standing at the Sugar Bowl the first time she went with us. In elementary school, Pam and her sidekicks, Dee Modica and Kaleigh McDonough, used to come by and aggravate me and the guys when we were playing hoop in my backyard. One day, when we weren't in the mood for girls hanging around, I told them to get the hell out of my yard. My mom heard me and came out. She didn't have to say anything, her face said it all. They were staying. The girls giggled with confidence. They knew my mom had their back. We tried a new strategy. Sal told them if they stopped bothering us, and just hung in the yard silently doing their own thing, they could go to the Sugar Bowl with us and hang out. They weren't allowed to go to the Sugar Bowl by themselves, so this would be a treat for them.

Pam was so happy at the Sugar Bowl. She enjoyed watching the old-timers reel in the fish but she was crushed when I told her they were going to kill those fish and eat them. One time, Pam was sitting on the sea wall outside of the fence. It was a really hot day; the sun was blaring and the heat unbearable. She stood up and jumped into the water and swam around. "Dee, come in! It's so nice." Dee shook her head. "No I saw a couple of jellyfish earlier. I hate them." Pam kept swimming around, having a blast. "C'mon Dee, have some fun for once." Dee put her shirt over her eyes and sat back, sunbathing. "I don't even think you're supposed to swim out here," she muttered.

When Pam didn't respond for a few seconds, Dee lifted the shirt from her face and saw that Pam was caught in a current. "Dee! Dee!" she yelled. Pam was a decent swimmer, but not a great one. She swam against the current, but stayed stagnant. She started to struggle. She was being pulled toward the locks. If she got caught in those, who knows what could happen. Dee seemed paralyzed, not sure what to do. Pam disappeared from sight. Dee screamed. The boys and I were skipping rocks on the other side. Kaleigh came walking down the runway with some hot dogs and drinks from Sully's. We looked over, concerned. Dee pointed to the water but only mumbled incoherently. We had no idea what was happening, but then we saw Pam's head pop up. She was gasping for breath. I jumped over the fence and ran along the rocks. I jumped into the water, holding on to the nearest rock for stability. I extended my arm. "Take my hand, I promise I won't let go. Take it now." She had no other choice but to trust me. She grabbed my arm and I pulled her in so she could grab onto a nearby rock. The guys came over and pulled us out. We stood up. She promised me she was done swimming in unsafe waters then kissed me on the mouth. I never expected that.

I saw the Sugar Bowl in front of me. I was getting nervous. There were fishermen on the seawall as always. I looked around and didn't see anyone else. Maybe I was wrong. She wasn't here. And then, an image caught my eye. Someone was hunched over on a bench with a wool blanket wrapped around her. That was her. I suddenly realized I had no idea what I was going to say.

Pam's head hung low and her hands covered her face. She looked miserable. It started raining lightly and the sky was getting dark. We walked up to her. "I thought it was going to clear up," I said. She was startled, so lost in her own world, she didn't hear us approaching. "You thought wrong." It took her a moment to realize who it was. "Jesus. It's you Johnny."

"Yeah, it's me."

I looked across the bay and noticed the islands again, surrounded by frigid waters. I hadn't seen them for years. I wondered if journeying there would magically transform our lives and restore our happiness.

But Happiness was laughing at me.

Pam stood up and looked away towards Castle Island. When she turned around, her eyes were heavy with grief. Tears began to slide slowly down her face. Every muscle tightened in her face and she looked like she'd been sentenced to death. She seemed separated from reality.

"He wouldn't listen…now he's dead," she said. "I had to leave my house, couldn't take it. I knew it would be cold out here. I didn't care. I needed to be alone."

"We stopped by your house earlier," Sal said.

"I didn't tell my parents where I went," she said. "How'd you guys know I'd be here?"

"Johnny knew," TK said.

"What are you gonna do Johnny…save me from drowning again?"

She sat down again and burst into tears. We didn't really know what to do. Then, without saying a word, she stood up and walked over to the sea wall. We remained silent for a few minutes then walked over and waited for her to speak. She said, "I can't believe he finally did it to himself."

Pam reached into her pocket and took out a pack of Newports. She lit a cigarette and took a long haul before continuing. "I begged him to stop using. He thought he was fooling everyone but he was only fooling himself. His promises were empty words. Christ, I even brought up the Pact that you guys brought up at the café but he just laughed and told me to calm down."

She started fidgeting with the buttons on her coat. A seagull suddenly landed next to us and started pecking at an old Dunkin Donut's bag on the ground. Sully almost jumped out of his shoes. We laughed nervously yet Pam wasn't amused. I thought she was going to lose it so I put my hand on her shoulder.

"You gonna be alright?"

"I don't know. I tried my best but he was too far gone…couldn't stop."

"Don't blame yourself."

She didn't respond. Her eyes grew heavy with grief. I thought she was going to say something else when Sal interjected, "We should go. Gettin' colder. It's gonna pour soon."

When we arrived back at the World War II Memorial the sky opened up and cried. I told the guys I wanted to talk with Pam for a minute. "We'll catch up to you guys in a bit." They continued walking, walking fast, then ran, as Pam and I found temporary shelter under a nearby tree. Pam needed to hear something reassuring. Her face begged for something to ease her soul.

"Just take it slow."

She looked away.

Recalling my dad's words I said, "Everything will be okay. Time will be your friend."

She nodded, choked up.

"I'll be around if you need me."

"Thanks…can always use a friend."

The heavy rain turned into a drizzle so we started walking again. The dark sky frozen in place. Pam noticed a homeless man hunched over and sitting on the ground near the beach wall. He had a sign placed in front of him. *Hungry Vet needs money to eat.*

"Poor bastard's passed out in the rain." She walked over and put the blanket she had on him. Then she put a twenty-dollar bill in his coffee cup.

I took off my jacket and wrapped it around her.

"C'mon. You need to go home and see your parents."

SIXTEEN

"Where the hell were you?" is what greeted Pam at the front door.

"Stop it," said her mom. Mr. Winkowski's head jerked back. He appeared somewhat apologetic.

"Sorry…just needed to be alone…probably should have stayed home."

The neighbors had left. The house was quiet. Suddenly there was a knock on the door.

Two men were standing outside the door. Mr. Winkowski opened the door and they identified themselves as Boston Police Department detectives. One was Detective James "Jamo" McDevitt. He was a Southie original, had been on the police force for over a decade and was well-known and respected in the neighborhood. McDevitt was street-smart as well as book-smart, two key ingredients for being a good investigator. His partner, Detective Timmy Guiney, was a twenty-year veteran who hailed from the Boston neighborhood of Hyde Park. He was considered a hard ass and not too bright. He wasn't well-liked.

"Sorry to bother you so soon. I'm Detective McDevitt and this is Detective Guiney."

"I know who you are," Mr. Winkowski said. "C'mon in."

"We know an officer was here earlier taking a report," McDevitt said. "We've just been assigned to oversee the new Drug Over-Dose Unit. Moving forward the BPD is gonna respond to all OD cases to try to discover whose selling this poison. Gotta attack this crisis at the core. "

"We're here to ask some questions about Pete," Guiney said.

96

After fifteen minutes of speaking with them in the front living room, Mr. Winkowski's face grew red with frustration as he glared back at the detectives. Being a veteran Boston firefighter, Mr. Winkowski wasn't a big fan of cops in general. "Listen guys, we told you all we know about what happened last night. He overdosed! He's dead! We don't know where he got the drugs! Let's wrap it up! You've asked the same questions ten times for crying out loud. I thought this was supposed to be an interview not an interrogation."

McDevitt stepped in. "Sorry about the incessant questioning. Been a rash of overdoses lately. We're trying to get to the bottom of it." McDevitt stood up and Guiney followed his lead.

"Here's my card," McDevitt said. "If anyone remembers anything that can assist us in this investigation, call me. We'd like to nab the guys selling that shit."

"Thanks for your time," Guiney added. "Sorry for your loss."

"Next time, don't be afraid to wait until after the body is in the fucking ground," Mr. Winkowski said.

The detectives left. Mr. Winkowski slammed the door. "Fuckin' cops," he whispered to himself.

Mrs. Winkowski gave Pam a hug. "I'll go get you some tea."

When I arrived home my mom was watching TV. She loved mysteries on PBS and those mushy holiday stories on the Lifetime Channel that lasted about five hours. She stood up and gave me a big hug. She knew I needed one. My dad was taking a nap in the sun room.

"I'm so sorry. What a sin! It's so awful," my mom blurted out, holding back tears.

"Why can't we stop this from happening over and over again?" I asked.

"God knows we've tried," she replied.

"And where is God when all this is going on?"

"You have to have faith…never doubt Him."

I looked at her hoping she could make all the pain go away. I knew that was impossible. I was too old now, too pessimistic to trust in something I couldn't touch. She hugged me again and said, "You need to be tough. Like the saying, tough times don't last, but tough people do."

"Tough times don't last?" I repeated. "Sure seems like that's all there is. I don't feel tough."

My mother wasn't about to give up. She was stubborn and had faith in God and Mankind's ability to move forward with steadfast optimism embracing the belief that better times are inevitable.

"Like a storm. It blows over and the sun comes out?"

"Sometimes it seems like I'll never see the sun again."

"Faith is always ready to open your eyes."

My mother's words sank in sharply, like a submarine penetrating the ocean's surface submerging to unseen depths. I needed something to grasp onto so that I could 'believe' that better days were on the horizon. I wanted to see the sun shining once again. I sat down and told her Pam just called me to tell me the police were at her house. Apparently they're investigating a string of overdoses. "Wow, cops in his house. That must have been quite the scene."

My mom knew Pam's dad since they were kids and understood his reluctance to deal with the cops. He had a few minor scuffles with the law when he was a teenager but it was the cops who were subsequently found overstepping their boundaries. Those altercations almost cost him the opportunity to qualify as a firefighter later in life, but luckily he was in the right. Regardless, he never forgave the force for their few rotten apples.

I sat for a few moments, silent. My mom knew I was drowning and once again attempted to put me at ease.

"Can't undo what's been done no matter how many times you wish it to be otherwise."

"I know but it just doesn't seem real. I feel like I let him down."

"All I can say to you is we need to get through this, be there for his family. I once read, 'The world is many-sided in its lessons and these lessons, if rightly learned, all sustain and complement each other.'"

I kissed my mom. "Gonna go upstairs and read for a bit," I said. "See you in the morning."

I never forgot that passage. Maybe we do go through hard times because it teaches us exactly what we need to know at that moment? But how were my lessons many-sided? What did I need to know? What do I have to learn because all I felt was loss and guilt? These questions would always haunt me.

SEVENTEEN

We knew Pete's wake would be painful for us and insufferable for his family so we met in front of the funeral parlor at 4 p.m. and walked inside together. We thought it would be easier that way. It wasn't. It was a beautiful day. It just didn't seem right. As a diversion I counted the steps walking up to the front door and reminded myself to be strong. I've done it countless times before. Not sure when my habit of counting started. For instance, Southie High has fourteen steps and The Golden Stairs, fifty five. This funeral parlor has ten. Numbers are definite. Numbers are logical. Numbers are a welcome distraction.

I walked into O'Brien's Funeral Home. The beauty of it all took me aback. The shiny silver casket, the beautiful bouquets of red and white flowers, the bright lights throughout the room, the spotless floor and polished furniture, sat in stark juxtaposition to the mood of the place. I almost felt guilty absorbing so much beauty during such a terrible moment. On the nearby oak mantelpiece was a collage of pictures. Pete in his Holy Communion suit standing outside the Gate of Heaven Church with his parents. Pete with his family on vacation at Old Silver Beach down the Cape. Pete scoring his first goal as a mighty mite in the South Boston Youth Hockey League at the Murphy Rink and proudly high-fiving his dad after the game. Pete smiling broadly on stage at his graduation. Each picture fondly remembered telling a story not easily forgotten.

I knelt down and looked at Pete. I thought to myself he didn't just kill himself. He destroyed a part of his family and friends and now he was another statistic. Another short obit in the papers for a few days, then forgotten by most people after they pause briefly to pray for him. It's as if the dead didn't exist in the first place. Life goes on as usual. What's the point? Death and pure wasted potential united. Pete was gone from us, our world, and as far as I was concerned, lost forever in oblivion.

What could I say to the family to truly ease the pain? Nothing really when you think about it. The condolences of friends are welcomed but our presence a sad reminder that we're alive and their son was dead.

Inside the casket, on the white interior linen next to his left shoulder was a crucifix of Jesus, a picture of Pete in his high school hockey uniform, and a pack of new baseball cards wrapped tightly inside clear plastic. He collected them throughout the years and always told us to back off when we teased him about it. He was wearing a clean, white shirt and a dark blue tie. Funny, I thought. Pete hated ties. Never saw him wear one his entire life. He was sort of a slob who really didn't pay much attention to what he was wearing. I recalled Pam giving him that "I can't believe you're wearing that" look on more than a few occasions.

I wanted to hug Pete. Wake him up. He didn't seem dead only sleeping peacefully. But I knew I couldn't. I knew he wouldn't wake up no matter how hard I tried. I said goodbye, softly touched his right shoulder, hoping as many prescribe, that I'd see him again one glorious day on the other side. I stood up, turned abruptly to my left and almost knocked over Pam.

Unable to speak, I just hugged her and cried. I didn't want to let go. "I'm so sorry," I said, in a low voice barely able to speak. "So sorry." "I know you are," she said. "You were a good friend.

Everyone knows that." I held her hand and kissed her on the cheek. Then walked away with a broken heart.

I don't know what happens after our time on earth is up. My thoughts change from day to day. Maybe nothingness. Perhaps a reunion with those we knew and loved who left this earth before us. I don't know, I want to believe but don't have a good feeling about it. I can only conclude right now that it's beyond my comprehension. I've been labeled as a non-believer. I could never buy into the theory that after we die, we go to Heaven or Hell, or perhaps have a short stay in Purgatory. Honestly, when all the soul-searching is done, when all the what-ifs are pondered, deep down inside I believe, at this point in my life, that once we are dead we are dead, from dust to dust, and that's the ballgame. Sort of blows your mind dismissing the idea of life after death but if you delve deep enough it may eventually alter your views placing belief on your doorsteps.

Everyone wants to be immortal. Nobody wants to die. All religions promise an afterlife to keep Hope alive in the minds of the people. During the Middle-Ages, the church promised people Heaven after Earth, that is, if they gave their money to the church. Life was short and miserable so people were only too happy, after experiencing such misery in life, to take the chance for a shot at happiness in Heaven. Death was only the beginning. We would all be reborn.

The supreme question concerning the existence of God has always been on the lips of Mankind. Did God create Man or did Man create God? For centuries, Man fought and killed without reservation in the name of their right and just God, defending their actions by declaring that their God was the only true God.

But, would an omniscient and omnipresent God let this happen? Would He allow this to happen over and over again? I didn't think so.

So I thought that maybe if we took the good in every religion and pieced them together, maybe we could end up with one pure religion, a true one, the One Religion for Man which would end misery in His name and on Humanity's behalf. And peace and happiness would follow.

But none of this, I didn't think, would bring Pete back to us.

The next day the funeral procession took a slow detour to Castle Island before going onto the expressway to Pete's final destination at the Cedar Grove cemetery in Dorchester. Just like I did at Tool's funeral, I counted the cars that passed in the procession. There were forty-eight. At the graveyard, Father Joe blessed the casket and exclaimed the wonders of the afterlife. He reminded us that someday we'd be reunited with those we grieved. Obviously, none of it made me feel any better. I felt the presence of Death. It was as if he were sitting right next to me. Ironically, I felt his heartbeat. It was terrifying.

Afterwards we went to the local VFW Post, ate and gulped down several drinks. Pam was in the corner sitting with her mom and dad, her head hung low. When I got a chance to talk to Mr. Winkowski, I took a deep breath, gathered my courage, and told him that I loved Pete like a brother. We all did.

"I know you did. You got a good group of guys. Good friends since you were running around the playgrounds with snots stuck under your noses." He forced a laugh and so did I. He took a sip of coffee and waited a beat before talking. "Pete was his own worst enemy. We knew it. I don't think we did enough. We were hoping things would eventually work out for him. I guess you could say we enabled him."

Mr. Winkowski felt like he didn't do enough? I knew the feeling…

"We always told him we'd do whatever it took to help. But he said he could do it himself. He'd be good for months. Everything would be fine and we figured he'd be okay. We were wrong. We'd notice erratic behavior. We knew deep within our hearts he was using again. Things went missing like jewelry and money. We didn't tell anyone, not even Pam."

Instead of summoning up tough love and throwing him out on the street, which isn't the greatest alternative either, Pete's family tried their best to help him fight his addiction.

"You did what you thought was the right thing to do for your son."

"Pete thought I hated him because he gave up on hockey. But he was wrong. Sure. I was disappointed but he was my son and I loved him. He just couldn't accept that. I don't know why."

He gulped down the rest of his coffee and then without another word got up, patted me twice on my left shoulder and walked towards his wife's table.

EIGHTEEN

After leaving the VFW Post we went to Calo's Café. We continued drinking and talking about Pete. That's what you do when someone dies. You eat, drink, and reminisce. We were getting pretty good at it. Also, we were getting pretty drunk.

One story which touched us centered on Pete when he stole the spotlight, which he often did, during a high school hockey game. Sully said to Sal, "Remember when he scored the winning goal against Xaverian in the championships and recruits came up to him? The first thing he did was introduce them to you, telling them to recruit you. That's the type of person he was."

"But Pete changed and you guys know it. It's been a long time since high school," TK said. "Let's not picture him as a boy scout for Christ's sake. You guys are acting like he just started messing around with drugs yesterday. He was doin' it behind our back for years and we all knew it."

"We've all done some stupid shit we regretted the next day," I said, looking at everyone.

"It's not like we didn't cross the line a few times ourselves," Sal said.

"Some crazy nights for sure," Sully said.

"Yeah we were lucky, we backed away," Sal interjected. "But we never stuck a needle in our arms. Never went that far…thank God. And I do thank Him quite a bit for watchin' over us."

"Save that for Sunday Mass will ya?" TK said. "Christ, I saw Pete a few mornings all coked up looking for downers but never told you guys. He didn't even try to hide it from me. He asked me if I wanted a bump. He didn't know when to stop."

"Great, so now you tell us," Sal said.

"C'mon, like I said…he wasn't a newcomer to the game," TK fired back. "When you're getting high it's usually not a secret! Eventually he secretly gave up on himself and just didn't give a fuck."

"What are you his post-mortem psychoanalyst?" I asked, pissed that our conversation was a moot point anyway. "Fuckin' Johnny, give me a break," TK said. "And ya can't say it was about him not making it in the big leagues. Blaming his dad is a cop out and you guys know it. So don't try to feed me that shit because I'm not eatin' it."

"You're a heartless bastard sometimes ya know that," I said.

"You guys are so naïve," TK said. "You act as if Pete was the only person in the world who had a dream."

Perhaps we were naïve. TK had a dream once. He learned how to fight, and I mean really fight after he got his ass kicked a few times by the boys from D Street. He worked out at Joe's Gym on West Broadway with a local trainer named Jimmy "Jimbo" Curtis. TK worked hard seven days a week and made it to the Golden Gloves Nationals in the middle weight division. He hammered his opponent in the championship fight. He fought five pro fights and won all of them. And he was only twenty two. He was being touted as a possible championship contender but a nagging knee injury abruptly ended his days in the ring.

We sat in silence for a few minutes then Sully piped in, "And Al was always there, happy to supply Pete with the poison."

That's all TK needed to hear to start his engine roaring. He opened fire. "He's going to get his. Our lives would be different if he never existed in the first place."

"Yeah, a lot more people would be alive too," Sully said.

"Guys calm down for fuck sake," Sal said, looking around nervously at the other customers in the café. It was packed. He leaned in, talking in a low voice, "Johnny, can you talk some sense into these guys? This ain't the place to talk about Al. Nowhere is really."

"No one fucks with Al and gets away with it," Sully said, stabbing his food with his fork.

"Why not, there's always a first time for everything!" TK exclaimed, refusing to back down.

"You guys remember the Durgin brothers who tried to cut into his turf," Sal mentioned, hoping to drill some sense into them. "The cops found Jeremy dead from an alleged overdose in an apartment at Old Colony, and supposedly James took off for Miami yet strangely nobody's heard from him in over two years. Who knows the real story behind that one?"

"So, what are we supposed to do, sit back and let things happen over and fuckin' over again," TK said.

Sal brought up the Durgin brothers to make a point. It backfired on him, only fueling TK's anger machine. The game was on the TV so I changed the subject and talked about the poor officiating in the NBA. I realized TK was ignoring me and slowly burning up with hatred. With each beer he drank, the quieter he became. I was just happy he wasn't ranting. We all had our share of listening to TK rant about this or that. No doubt he was a hothead and had been since he was a kid. One time playing youth hockey he was hit from behind. He got up, ripped the kid's helmet off and hit him over the head with his stick. He was suspended for the season. Another time, in high school, Rocco DeMatteo, stole his girlfriend. TK was pissed, took his belt off,

107

strolled up to Rocco in the schoolyard, and cracked him in the face with it several times. It was an ugly scene. Bloody. He was suspended from school for ten days.

The basketball game went to commercial and TK broke his silence. "One of these days I'm gonna punch Al in the fuckin' face."

NINETEEN

A week after the funeral, I met Pam for coffee. I picked her up, drove down to the Lagoon, and parked along the strip. The sun was shining brightly on the water. Pam seemed distant and preoccupied. She didn't have any make-up on. Her hair, somewhat unkempt, was pulled back. She was wearing an old jacket and jeans and appeared uncharacteristically disheveled. She looked exhausted. Defeated. She sipped on her coffee and nibbled on the blueberry muffin I bought for her from Joseph's Bakery. I could tell she didn't have much of an appetite.

"They're the best muffins in Southie but I like their 'fat-free' Danish pastries," I said, jokingly.

Pam tried to laugh but couldn't. "Fat-free my ass," she said. "They're about a thousand calories."

"But they're delicious."

"They should be...they're a thousand calories."

Relief momentarily surfaced as Pam smiled but sadness didn't entirely take leave of her.

"What was it like in New York? Meet anyone there?"

"No. Not really. Met a few young ladies but wasn't ready to settle down."

"Why?"

"Too young to die," I said, laughing. Then I realized what I said. "Sorry. Pretty stupid huh?"

She took my hand. "Johnny, I'll have to admit. That's probably one of the first times in your life you did say somethin' stupid but don't worry about it."

"Thanks."

"Just don't let it happen again."

We laughed simultaneously as if air was coming out of a tire to relieve unwanted pressure. We finished our coffees and then walked out to the Sugar Bowl. We arrived at the Sugar Bowl and sat on a bench. Pam momentarily looked up to the sky as a plane passed overhead. She took out a cigarette and I lit it for her. She took a puff then exhaled it in the other direction. She knew I hated cigarette smoke. In the distance a cruise ship could be seen behind the castle heading out to sea. Another plane flew overhead towards the airport. Then another. Unbelievable how many pass by in a short span of time. We sat silently looking at the people walk and jog past us. Some were riding bikes and rollerblading. One teenager on rollerblades fell down and banged his head. He was lucky. He was okay but we had the feeling next time he'd wear a helmet. We even saw a dog-sitter with six dogs jogging by. We laughed again.

"I just wish Pete could've been stronger...I really miss him," Pam said. I didn't know what to say, so I said the first thing that came to mind.

"Hey, why don't we take a ride out to Cedar Grove?" I asked. "Can be there in ten minutes."

She nodded and we returned to the car and drove to Dorchester. She didn't say a single word on the way. I didn't put on the radio. When we got to Pete's gravestone, which had fresh flowers and several small American flags in front of it, Pam stopped several feet away, and for a few minutes, stood motionless like an ageless Greek statue. I didn't say a word and waited for her to speak. With great effort, she finally approached and put her hands on top of his gravestone. Tears flowed freely down her face. I noticed one fall on the flowers. It was an oddly

110

beautiful moment. She reached out in search for my hand. I held it tightly.

"I've dreamt about Pete dying. I'd see him sitting in that bathroom over and over and over again. Sticking that needle in his arm and thinking he was gonna have the high of his lifetime…yet not realizing that this was it. That it was all over. That he'd never wake up. Then I wake up, shudder, and think it was only a silly nightmare. Then I realize it's for real. I close my eyes again hoping everything will change. But nothing changes. It never does. It never will."

After that there was only silence as Pam stared at the gravestone. Then she bent down and picked up a red flower. She softly kissed it and then placed it on top of his gravestone. Suddenly, and without warning, she fell to her knees and started clawing at the ground. Dirt and grass was flying to the left and right of her.

"This wasn't the way it was supposed to end," she screamed. "This shouldn't have happened to him! This can't be real." I wanted to grab a hold of her, help calm her down. But then I realized whatever she was going through, she needed to go through it. She screamed an ungodly scream. She clawed some more at the dirt and finally collapsed on the ground.

I knelt down beside her for a few moments. Finally, I grabbed a handful of dirt and grass. I placed it in Pam's hand. "Here, take this and put in down right there," I said, pointing right in front of Pete's gravestone. Then I scooped up two more small piles of dirt mixed with grass and gave it to her to spread on the ground. Pam ran her fingers gently through the earth then began patting the ground in front of her as if she was rubbing someone's back. "Pete's here and glad you came," I said. "He's at peace now with himself." She didn't answer just continued caressing the ground as if searching for answers to her grief.

I gently picked her up, and once again, tears streamed down her face. She wiped them away, looked at me. She tried to smile, couldn't. Her eyes grew empty with pain. Then a sudden calmness engulfed her and she said, "Time to go. Don't have any more tears for today."

We drove home. I parked the car in front of her house. She randomly asked, "You ever watch "Changers" on the Syfy Channel?" Puzzled, I replied, "No, not really, I—"

"The Changers are people who have special abilities. One of them, Tina, this hot cougar lady, curly red hair, can *push you*, using her mental powers along with verbal commands to make you do or say things you wouldn't normally do. It's kinda like mind control. I could have changed Pete and he would have stopped taking drugs."

"I'd like to be able to do that," I said.

"She can also make you forget! I wish she'd do that to me. Just forget with a simple voice command or the snap of a finger – imagine? But I guess that's only science fiction."

"Yeah, unfortunately life's not as obliging."

"Would it be right though? To erase feelings or past events and still be whole?"

I didn't have a good answer but felt I had to say something.

"I really don't know if that's possible. If we could it would certainly help a lot of people. But that's not gonna happen unless you know a good hypnotist. We can only try to forget and move forward."

Pam wasn't overly receptive to my lame response. "Remind me not to sit on your couch for any counseling sessions," she said. Then she laughed. At least I got her to laugh again even though it was surrounded by Sadness. But at least it was a good start. One step at a time.

She continued, "I was hoping against hope he would stop, but it doesn't matter now." She turned her head and looked out the car window.

Pete was no longer the kid we knew growing up. Drugs had taken control of his life. He was consumed with the high. Nothing else mattered. She hoped he'd change but that opportunity was gone just like Pete, never to be given another chance at life.

"Why blame yourself?" I asked.

"He was my only brother...I should've done more."

"You didn't stick the needle in his arm."

She didn't answer. I didn't know if I was trying to convince Pam or myself whether or not anyone should feel guilty concerning the behavior of others. I knew I wrestled with doubt every day yet wanted to free her from the prison she found herself locked within.

Darkness surrounded Pam. As she was about to get out of the car she leaned over and kissed me on the cheek. "Thanks Johnny."

"Wait, let me get the door."

"Wow, chivalry isn't dead after all."

I opened the door and I watched her walk up the stairs. She turned abruptly, meekly waved, and vanished behind the heavy, brown exterior door. As she shut the front door, I realized I tried to stay strong for her and was holding back my own feelings of hurt and loss. Suddenly, a wave of emotion struck me. Dazed, I sat uncomfortably in the car, still parked in front of her house. I felt alone. I didn't want to move. I just wanted to sit and feel it. Then I cried until I could no longer clearly think why I was crying in the first place.

TWENTY

I arrived at the Café at 8:00 p.m. The place was crowded. The clock still hanging in the corner crooked as hell. Someday I was going to mention that to Calo. I sat down with the guys. They were drinking red wine, eating baked haddock and watching the Celtics playing the Knicks in New York. I ordered veal parmigiana with a side of pasta and a salad.

Two men walked into the café and ordered three large pizzas. We had never seen them before. Must be yuppies. When they left, Calo sat with us and quietly said, "Little light on the loafers don't you think?"

"Who cares," Sal said. "Are all you old guys homophobic?"

"Hey, won't be long when some wise ass – someone younger than you - busts your balls. Like my dear mother used to say, 'Don't spit in the wind cuz it will hit you in the face.' Don't forget I told you that."

"Words of wisdom from an old Italian goat?" TK said, under his breath. We laughed. Calo didn't. He said, "What? Ya gonna defend those twinkle toes? I'm telling you, homosexuality is a disease." We looked around, not sure what to say. I chimed in. "You're too old school man."

"I'm just telling the truth. Ah, whatever. Sometimes I can't talk to you guys. Even TK's too liberal for me. But I can tell you one thing. I can't deny there's nothing like a good lesbian. That's not homosexuality, that's okay." With that ridiculous statement, Sal laughed uncontrollably. I could tell Sully was trying to think of some stupid joke to say. It wasn't a joke but he didn't disappoint us. "What are you talking about? Lesbians and homosexuals is the same thing, aren't they?" Sully asked.

As if he knew what he was talking about, Calo shot back, "No, they're not!"

"Sure you're right," Sal said, with a fake laugh.

"You're insane you know that?" TK said. "Ya gotta be shittin' me?"

"You fuckin' guys…you guys call me crazy. Homosexuality is banned in Russia and a bunch of other countries that know better. It's a sickness. It ain't natural."

"That's highly debatable," I interjected. "Homosexual activity occurs in a variety of species with a lot of animals. So even if you think it's an aberration in nature, there are many aberrations in nature, and that doesn't mean it's a sickness. Perhaps aberrations in nature are the norm, an integral part, and actually not an aberration at all. There's nothing wrong with that!"

"Who are we to judge?" Sal asked.

"Judge. Smudge. It's gross. Makes me sick."

"Calo…you're a religious man," Sal said. "Didn't God make all of us?"

"God didn't make *them*."

"Hold on," TK said. "There isn't anyone in this café or in Southie who doesn't have a friend or family member who is gay. So who gives a fuck? Live and let live as long as they don't try to shove their lifestyle down our throats. I'm alright with that."

TK always surprised me when I didn't expect it but I couldn't just sit there and listen to Calo's rubbish. Like my mom always told me, everything happens for a reason and it happened that one of the halftime stories featured a Celtics forward. His image appeared on the TV screen.

"Hey, Calo, isn't James Smyth one of your favorite NBA players?"

"Yeah, he's having a great year. Great trade for the Celts. Why?"

"That's funny. Do you know why?"

"No I don't."

"He came out yesterday."

"What are you talkin' about?" Calo asked.

TK roared. "Breaking news last night, he announced he's gay. Came out of the skin closet."

I smiled. Calo stared, speechless. His facial response, priceless. In that moment, he represented Old Southie to me. Old America too. Old beliefs, old prejudices.

Every town has older people who are firmly entrenched in their own bias. It sits beside them on their couches. It goes out with them when they take walks. And it will keep them company until the day Death knocks on their door.

Sully couldn't resist. "Hey TK. Skin closet? That's a new one. Maybe I can figure out a joke about that."

In unison everyone told him to shut up.

Politely that is.

"Hey I got a good one," Sully said, undeterred. "How do you make a hot dog stand?"

"Don't know. We give up," I said.

"You take away its chair."

No one laughed.

"Your jokes are terrible, Sully," Sal said.

TK said, "They get worse every time."

As soon as TK's last few words found air, the door of the café opened and in walked Pat and Jaws. They were carrying duffle bags filled with goodies for their clientele.

"Homeboy network right on time," Sully said.

"What ya got in the bag?" Sal asked Pat.

"Yeah, it's nice to see you too!"

"Oh…sorry… should've given you a big kiss."

"Damn right you should've," Pat said. All the guys laughed.

Jaws interjected, "Let me show ya what we got." He dug into his bags like Santa Claus.

Suddenly I drifted back to an unforgettable experience. Once, after a morning hockey game, back when Jaws was still an amateur thief, he asked me to go shopping with him. I went, not realizing his hobby. He asked me to go downtown to the clothing stores. When I saw him snatch a bunch of shirts, I started to worry. What the fuck did I get myself into? Walking out the front door I was sweating bullets. Suddenly I felt a tap on my shoulder. My heart literally stopped.

"Excuse me, sir." I turned around and saw the salesperson. I thought I was in for it. "You dropped this." She showed me my wallet. I took it, exhaled a thank you, and walked away. Once we got outside Jaws couldn't stop laughing, "Man you should've seen your face! You didn't even steal anything! You looked like you were gonna faint. Whatdaya think we wus toast?" When we sat down on the bus he shook his head, roared, and asked why I doubted him. I didn't answer and wiped the sweat from my forehead. He laughed again. It was my last excursion of that nature with that crazed thief.

Jaw's sales pitch woke me from my thoughts. "North Face spring jackets man, worth $240 in the store. See, price tags right on them. Give em' to ya for eighty bucks each."

"I'll give you fifty bucks," Sal blurted out. "That's a good deal."

"Sorry man, no fuckin' way. I know I can get sixty to eighty at the bar," Jaws said.

TK asked, "What size are they?"

"XL's," he said.

"Any smalls?"

"Next week."

"Save me one for my sister!"

"I will."

TK took another look at the jackets. "If you don't get any buyers across the street, come on back. I'll buy an XL."

"Me too," Sal piped in.

"Okay, but let me show you this bad boy before we leave." Jaws dug into his inside coat pocket and produced a small, black, velvety box. He carefully opened it as if he was handling a precious little baby. "Look at this. It's a Cartier watch worth 15k. She's a beauty. I snapped it up in New Hampshire yesterday. It was worth the trip. Security was everywhere but we were too slick for them. It was like Mission Impossible."

"Wow, you got big kahunas," Sully said.

Jaw said, "I call it *Balls of Courage.*"

Everyone laughed.

Pat and Jaws looked at each other and smiled. They made a great team. They spend their time preying upon the Braintree Mall and other locations, stealing suits, coats, leather jackets, pants, dress shirts and whatever they can get their hands on. They cleverly remove electronic price tags, put the soon-to-be stolen merchandise in army duffle-bags then strut out of the store as if they own the place. They go into fancy stores on Newbury or surrounding streets in Boston and steal expensive sunglasses or wine. They could steal five or six expensive bottles of wine without being noticed or snatch several pairs of expensive sunglasses at a time. They do all of this without fear or hesitation, remaining cool and calm while walking out without being detected. It's as if they are invisible. The key they said, was relaxing your heart rate. Keeping it as low as possible. If you could do that under pressure, you could do anything.

Obviously no one had the cash to buy that watch so Pat took out three bottles of red wine and put them on the table. "Got them last night," he said. "Primo fucking wine for the boys."

"I'll be the judge of that," Calo said.

"See the price. Eight hundred apiece," Jaws said. "It was a good year."

"Jesus, eight hundred bucks for a bottle of wine? Who can afford that?" Sully asked.

"How much for all three?" TK asked.

"Need at least three hundred apiece," Pat said. "That's a good deal. Ya know stealing wine isn't easy. Gotta be a pro ya know. But for us sometimes it's totally ridiculous."

"How do you do it?" Sully asked.

"Easy," Pat said. "You target a busy store with only one or two people working and when there's a bunch of customers buying shit you go in. I work with a partner, usually Jaws, sometimes others. We usually take turns to keep our skills fresh. Ya know what I mean."

"Yeah we certainly do," TK said.

"I'll make a few slick statements about certain wines and then ask the worker to show me his best merchandise and then ask questions. Meanwhile my partner drifts away and does his thing. You can stick a couple of bottles of wine down your pants or inside your coat in an instant then walk calmly out of the store. Haven't got caught yet."

"You sure got balls...balls of courage like Jaws said. I gotta remember that one," Sully said.

"Hey you guys should teach a course and make even more money. Call it Hot Wine 101," TK said. "Be a big fuckin' hit. Your American dream."

"Hmm," Pat uttered.

"You can think about that later," Calo said. "Let's take a closer look at the wine."

Calo, the wine connoisseur that he was, put his reading glasses on to take a closer look. "Nah, too much, overpriced, give ya six hundred for them."

"C'mon, no way, you can't be serious," Pat said.

"That's a fair price."

"Are you crazy?" Pat responded. "I don't know about Jaws but I was born at night but not last night."

Jaws playfully punched Pat on his arm.

As usual, Calo enjoyed chiseling any junkie down. "Okay...I'll give you seven hundred."

"Ya killing us dude," Pat said.

"Always Jewing us down, hey Calo," Jaws replied.

"Nothin' personal."

"We can get more across the street but we came here first. We take care of you guys and you take care of us. That's the way it goes," Jaws said. "So....what's your price?" Calo asked. "Hold on one sec," Pat said. Pat and Jaws took turns whispering to each other. Pat said, "Eight hundred, two packs of smokes... two slices of pizza...and two cokes."

"Seven-fifty. And you pay for the food."

Pat and Jaws exchanged glances then nodded. Calo grinned. The deal was complete. Calo winked at us. Mission accomplished. He could always count on any junkie selling their expensive merchandise cheap. They need to get fucked up so they're willing to sell their wares for practically nothing.

Sal said, "Hey, we'll split the bottles and drink one right now. Give them the smokes and food and put it on my bill."

"Forget about that. I'm not making them pay for the food. Just giving them a hard time."

"Hey…a personal discount," Sully said.

We laughed.

Even Pat and Jaws smiled.

I felt a little guilty seeing my friends support their drug habit but everyone likes to take advantage of a "good deal cheap." Even though everyone in Southie knew they used the money to buy drugs, it wasn't their concern. They rationalized that if they didn't buy the stolen items, someone else would. It was a faulty premise yet conveniently placated those who harbored the tiniest remorse. Funny thing is; the thievery in itself didn't bother me or anyone else it seemed. My thoughts were interrupted. "Johnny, you want a glass?" I declined, but Calo said nonsense, and poured me one anyway. I took a sip. It was the best wine I ever had.

They must have noticed the expression on our faces. Pat said, "Like Jaws said it was a good year for that wine." Calo gave two thumbs up.

TK was impressed. "How do you two clowns know so much about wine?" Pat chuckled. "We're practically sommeliers, bitches. Study online every chance we get."

Pat and Jaws ate their slices of pizza in five seconds. And as soon as Pat got the money, Jaws gave him the high sign. "We gotta go guys," Pat said. "Gonna sell those jackets. Time to make more money."

They walked across the street and into the Hub Bar. Pat got a phone call and went back outside to get better reception. Jaws stood at the bar. He noticed Kaleigh McDonough who was drinking vodka straight up. She loved to drink and it was starting to show. The drugs didn't help either. She was another example of how promises aren't meant to be kept since she was also part of the Pact. She looked much older than she was. And it was too bad because she was beautiful in a specifically Irish way. Her red hair was dry at the ends and her eyes had tired, dark bags under them. She appeared distraught, completely consumed in thought. Jaws would change that.

"Hey young lady, how ya been?" Jaws asked.

"Just looking…need a fix. Know anyone holdin'?"

"Nice to see you too," he said.

She put her arms around him and gave him a big hug. "Sorry, forgot you were the sensitive type."

"That's betta Kaleigh."

Her mind was only on one thing though. "So…what's happening?"

"There's Oxy floating around for eighty-dollars a pop. Some young burnouts down at Andrew Square are making a killin' I've heard."

"I could use some percs can't afford OC's anymore."

"I know the feelin'," Jaws said.

She looked away. She was anxious to score and had to keep moving. She finished her drink.

"Okay. Well. See ya later big guy."

"Yeah take care," he said. "Hey...wait a minute. Maybe I can help out. Might have a few percs floating around. I've got a couple of 'reserve bags' stashed away for moments like this."

"Oh yeah, what moment is that?"

"I get you high, buy you as many drinks as you like and we have some fun."

He didn't have to say anything else. She understood. He could see her mind racing a mile a minute. Acting like she was an innocent school child, she declared, "I've never done that before."

"Always a first time for everything."

"Hmm. I tell you what. I'll give you a hand job and that's it. I'm not puttin' my mouth on your dirty dick."

"Hey. Hey. It's big not dirty. You're gonna like it."

She punched him lightly on his right arm. "You're gonna like it not me. Let's go, asshole."

"We'll see who likes it," he said. "We'll see..."

TWENTY-ONE

Thanks to all the yuppies and the booming business, most of the Southie bars have been recently renovated. The Hub Bar was our spot. A few years ago, it was a hole in the wall, dingy and uninviting. Now it had big screen TV's, modern décor, and revamped menus. Entering the bar we automatically, from habit, headed toward the far end. The place was packed but there were empty seats available in the corner. We never really talked to anyone else so we sat down there.

Robbie Fallon, a local guy who's a fixture at the Hub, walked out of the men's room. Sal had previously filled me in on a few of the boys, and Robbie was one of them. Life was good to Robbie when he was younger. He got married and worked as a Union laborer but injuries found him on workmen's comp. He got hooked on Percocet and started drinking vodka for breakfast. His wife had had enough so she moved to East Boston, aka Eastie, with their daughter to live with her mom.

"Hi guys, how ya hittin' em?" he said, slurring his words.

"Good, all's well," Sal said. "Good to see you, Robbie."

Hoping to change his luck, Robbie grabbed some lottery slips and limped back to his seat. He was drinking more than ever and certainly eating too many painkillers.

I stopped to say hello.

"Jesus, Johnny. How the hell are ya?"

"I'm fine," I said. "Are you okay?"

"Yeah why?"

"Just asking."

"What are you the newly ordained neighborhood

Samaritan?"

"Just concerned that's all."

"Thanks, but I'm okay. Couldn't be betta."

I silently accepted that rationalization.

He looked rough.

Robbie measured his life in a twenty-four hour period. Ironically I guess that's where the AA quote originated, 'one day at a time.' He'd wake up every morning and have a cup of coffee and then take two percs for the pain and two alprazolam for anxiety. After watching TV every morning he'd journey on down to the Hub Bar for a few beers and more pills. Lunch was usually a small sandwich from Paul's Sub Shop, which is directly across the street from the bar. Calo's Café is on the other side. After a short respite back home he'd revisit his medicine cabinet and conclude his day with yet another trip to the bar. Robbie drank every chance he got. It was like a bad dream that he could never wake from because it was his life. Passing out was the best. No dreams, just blackness. No sound, just silence. No pain, just emptiness.

He was caught in the throes of déjà vu. He wanted to change. He wanted to wake up one morning and start anew. He'd throw his pill stash down the toilet. No more pills. He'd stop going to the bar every day. No more booze. He wouldn't feel crappy in the morning or depressed in the evening. Life would be good and he could smile once again. Maybe have a rapprochement with his wife and see his girl again. Yet that morning never came. I could see it in Robbie's eyes that he understood his predicament but didn't know how to fight against it to end his cycle of despair. He was lost and resigned to his fate. I felt the urge to scream but what good would it do? I felt the urge to tell him to smarten the fuck up. But who am I?

"Hey Johnny. Sorry. I was being a dick," Robbie said.

"No problem."

"Let me buy you a beer."

"Sure. I'll take a Heineken if you don't mind."

"You gamble at all Johnny?"

"I do once in a while."

"I'm playing Keno," Robbie said. "You wanna give it a shot?"

I knew that was my cue to leave but I didn't. I filled out a slip and put a c-note on one number, number 11. Joey Westfield, a big, lanky Lithuanian was behind the bar. I handed him the slip and the money. "High roller, hey Johnny," he said. "Wow, that's bigtime. I usually play a buck or five bucks a game," Robbie blurted out. I played four more games and lost all five games along with five hundred dollars. Joey gave me a free beer. "Hey guys," I said. "Do me a favor and keep this to yourselves. Don't want to listen to my friends busting my balls."

My mind flashed back to my time in New York. I was sleeping and the doorbell rang at 2 a.m. I didn't know who the hell it could be, possibly a co-worker needing a place to crash for the night. I looked through the peephole and saw Jason Finn, my friendly bookmaker. I let him in. I had been ducking him for two weeks and owed him three grand after two dismal weekends betting on NFL games.

"Johnny. Johnny," he said. "Listen. When you win I pay up…and when you lose you pay up. Right? That's the way it works. You know that."

"Been meaning to stop by the bar to pay you."

"Well, I'll take a check right now. I'm not fussy. I know

127

you're good for it."

I handed him the check and said to myself I'd never gamble again.

My thoughts returned to the present and I walked back to my friends. I was pissed. I had that sick feeling in the pit of my stomach. Déjà vu smacking me right in the face. Never again is such an empty promise to oneself. Joey shot me a sympathetic glance. Five hundred down the toilet bowl. I grimaced, unnoticed. I took a deep breath and silently counted to twenty.

Sully turned to Joey. "Hey, what's the score of the game?" He said, "The Celts are up by twenty. Bradley's having one of those games. The Knicks suck and so don't the Jets."

"Yeah, I hate New York, fuck New York," Sully said. "Did ya hear this old one? Why do ducks fly over Yankee Stadium upside down?"

"I don't know, tell us," TK said.

"Because there's nothin' worth crappin' on."

Sully never told any original jokes. Thank God. They probably would've been even worse than the shitty ones he stole from others off the internet.

"I don't really hate the Yankees," Sal said. "Don't want them to win, but don't hate them like I hate the Jets."

I said, "Everyone in New England hates the Jets.

"No shit," TK said.

"We all hate New York, we always have, yada, yada, yada," Sal said, bored with the conversation.

"And we all hate Sully's jokes too," TK said.

Sully ignored him. He said, "So what else is new in Beantown?"

TK had a look of disgust on his face. He said, "I don't know about Boston, but in Southie there's always something new. New condos, new bars, new people. Everything's new. Out with the old and in with the new."

I said, "You can't stop change."

"You're always playing the good guy," TK blurted out.

Sully laughed. He said, "That's our Johnny."

Sal changed the subject. "Your turn to buy you cheap Irishman," he said to me.

"Hey meatball. Don't be afraid to reach into your pockets once in a while," Sully shot back.

"Fuck you...you Irish mother-fucker, call me meatball one more time and see what happens." Sal looked at all of us, "Fuckin' TK, Sully, Mac... What is it with you Irish guys? You all have corny nicknames. Big D, Anvil Head, Wacko, Neezo, Fitzy, Okie, Obie, Dee-Man, Bubba, Spunky, Lal, Monka, Flabo, Edso, BoBo, Bouggie. It never ends."

"Fuck you," said Sully. "What do the Italians got for nicknames? Fuckin meatball, meatball, meatball..."

"Keep the shit up, Sully, and you're not coming to Ma's house for dinner on Sunday. You never turn down a meatball there."

"Okay, I'm done," Sully said. Everyone laughed. Sal got him. Sully looked to us. "What? I love her cooking."

We laughed again and I was about to order a round when TK grabbed my arm. We followed his glance and saw Al walk in with his boys, Joey and Ryan Murphy.

My thoughts zeroed in on Al. He wasn't a good person. When we were young, we hung with him. We tolerated him but we really never trusted or respected him. TK never trusted him. He saw his dark side, hidden behind his façade, only leaking out in whispers, low voices.

Even as a kid, Al was a bully. We were at Little League practice once. A boy from Savin Hill, the neighboring community, had just joined the team. Al didn't like that. He told the kid, and bragged later about it, that if he showed up for another practice, he was going to follow him home, kick his ass, and throw a firecracker down his pants. We never saw that kid again.

Sal had updated me on Al. Al spent a few semesters at UMass, Boston; lost interest and dropped out. After that, he saw an opportunity to sell drugs and consciously chose it. He filled the void of the old guard drug-dealers who were either dead, in Florida hiding from the law, or eating three square meals in federal prison. Al's motivation to join the drug game wasn't financial. He didn't need the cash. His mother made big bucks working downtown in finance and his father owned real estate all over Southie. It was about power, pure and simple.

Several minutes later, Pat and Jaws entered the bar. Dee, Kaleigh, and, to my delight, Pam, were behind them. Pat and Jaws went right over to Al and the gang. Pam said something to Dee and walked towards us. Dee and Kaleigh stayed with their guys.

Pat and Dee had been dating off and on for a few years and had a child named Patrick. They had that classic love-hate relationship. They were junkie buddies and occasionally she'd go out with Jaws and Pat when they went shopping. That is, five-finger discount shopping. Kaleigh and Jaws were relatively new news.

TK said, "Perfect way to fuck up a night."

No, the perfect way to fuck up a night is to lose five hundred, I thought.

It didn't take Al long to open up for business. He passed Pat a small plastic package. TK's eyes almost popped out of his sockets. 'What the fuck' he said to himself. Then he looked at Sal. "Stuff has to change around here before more people die," TK said. "What do you mean, *stuff*?" Sal asked. Exasperated, TK said, "Open your fuckin' eyes. Al just handed Pat some dope."

"Let's just watch the hoop game, fuck 'em all," Sully said.

Sal wanted to ease the tension. Settle TK down. He turned to the bartender and said, "Hey you big lug, we'll have another round of beers over here. And Pam will have a Chardonnay. TK's buying."

"Watch it…I'll big lug ya with a bear hug and a right hook," Joey responded. "Or I just might shut you off."

Playfully busting his chops, Sully said, "Hurry up with those beers before I complain to the owner. You don't want to lose out on any tips."

"You're a funny guy," he shot back. "You guys think Tipping is a city in China."

"Who's the comedian now?" TK responded, forcing a smile.

"You and Sully gotta stop stealin' other people's jokes," Sal said.

"Yeah, no kiddin'," Pam said. She looked like a million bucks. She was wearing tight jeans, a beige blouse, and a brown leather jacket. I noticed my heart beating faster.

Although Pam was right next to me I subtly turned my attention to the other end of the bar. I couldn't stop watching them. I noticed Al and Dee exchange cold glances. She was irritated.

Dee was fried. She had the look. It's impossible to disguise the look. White-skinned, sunken, glazed eyes devoid of liveliness accompanied with a scary, disconnected stare of a person lost from the moment, lost from reality and seemingly imprisoned a thousand miles away. She stood there silently for a few minutes, fidgeting with her IPhone, ignoring everyone. Her thoughts brought her back to that fateful night, that ugly night years ago when she was drunk and found herself with Al in a hotel room in Dorchester. Al took out his kit and showed Dee his works. "You're gonna like this," he said. "Best high ever."

Dee hesitated but not for long. That was about all she remembered about that night. She wasn't even sure if he gave her a roofie before she arrived at the room because she was so banged out. After that night, she played the game on the surface but deep inside hated Al for what he did. What he started. How he changed her life.

Al was facing the door. I assume so he could see everyone coming in and going out, sort of a modus operandi commonly followed by drug-dealers and other low-life types. His boys were right next to him. Although Al was tough and could handle himself, he was smart enough to have reliable back-up. Golden Glove champions and feared throughout Southie the Murphy brothers were his muscle and go-to boys when trouble arose.

It didn't take long for Al to notice me. "Hey Johnny! I thought that was you? Johnny Mac… I'll drink to that." He took a sip of whiskey. I nodded in his direction, and took another gulp of beer, hoping that was the end of it. He called to me again, "Hey Johnny, c'mon down…let me buy you a drink." TK was bullshit. Sal momentarily sidetracked him to avoid a confrontation. He told him Paul Pierce was better than Larry Bird. TK's expression changed in a heartbeat. He loved Bird and thought no one could touch him. "O boy," Sully said. "Here comes the Paul Pierce-Larry Bird debate again." TK said, "Pierce couldn't wear Bird's jock strap!" "Yeah right," said Sal. The debate was on.

Al persisted. "Hey Johnny," he said, loudly. "Don't be a stranger. Your boys will be okay for a few minutes without you." TK wasn't amused. He turned to me. "Tell our local drug dealer he's a great guy," he said, a little too loud. "And while you're at it, ask him how Pete and Tools are doing." This angered Pam. TK murmured, "Sorry."

As I approached Al, I put on a fake smile and told him I was drinking Heineken. He shouted the length of the bar to Joey, "Hey. Get my man his usual. And give everyone else whatever they're having."

"Thanks," Kaleigh said. "I'll have Merlot."

Dee said, "I'll have what she's drinking. Black out Friday am I right?!"

The bartender knew what everyone else was drinking. I said, "Hi Dee, how you doing?"

"Good, thanks." She smiled and gave me a big hug, a kiss, and surprisingly a pinch on my ass. Dee's flirtations didn't seem to bother Pat. He just smiled.

Kaleigh said, "Dee, you're an animal."

"What are you jealous?" Dee asked.

I had had enough of their small talk. I looked at Al. He put his hand on my shoulder and said, "Long time no see."

"That's for sure."

"How you doin' Johnny?"

"No complaints here."

"I just got into the real estate game thanks to my Dad. Just bought a few properties."

"Good for you."

"Well thanks. Lotta people in Southie don't like to see people doing better than them. It's a Southie curse."

"I think Southie is cursed in different ways."

Al laughed. "So what are ya doin' these days to keep busy?"

"Was thinking about writing for *South Boston Gazette* but started teaching again."

"No shit," he said. "That's too bad. You could've written an article about me. *'Southie's next real estate baron.'*"

"Oh I'm sure you'll end up in the papers one way or another."

And there it was, the defining moment when I decided I wouldn't play nice with him. I think I caught him off guard. Al pulled at his shirt collar. A nervous reaction I presumed.

"Okay but just say the word if you need to make some more money," he said. "Could use your intellectual talents for something."

The last thing I wanted to be was allied with Al. Although I enjoyed it, I grew tired of this disingenuous exchange. "Thanks for the beer," I said. "Good to see you."

I walked away, realized how hot it was inside the crowded bar, and asked Pam to join me outside. She nodded and said, "It's about that time to light up."

I held the door for Pam and we went outside. The song "When Irish Eyes Are Smiling" came rushing out of the jukebox but the music faded as the door closed shut. It was cold and beginning to rain, the kind of raw, chilly night New Englanders were accustomed to throughout their lives. The moon was nowhere to be found and the only light reflecting off of Pam's beautiful face emanated from the newly installed corner

134

streetlight. I had time to gather my thoughts as she lit up a smoke. I looked away distracted by a taxi speeding through the nearby red light. I looked at her. She knew what I was thinking. She took a long haul of her cigarette, a classic delay tactic. I didn't want to say anything, wanted her to speak first. A few minutes went by that felt like eternity. She took several more drags then finally spoke. "My father told me a funny story about him getting caught with cigarettes when he was a kid. 'Member when they had mom and pop stores? Families had cuffs. His corner store was on N and Sixth. One day he cuffed a loaf of Wonder Bread, a great misdirect, and a pack of cigarettes."

"Clever," I said.

"Yeah, he thought he was slick. But his plan unraveled when my grandfather stopped by and cuffed milk and cigarettes. Mrs. Moore innocently noted that his son was in the store earlier. The rest was easy to figure out. He was busted. As punishment, my granddad made my dad smoke a whole pack. He turned as green as an apple after three." Pam laughed, "I wish my dad did that to me. Wouldn't be chained to these things…"

She threw her cigarette butt on the ground and stepped on it. "Maybe that should be the last cigarette you step on," I said. "Wishful thinking," she said.

Wishful thinking about a lot of things I thought to myself.

I said, "I'm glad you're here."

"Me too," Pam said. She gave me a quick hug.

"By the way what's going on with Dec and Kaleigh? "I asked. "They're all messed up."

"Those two have been messed up on and off for years," Pam said. "You just haven't seen them much lately. Don't forget you were in school and then in New York, kiddo. One week Dee's fine...she looks okay. Then another week, forget it. Same with Kaleigh. They're "BDFF"s-best druggie friends forever."

I wondered if I'd go through life asking ad infinitum, ad nauseam why people-my friends-were hooked on drugs and destroying their lives. I wondered if heartache, abuse, and untimely death would ever cease and happiness prevail. "Better way to live than that," I said, my heart throbbing with disbelief as to what life had drawn for me on that blank canvas. The rain intensified and the wind picked up. "It's getting cold," Pam said. She shivered. "Gonna go back inside."

We went back inside and as we walked past Al and his entourage, he called my name. I stopped. He leaned towards me and whispered. "Beautiful girl. You got taste."

Pam intuitively kept on walking towards the guys.

TWENTY-TWO

Old Man Winter officially arrived. It was freezing outside and people were huddled inside their warm apartments. The latest snowstorm had dropped over a foot of snow on the local landscape two days ago. People weren't thrilled with Nature's latest antics. TK stopped by his dad's house before going to the L Street Bathhouse for a workout. He dropped off the paper to his dad and had a quick cup of coffee. His father opened the newspaper right away and turned to the obituaries, aka the 'Irish Funnies' - hoping he didn't know anyone listed today. While drinking their coffee, the topic turned to Mother Nature and inevitably parking spaces now that winter was firmly back in town and snow had fallen. Finding parking spaces in Southie had become a daily challenge, to say the least, and the problem was exacerbated every time snow fell, leaving fewer places to park. This angered many Southie residents to the point of utter frustration.

The Southie tradition was that you shoveled out your own spot and you owned it for a few days. People placed various personal objects - old chairs, cones, buckets, boxes - anything to easily identify that it was your spot. No one is supposed to remove those objects and then park his own vehicle in that spot. It's an unwritten rule in Southie. If violated, people took matters into their own hands and sometimes it got ugly. Just recently, an older man was assaulted by a young punk on East Eighth. The old timer took umbrage when the guy parked in his spot after he spent two hours shoveling it out. The old timer argued his point and ended up in the emergency room.

TK was sitting in the living room and looking out the window when he saw a guy, unmistakably a yuppie, in his late twenties pull up to his sister's parking "spot" she and her dad had painstakingly shoveled out in the numbing cold. His sister, Alanna, left for work earlier and put her cone out. The guy looked around and then threw the cone aside, parked his car, and dashed inside his condo. TK couldn't believe his eyes.

"See what that yuppie did?" TK asked his dad. "Can you believe that? That arrogant fuck."

"Uh...Uh...you know my rule."

Indeed TK did. TK never heard his dad swear nor did he ever see him drink. His dad wasn't overly religious but always made it a point that swearing and drinking in his household was forbidden. He simply followed this rule in honor of his deceased wife, Margaret, who couldn't stand it either. The boys loved it when TK's mom chased him around the house after he let a bad word, as she called it, slip out. TK would run into his bedroom and hide under his bed. She'd force him out with her trusty broom and then whack him on the butt with it.

"Sorry," TK said, in a huff.

"Calm down," his dad said.

"See what I mean about these people?"

"Relax."

"They know the deal."

"Don't start any trouble."

TK paced around the room.

"You won't find him anyway. He could be living in any one of those condos," his dad said.

"Like those faceless condos, these faceless yuppies don't give a fu—a crap about tradition, only about themselves," TK opined.

138

"They might as well live in the projects living in those buildings they call condos. What a joke. The only thing missing is the cockroaches."

"Don't get all riled up, can't do anything about it now."

"Yeah, maybe you're right."

His dad excused himself and headed to the bathroom. TK snuck into the kitchen, grabbed a gallon of water and a dozen eggs. He went outside and poured the water on the front windshield and back window. It practically froze in mid-air. After that, he smashed the eggs all over the windows. He considered it a masterpiece. "Have fun cleaning that off," he yelled towards the building. "Next time you'll think twice before pulling that shit." Then he looked towards the house and saw his dad standing at the window. At first his father didn't know whether to approve or disapprove of his son's antics. TK looked to his dad, who waved for him to leave. He shut the curtain so his son wouldn't see him smiling.

TK poured the last of the water on the car for good measure.

Nobody was going to mess with him or his family.

TK walked into the L Street Bathhouse. We were working out in the gym.

"What are you smilin' about?" Sully asked, looking at TK.

"Ah, just taught a yuppie a history lesson."

"I can only imagine," Sal piped in.

"Yeah, last time he'll park in someone else's spot. Gotta respect that or suffer the consequences."

"*What did you do?*" I asked.

"I'm gonna take the fifth on that."

"Betcha you told him this is how's it's done in 'Southie' not in 'SoBo' as they like to call our town," Sully said.

"No comment," TK added, with a sly grin. "Hey, I think I'll go punch the bag for a bit. Don't leave town without me."

Half hour later TK walked back into the main gym. We had just finished our workouts. I looked out the gym window towards the beach. The sun peeked out from behind the clouds, like an innocent child. White, simmering rays of sunlight rippled across the surface of the clear, cold water. In the distance, three lifelong Southie guys, naked from head to toe, ran down to the water's edge. Part of a group known as the *Southie Brownies*, they're die-hard guys who love taking plunges into the frigid ocean during the winter. I guess it relieves stress, invigorates the body and soul. It's a refreshing experience, free of charge, which helps them face the day. Some people think they're crazy. Many wouldn't have the nerve to do what they do but they swear by it. I got cold just looking at them. They bent over, sprinkled water on their faces, and then ran into the water and disappeared under the small waves. They swam around for several minutes, stood up, dove in again, and then returned to their towels.

Sully turned to me. "Hey, are ya finally gonna take a dip today?"

"Yeah, are ya, punk-ass pussy boy?" TK added.

"I'd rather jump off of a three-decker. I'll stick with watching you crazy bastards turn blue, pretending you actually enjoy this foolish rite of passage. Making believe so you can say you're Southie through and through."

"What's wrong with being a Southie Brownie?" Sal asked. "Lots of people enjoy it."

"It's tradition," TK said.

140

"When you gonna join and start going in every freakin' freezin' day like a *real* Brownie," I asked. "One or two winter swims a year doesn't make you a brownie. I'd love to see you freeze your balls off."

"Speaking of balls," Sully butted in. "Why don't you jump in and show some yourself?"

"No thanks. I'll take a pass. Leave the fun to you crazy fucks."

"Well," Sal said. "If TK and Sully can do it, anyone can. I need to get the cobwebs out from last night anyway. Too much booze. Should jolt me back to reality."

Once on the beach, Sal, Sully and TK, along with several die-hard Southie Brownies, ran into the frigid water. The regulars dunked and remained immersed in the uninviting water for several minutes. TK, Sal, Sully hurriedly ran back onto the shore and grabbed their towels.

"Boy," Sal shouted. "Boy. That's fuckin' cold."

"Nah," TK said. "Piece of cake."

I said, "Really, so how come you ran right out?"

"Fuck you. Watch and learn."

TK ran back headlong into the water. We watched and waited as he re-surfaced. He turned, laughed, and then waved as he dove under the surface again. Sal put his hands up in surrender. "It doesn't bother him 'cause he doesn't have a heart."

We all laughed as we watched TK swim about.

"TK's the man," Sully said.

"Right," Sal said. "Why don't you go smoke some weed and kiss his ass?"

"That reminds me," Sully said. "Didya hear the joke about the..."

I refused to let Sully finish. "I've had enough of this. I'm freezin' out here. And I'm the only one with clothes on."

TWENTY-THREE

It was a Sunday evening and Billy "Big Kane" Kane, TK's uncle, was in Murray's Market, a nearby corner store, ready to buy his lottery tickets for the week. He enjoyed playing the lottery hoping beyond hope that someday he'd hit it big and take care of family and friends. He was careful and never spent beyond his means, never spent too much that he'd regret doing afterwards. I wish I could have maintained such control of my finances without gambling them away but my impulsiveness disallowed it. On more than one occasion I rationalized it by thinking that it was the last time I'd be so stupid, so foolish; so repetitive in nature and I'd recuperate. No harm, no foul...another day would come and the losses would fade from memory. Pick up the pieces and make believe everything was okay.

Yet it wasn't.

Why was there such a void in my life?

I didn't have an answer.

Big Kane filled out his new slips on a nearby countertop and walked over to place his bets. Optimism was beside him ever ready to prod him on. "How ya hitting them tonight?" Sean Murray inquired. He was the owner of the store and also an ex-marine.

"I'm doin' good," Big Kane said, always positive.

"You feelin' lucky hey," Sean asked. "Course. Luck of the Irish."

"Getting ready for the parade?"

"Yup can't wait."

"It will be here before we know it. Time flies for sure."

Pride flashed across Big Kane's face. "Gonna be my twenty-fifth year marching and rumors have it that I'm going to be selected by the parade committee to be the Grand Marshall."

"That would be somethin' hey. You deserve it for all you've done for the vets in Southie."

"Thanks. I only do it because they deserve to be treated fairly and get the benefits to help them in civilian life. Somebody's got help them the fuckin' government isn't."

"It's shameful how the politicians turn their backs on us when we need them. Glad you're fighting for us."

"I don't need any pats on the back."

"Ya know I'd like to kick you in the ass for being so humble."

Murray was a big son-of-a bitch. Big Kane readily acknowledged his disadvantage with a smile. "Jesus, I wouldn't survive that."

"Not to worry," Murray replied smiling. "I got your back."

"Take care. I'll see you later in the week," Big Kane said, putting his lottery tickets in his front pants' pocket for safe-keeping. "I hope you have enough money to pay me off tomorrow," he said, leaving the store. "For you of course," Murray said. "Semper Fi."

"Semper Fi indeed," Big Kane said.

"Be safe. See you soon," Murray said.

"Big Kane" as he was respectfully called, was sixty-six years old. Aside from his two stints in Vietnam, he lived in Southie his entire life. His left leg was smashed up during a fire fight when his patrol was caught in a jungle ambush. When he returned to the states he walked with a cane.

Big Kane walked out of the store. He always played his

144

lottery numbers no matter what the weather brought. Tonight it was snowing. It was cold. He was tired, sore, his war injury always a painful reminder of the past. He took a shortcut into M Street Park and was near the basketball courts when he suddenly heard a voice call out to him from behind, seemingly out of nowhere. "Hey mister, got a few bucks you can spare?"

Big Kane turned around and was struck in the head. He fell to the ground. The assailant hit him three more times with a golf club. Blood was everywhere. The snow turned red. Big Kane lay motionless. The cops happened to be driving by the park. The park lights were on and they saw a body on the ground with someone hovering over it. They got out of their cruiser. "Hey you," yelled one of the officers. The culprit looked up and started running. They nabbed him at the top of the park and arrested him. Boston EMS brought Big Kane to the Boston Medical Center. He never regained consciousness.

TK called me later that night. "Hey Johnny," he said, his voice disconcerting. "Everything all right?" I asked.

"My uncle's dead."

"Jesus. What happened?"

"What do ya think happened? Fuckin' junkie killed him in the park looking for an easy buck to get high."

"Jesus. Sorry. How's everyone?"

"My sister's sorta okay…but my Dad…I don't know what to say to him."

"They were close," I said.

TK welled up.

"Can ya do me a favor?"

"Shoot."

"I'm gonna stay at my dad's house. Call the guys and tell

145

them. I can't talk about it right now."

"Sure. We'll see you tomorrow."

TK hung up. I called the boys then sat down on my bed. It was close to midnight. I closed my eyes. I counted to one hundred. I wanted to go outside and scream to the Heavens. What a shame, a distinguished United States Marine war hero, who survived Hell in Vietnam, only to be beaten to death in his own neighborhood. I wonder what thoughts crossed his mind during those final moments.

I could still see Big Kane sitting in the park watching us play basketball. He'd watch and smile, occasionally shouting out a few hoop tips. He knew the game and played on the Southie High varsity squad. When he was leaving, he'd always walk by us when we were standing on the sidelines taking a break between games. He'd laugh and say, "Hey you knuckleheads, spread out, one grenade will get all youse guys." We'd laugh. He'd smile again, salute us as customary, and raise his cane in the air as if signifying victory. And all was right in the world.

Monday morning the story was all over the city's two major newspapers and being talked about in every kitchen in Southie. Eamon Duffy was the one arrested. He was seventeen and well-known in the neighborhood. He was a local junkie. He was from a good family but good families don't always produce good kids. Unfortunately it's beyond their control.

Later that day I went to TK's house with Sal and Sully. We conveyed our sympathies to his dad and sister then sat with TK in the living room. "Not gonna be a wake," TK said. "Only a Mass at Gate of Heaven. Burial services at the Bourne military cemetery on Cape Cod are gonna be private." As he was

146

conveying these details, he was calm, but soon afterwards became angry. "Duffy's a fucking bum," he said. "He's already overdosed four times. They brought him back to life using Narcan. Should've left him for dead and my uncle would still be alive."

The details of this heinous crime were the daily topic of conversation. Duffy confessed. He didn't have a choice, he was caught red-handed. He admitted he was messed up and needed money to buy drugs. He said he attacked Big Kane, grabbed his cane and hit him with it. He told the cops Big Kane started yelling for help. He said he just wanted to keep him quiet and didn't mean to kill him. He caved his skull in with repeated blows. But he was so messed up after the fact he still didn't realize he killed Big Kane with a golf club and not the cane.

According to media and neighborhood rumors, Duffy initially refused to roll over on his drug sources, but was reminded he was facing a murder charge. He started talking. Supposedly, right before the incident, and using an untraceable, burner cellphone, he contacted someone named Finbar from 'Dirty Dot.' Dirty Dot was one nickname for Dorchester, a section of the city that borders on Southie. Duffy planned on meeting him at Jerry's Bar on Dorchester Avenue near Town Field. The cops had Duffy call him several times but he didn't answer. Finbar must have been tipped off. That's if there ever was a Finbar. Rumors were floating around the community that the police weren't buying. Would Duffy now be willing to cut a deal and roll over on Al, his real supplier?

Southie residents were saddened by Big Kane's death. And they were worried. Who would be the next victim of some strung-out druggie looking for a quick way to make a buck?

Would it be your uncle, your mother, son or daughter?

Tragedy struck again sooner than we ever imagined. Less than two weeks after Big Kane's death, a young, single woman named Tina DeMarco was murdered in her apartment on East Second. Within three days of the incident the cops had their murderer. Her neighbor, Jason O'Keefe, confessed. O'Keefe was unemployed. He took Tina's garbage out and occasionally helped with the shoveling after snowstorms. He lived with his elderly mother and never bothered anyone. Tina knew him for about five years. She knew he had a drug problem but he was polite to her and she was kind to him. She trusted him and didn't see him as a threat, just a kid with a problem.

Desperate for money to buy a bag, O'Keefe told police he broke the lock on her back door. He thought she was working. Unfortunately she took a vacation day and was home. He said he knew she kept money hidden in the kitchen because one day he saw her put money in a bowl and place it inside one of the cabinets. O'Keefe said she came into the kitchen unexpectedly. She must have heard him rummaging through her cabinets. He said she screamed and then yelled at him. He admitted he panicked and picked up the crowbar he used to snap the lock and smashed her on the head. According to police reports, she died instantaneously.

Crime hadn't been this bad since Michael "Mad Dog" McCarthy presided over Southie's clandestine drug culture in the eighties. When he was finally charged, he fled Boston, avoiding prosecution. He was christened public enemy number one by the FBI. For over a decade he escaped the tentacles of the law. But people didn't buy it. We could blast rockets into outer space but couldn't nab Mad Dog? Nobody said anything. Skepticism hid behind closed doors. As time would tell, he was in bed with the Feds. He finally made a mistake while visiting friends in Las Vegas one weekend last May. He was found, not by the feigned diligence of the FBI, but by the keen eye of a lowly city cop. Now Mad Dog is waiting in prison to face his accusers and ultimately answer to God.

How much worse were things going to get now? Was Al our generation's Mad Dog? Drug-fueled murders started happening one after another. A jealous boyfriend, all strung out, beat his girlfriend to death with a tire iron because she wanted to leave him and start anew. He left her body inside their apartment. She was found by her daughter three days later. Another incident ended in a woman being burnt to death in her apartment over a drug deal gone south. A homeless junkie stalked and murdered a yuppie one day who was on his way home from work.

People in Southie didn't feel safe anymore, not walking around in their own neighborhood, not even in their own homes. Residents no longer had the luxury of conveniently dismissing the obvious. The collective consciousness of the community wouldn't allow it. It was official; Southie had a major drug problem which wasn't going away tomorrow because it didn't start yesterday.

It was time to act.

TWENTY-FOUR

The Tynan Community Center school cafeteria was buzzing as people streamed in and took a seat. People were standing in the back and upstairs on the balcony. The politicians and law enforcement representatives were seated up front.

"Good evening," Representative Mike Conroy said into the microphone. "We'd like to thank you for coming and we'd like to start in a few minutes. I'm Representative Mike Conroy. We have a few speakers who will discuss what they plan to do and then we'll be open to a question-and-answer portion of the meeting to close it out."

Representative Conroy gave Boston District City Councilor Bobby Lane the mike. "Hi everyone," he said. "For those of you who don't know me, I'm Councilor Bobby Lane." He turned to the front table. "I'd like to introduce everyone sitting here. We have Congressman Stanley Lewis, Senator Dianne Forbes, City Councilor Steve Murray who sits on the public safety committee, John McNabb from the South Boston Drug Rehabilitation Center, Boston Police Superintendent Bernard McLain, Captain John Garfield from BPD C-6, and Drug Enforcement Agency special agent, Jonathan Cross. We'd appreciate it if you listen now, don't interrupt the speakers and you can ask questions afterwards. Thank you."

Councilor Lane passed the mike to Congressman Lewis. "Thank you everyone for being here," he said. "My heart goes out to the families of those who lost loved ones. These are indeed dark days in South Boston. Drugs affect everyone and we know no one is safe. We have to be vigilant. Aware of our surroundings. We are going to use all the resources at hand to keep everyone safe," he said. "We are going after the drug dealers and hunting down their sellers on the streets. I've called in the DEA to collaborate with the BPD. John McNabb from the center will be working with Senator Forbes and city officials to secure more money for his rehab facility. We have to attack this epidemic on all fronts. But we also need your help. If you see or hear anything, please contact the police. You can call the station or just leave your information on the BPD's anonymous drug hot line. Together, we will win this battle. Thank you."

Superintendent McLain spoke next.

"We've assigned more uniforms in Southie to conduct what has long been touted as 'community policing,'" he said. "Instead of seeing faceless officers drive by in police cars, we've got boots on the ground, walking around the neighborhood and interacting with the residents. Additional undercover drug-unit officers have already been re-assigned to the day shift to nab street-level addicts and suppliers."

Agent Jonathan Cross was the next to speak.

"Hi everyone," he said. "Glad to be here in Boston but of course not under these circumstances. Congressman Lewis asked if we could help out and we are going to use all of our resources to tackle this drug problem and keep folks safe. We'll be working with the BPD undercover units in Southie to gather Intel to build cases against those involved in dealing drugs. I arrived yesterday so I'm eager to start. Thank You."

Councilor Lane took the mike and opened up the meeting to questions and answers. There was a mike in the middle of the center aisle for the residents to use.

"I'm John Darcy. This is for the BPD. I live near M Street

Park where Billy Kane was attacked. What measures have you implemented to keep our parks safe?"

"We've increased patrols at all the parks in Southie," said Captain Garfield. "We have additional manpower starting as early as tomorrow so we'll have officers actually stationed within the parks to monitor activity and rapidly respond to any situations that might arise."

"Hi, I'm Joanne Doherty. I've know people who have tried to get their kids into rehab but there ain't no beds anywhere in Southie. Or anywhere else for that matter."

"John," said Councilor Lane. "Could you answer that question?"

"We know there's a shortage and I'm working with our city and state officials to secure more funding for additional beds," McNabb said. "We are hoping more money will be allocated soon. I know it's frustrating for people. It's very frustrating for us too."

An older woman, a Southie lifer named Maggie O'Keefe grabbed hold of the mike. She was a classic Mouthy from Southie woman. We knew this wasn't going to be the short version.

"Why can't we talk about the good things that are going on in our community? We are so giving. We have fundraisers all the time. A family loses a dad unexpectedly or a child is sick, we all rise to the occasion and lend support. Always willing to help others… BUT people don't want to read about that. It's too boring and un-newsworthy. The city papers focus on sensationalism and rarely spotlight good stories. Why write about people who are generous to others? Can't make Southie look good. Heaven forbid they shed any positive light on our community. They love going to our beaches and using our boulevards for everything from strolling along to running road races. It's a place they hate to love and love to hate."

The room erupted. People cheered and clapped their hands.

"That's true," Councilor Lane responded. "And your question?"

"That's all I got to say about that!"

Again, cheers reverberated from one end of the room to the other.

"Okay let's get back on track. Next question please."

"I'm Kathy and live near Andrew Square. I don't see any police presence around the square and there are plenty of dope deals being made there every day for cryin' out loud."

"We have undercover drug units there," said Captain Garfield. "We are compiling a list and taking photos in a nearby police undercover vehicle. We'll strike soon. I can promise you that."

A little old lady shuffled up to the mike.

"I've lived in Southie my entire life. I live next to the Old Colony projects. I'm afraid to go out of my house. See drug deals or something happenin' in broad daylight. Never see any police doin' anythin.'"

"Ma'm," Captain Garfield said. "After the meeting please see me. Like to get some more info and we'll take care of it."

"Well you betta not say things you don't mean. Sick of empty promises especially from the politicians. Most times they don't even call me back."

Everyone roared in approval.

She struck a nerve.

People were fed up with inaction.

"Yeah, we get lip service and then after everyone goes home, everything's back to the same old crap," a man yelled out from the back of the hall.

People cheered again.

"He's right. We need to know we can be safe in our own neighborhood," said a lady sitting down at the front of the cafeteria.

Representative Conroy stood up. He was handed one of the mikes.

"Ladies and gentlemen. We know people are worried. I've lived in this community my entire life and like you, I don't like what's going on. But we will prevail. We will work with the police, the courts, the rehab people, and with YOU to make sure Southie is safe and people feel safe walking in the streets, the parks, and while in their homes. If anyone needs our contact numbers, please come up to the main table. Thank you for…"

"Hold on," said a local guy from the rear of the room. "I've got something to say."

"Okay, one more question," Representative Conroy said. The man walked up and Conroy handed him the mike. "Hi, I'm Bubba Burke. I want to know why if we know who the drug-dealers are how come the cops don't? It's ridiculous. I wonder sometimes if certain druggies are somehow being protected. I just don't get it. I've called the cops and told them my neighbor has more traffic at his house every day than the local T does. I don't see them doing anything about it. Could you explain that to us?"

Captain Garfield stood up. "Just to clarify one point. I can assure you that none of my men are on the take if that's what you are insinuating. We investigate all tips but you've got to understand that it takes time to build a case. Don't want the judge to throw it out on technicalities."

"That's baloney," Burke said. "If it walks like a duck and looks like a duck…guess what…it is a duck. Just arrest the sons-of-bitches and put them out of business."

The room exploded with approval.

"All I can say is, we do take every tip seriously, and we'll look into your situation if you just stick around after the meeting."

Disorder was peeping in on the meeting.

"Get them out of our neighborhood," shouted one lady.

"Yeah, get them off the streets and away from our kids," said another.

"Like Bubba said," a frail old man said. "We know who the players are, put them behind bars."

"This is a good start but it's getting late so we'll end this meeting now," Representative Conroy said. "Thanks for coming everyone."

The meeting was electric. The people angry, aroused. Law enforcement and city officials were now in a proactive mode and ready to eradicate the poison decimating the community. I left the meeting hopeful that things might finally change. As I drove home I thought about the not-so-famous quote, that "With public sentiment, nothing can fail, without it, nothing can succeed."

I was hoping we could prove its validity.

TWENTY-FIVE

I was sitting at the kitchen table drinking a cup of java and reading the local paper, *South Boston Gazette*, on my laptop. I turned to the editorial pages and two stories jumped out at me, only proving once again that the tentacles of drugs are endless. Their impact devastating.

My dad walked into the kitchen and poured himself a cup of coffee. "Good morning," he said.

"Dad. Sit down and read these two stories. One's from a young girl, another from distraught parents."

My dad grabbed his reading glasses. Although I didn't ask he read the first story out loud.

"Dear mom.

I want to tell you I need you always. Please stop drinking. It's not good for you. Sometimes you fall down and that's not good for you. When you drink, you seem mad and don't talk to me. And all those pills you say your doctor gives you. I don't think they're good. You yell and say bad words. I'm scared you will get really sicker and go into the hospital and I will be all alone in the world. Please stop so we can have fun again like we used to. We can play games and watch TV. You haven't read a story to me in a long time. I miss that. I cry a lot at night when I am in my bed. I have an ache in my belly that won't go away.

Love you as much as the blue sky.

Ella"

I could tell my dad was emotionally moved by this young girl's plea for normality-for happiness. He took off his glasses and discreetly wiped his eyes. "Her mother better wise up before it's too late. God don't like ugly."

"Sad. Really sad. But read this story too."

Again. He read out loud, the words powerful and disturbing.

"We buried our son last week. We listed it as a recent illness but that wasn't entirely true. He was battling the demons for several years. He went to rehab numerous times and seemed to be back on track. Then he went back to his old habits and started using again. If it wasn't heroin he was taking uppers and downers, whatever they were, and he looked awful. Like he was already dead. Broke my wife's heart. Three days before he died, we found him comatose in his bed. We couldn't wake him up. EMS took him out. I'll never forget the look on my wife's face when she realized our son was gone. We want to tell the people of Southie and everywhere else that we all need to pray, to stick together and help each other out. Don't wait for it to happen to you. Keep a watchful eye on your children. There are a lot of good kids. Lots of good dead kids. This is a tragedy we needed to let people know about. Can't let things go on like nothin's different. Like nothin' horrible happened. Our sons and daughters aren't just statistics. We don't mourn statistics. We mourn for our loved ones dead before they should be."

The parents didn't sign their names but they left their hearts in their words. Mr. O'Toole's words *before your time* shot through me like bullets. We lost Tools. Pete was dead. With this latest round with Death, including TK's uncle, I felt I could no longer sit on the sidelines and let life pass by without trying to make a difference. And then after attending the meeting at the Tynan and reading these two stories I realized more than ever that I needed to do something. But what could I do?

"Dad. Have to do something to help others with this drug problem. But I'm not a politician or a rich guy with money to help out. What can one person do?"

"I don't know but everything in life happens for a reason and one day you'll wake up and have the answer."

"Sure, yeah, everything happens for a reason, including me putting peanut butter on my toast."

"Oh, quiet down and hand me the cream," he said, as he slapped me on the right shoulder. "Also, you're more spiritual than you think."

Two days later after work I went to the new rehabilitation center, the Joseph P. Long Rehabilitation Center on East First. The center was named posthumously after a former representative.

"Can I speak to Director Holmes," I asked the receptionist. "Of course," he replied. I sat down and five minutes later, he appeared in the hall. I knew Paul for a long time.

We shook hands. He looked good…lean and in seemingly good shape.

"It's been a while," Paul said. "How's everything going with you."

"Fine…every things fine."

"Ma and dad?"

"Still going strong on Marine Road."

"That's good. Tell them I was asking for them."

"Sure will."

"So what brings you to this neck of the woods as my dad used to say?"

"I'd like to volunteer a few shifts in the evening," I said. "I noticed in the local paper you were looking for volunteers."

"We'd love to have you as a mentor," he said. "How do you think you could assist our clients?"

"I don't have much experience in this field but I'm willing to help out in any way I can. I just want to give back to the community. Help out."

"We can use all the extra help we can get. These alcohol and drug-related problems aren't going away. Only getting worse. I've never seen it this bad. I appreciate you thinking about us. Next time you come by I'll take you on a tour of the center then we can set you up with a schedule."

"That would be great," I said. "Looking forward to it."

"I hate to cut you short but I have a scheduled meeting with my staff so why don't you talk with my receptionist and pick a time to come in and we'll take it from there. How does that sound?"

"Okay…sounds good."

"Oh Johnny…again…thanks for coming in. Every ounce of assistance is needed in this fight. See you soon."

I left.

I felt good.

I was going to help others in need.

It was the right thing to do.

While I was honing my mentoring skills and helping clients at the center fight their demons, the police were busy busting the bad guys. The opening salvos netted over three hundred arrests for a variety of drug offences. All cannons were being fired point blank and word on the street was, "Stay out of Southie" because the place was just "too hot" to do business. Residents also got involved taking advantage of the anonymous hotlines to alert police about possible drug deals going down or the names of possible drug dealers and drug-abusers living near them. The concerted measures were effective and people were happy as well as confident the situation was under control. Many of the "bad guys" had been rounded up. Al was the smart one who disappeared. With plenty of cash he could afford to wait it out. Rumors had him vacationing down south, Ft. Lauderdale to be exact. He wouldn't return until he heard from his boys that the pressure was off.

TWENTY-SIX

Winter was slowly walking out the door. The weather was becoming friendlier. We were all busy with our jobs during the week. Fridays was still our night to meet at the café for food, drinks, and intelligent conversations. And then a few more drinks at one bar or another, but mainly at the Hub Bar.

Saint Patrick's Day was around the corner so the topic of conversation on this particular Friday night turned to a familiar subject.

TK said, "Hey Sal, we'll call you 'Patrick,' *an Honorary Irishman,* for the entire weekend and not make any disparaging remarks about your ancestry."

"I don't mind being an honorary Irishman on Saint Patrick's Day. I'll even do a jig," said Sal, with a shit-eating grin. "And, I'll pray to Saint Patrick for you guys. You need it."

"Yeah, Yeah that's great…we could use a little help from upstairs," TK said. "But that's all you get: one day. Make it count."

"Believe me that's all I want. I can't wait until you guys go to the North End during the August feasts. My Italian friends are gonna terrorize you. They can spot potato-heads a mile away. They won't be handing out any honorary Italian reprieves for you guys."

"Like we might go into "da not end" with you," Sully said, sarcastically, making fun of the local Italian accent.

"Your loss. The food's great," Sal said. As an afterthought, he added, "Food's better than sex."

Sully laughed. "How would you know?" he said.

"That's not funny!" Sal said.

"Sure it is," TK blurted out. "I think it's hilarious."

"Not funny coming from a guy who didn't have his first slice of pizza until he was twenty one."

"So?" Sully shot back.

"So what planet did you grow up on?" Sal asked.

"Hey, sorry I didn't like the way it looked," Sully responded. "Sorry my claim to fame isn't that I ate two whole HiFi Pizzas with extra roni down at the Castle Island parking lot when I was eighteen."

"Every meatball I know talks about food all the time," TK said, enthusiastically. "Let's go eat here, let's eat there. Do you know the best way to cook this food or that food? Food, food, food, morning noon, and night. Geez all *you* people think about is food."

"*You* people?" Sal shot back.

Oh boy, time for an intervention I thought.

"I was watching a documentary on television," I interjected.

"Oh no, here comes another yawner from our Johnny," TK said.

I continued. "During World War II a search and recovery plane crashed in the Pacific. Eight of their crewmen died and three made it to life rafts. One of the airmen eventually died and they had to throw his body overboard. The other two were adrift for forty-seven days. It was a record for guys being afloat at sea on a small life raft. They survived a typhoon, machine gunning from a Japanese bomber, shark attacks, and hunger. Then, the two poor bastards finally discovered an island but soon found out that it was controlled by the Japs and became prisoners of war."

TK interrupted again. "Is this a long story?"

162

"Put a lid on it," Sal blurted out. "Are you afraid of learning something?"

I said, "One of the sailors was Italian. Guess what he brought up to get their mind off of their dilemma? It was food. He started talking about different recipes. You would think that would just torture them more but ironically, it preoccupied their senses, somehow dulled their hunger pains, helping them to cope."

"Well we all know only an Italian would have brought up that subject in such a dire situation," TK replied.

"Did he survive?" Sully asked.

"Yes he did. He spent two years in POW camps but still made it home," I said.

"Too bad," TK said. He laughed cautiously.

Sal gave him a nasty look. He blurted out loudly. "His name was Louis Zamperini. He ran the 5000 meters at the 1936 Olympics held in Berlin."

I shouted out, "Wow, you're stealing my thunder. So you know about this guy?"

"Yeah, of course, I read. The name of his book is *Unbroken*."

"Very good," I said.

"You're not the only Southie intellectual," Sal said.

"You mean pseudo-intellectual don't you?" TK said.

"Fuck off," Sal said. He said. "Zamperini was mentally strong and didn't want to die. He was determined to survive against all odds and he was the main reason the other sailor lived through the ordeal."

"Are we supposed to believe that fairy-tale," TK said.

"It's a true story you Neanderthal, read the book!" I said, with a sense of satisfaction, hoping he'd get the message and shut up. He didn't.

"Ya...ya...ya...whatever," TK said.

"Well, the book might be too much for you," Sal said. "Just watch the movie so you won't burn too many brain cells."

What ensued was the newest chapter of our classic Irish versus Italian debate to add to our memory collection. And Calo started it off in grand fashion.

"I'll tell you a story," Calo said. "Back in the sixties, my cousin Joey Bianca was about nine years old. This kid Jack McCarthy used to terrorize him every day after school calling him a guinea. He went home crying and told his dad what was going on. His father told him the next time it happened he needed to knock some sense into the bully. The following Monday after school, sure enough, McCarthy approached Joey, but he was ready to act. Not expecting to meet any resistance, Joey surprised him. He grabbed and then smashed McCarthy's head into the school's nearby rod iron fence, frantically yelling at the top of his lungs, 'Who's the guinea now? Who's the guinea now?' Nearby nuns separated them. Joey had to face them the next day. His father went with him and told the nuns it wouldn't happen again as he discreetly winked at his son for a job well done. The bullying stopped and Joey's dad told him he didn't want a repeat performance since the message had been sent."

TK couldn't resist. "Fuck talking about made-up stories. The Irish had it just as bad as you guys, taking shit from the Yankee establishment. Remember they considered the Irish no better than wild animals. They left Ireland back in the 1850's seeking a better life but found only poverty, resentment, and subhuman living conditions. It wasn't the mental picture they had so gladly etched within their minds when sailing across the Atlantic. They lived in cellars and shanties, almshouses…that's a poorhouse, for you dummies. They begged on every corner and many became sick and died at an early age. Their dress, accent, and illiteracy provoked disdain from every quarter. They knew nothing was going to be given to them, that they would have to strive to earn the respect of the establishment and they did. The Irish were tenacious. They didn't work the land because the land had deserted them. That's why they left Ireland in the first place, on the aftermath of the 'Potato Famine.' The blacks were the first ones to call the Irish 'White Niggers.' Destitute, they took the tough, no, the dangerous jobs, working on buildings, bridges, canals, and railroads, and the saying was born that there was 'An Irishman buried beneath every (railroad) tie.' The women worked as chambermaids, cooks, and took care of the rich kids. Unity became the Irish's calling card and through their organizational skills they grew strong and then gained power and acceptance. Their faith in themselves and their determination in seeking the good life in a new land were eventually realized."

We were amazed at TK's startling pronouncements, transitioning from blue collar birdbrain to historian. All Sal could say was, "Okay, we get it, everyone's had it hard. Why are we arguing about it?" TK said, "Because you're jealous. You wish you were Irish."

Everyone laughed.

Our Irish-Italian debate abruptly ended when three women in their late twenties walked into the store to peruse the menus. They were undoubtedly yuppies, dressed to the max, and beautiful. Calo immediately sprung to action and walked behind the counter. "Wow," Sal said, in a hushed voice. They ordered slices of pizza and were gone in a heartbeat. We would've liked to have left with them. We felt dissed when the tall blond, with pearly-white teeth and legs which never ended, nonchalantly glanced right through us as if we weren't there. Calo came back to our table and I thought he was going to have a stroke. "Did you see that?" he said. "Oh my God they were beautiful."

"Relax," Sal blurted out. "Leave that shit for us younger guys."

"Fuck no," Calo said. "Never gonna give up the chase."

Feeling like we had no chance with those girls was tough, but listening to his declarations all we could do was laugh.

I said, "You're right Calo, never give up the chase."

TWENTY-SEVEN

Jaws was sitting in the kitchen watching the news as Pat walked in. For unemployed guys they lived pretty well with TV's in almost every room. Pat poured a glass of orange juice. He drank it all at once and filled the glass again.

"What ya watchin'?" he asked. Jaws picked up the clicker and pressed pause. "The news. Woman down in Texas killed her husband and two kids. Then shot herself. People are crazy."

"Who cares," Pat blurted out. "I don't give a flyin' fuck. Let 'em kill each other. Less people on an overcrowded planet suits me just fine."

Jaws wasn't surprised at Pat's negativity but he wasn't going to go there. "What, no comeback budso?" Pat asked. "Nothin' about the goodness in everyone you like to bring up now and then?"

"Not in the mood to listen to you and your bullshit. You should watch what you say and do because sometimes you're a fuckin' complete asshole. I hope you know that."

"Know what?"

"Exactly…"

Pat said, "Fuck everybody."

Jaws didn't bother to respond. "Tell me somethin' I don't know *budso*," Jaws thought to himself. He knew it was a waste of time to try to reason with his pal. Jaws still at least lived in the real world, sometimes. Drugs, however, had totally corrupted Pat's mind and ravaged his body. Indifference became his best friend. He didn't care about anyone but himself. He was beyond the point of reason, oblivious to reality, devoid of compassion or love.

"Hey I've got an idea," Pat said.

"What's that? You wanna rob a bank you crazy bastard?"

"You're a funny prick. I was thinking."

"Man. You shouldn't think too much your brain might explode."

"Can I tell you what I want to do without being interrupted?"

"Lay it on me."

"My Aunt Kay goes to Mass almost every day. And if she ain't goin' to pray, she's walkin' around Southie. Should run for office. Knows everyone. Fuck. She shops at that goodwill store for fucking house trinkets all the time. You know those little decorations you put on tables and shit? She has a bunch of glass ducks. Why do you need 20 glass ducks? Shit's stupid. Anyway –"

"Is there a point to this?" Jaws asked.

"Point is," Pat said, "She's everywhere. Never home. Her house would be an easy score."

"You wanna rob your aunt?"

"Thinkin' about it?"

"Man, you oughta start looking at yourself a little more," Jaws said. "See who you really are."

"Okay, every day I'll spend thirty minutes in front of the mirror."

"Not funny."

Pat continued on about his plan, appearing as cold as an icicle in February. "She keeps money in her living room in a small desk. I've seen her take it out during family events. Gives money to all the kids."

"Yeah old people got cash on them all the time. Weirdos."

168

"I'm talking c-notes not dollar bills."

Jaws had his doubts. Pat's latest scam seemed too low, even for Jaws. Where does one draw the line he bandied about in his mind? "I don't know if I want to be part of that. We don't rob from our own."

"Nah, she won't even know it's gone," he said, matter-of-factly.

"Fuck you she won't. She's got more marbles left in her skull than you do you nutty fuck."

"I just need you to keep an eye out in front of the house. Nothin' else. Nobody's gonna get hurt."

Pat walked over and patted Jaws on the back. "C'mon. I'll take care of everything. You stand outside and look pretty. If you see my aunt coming, text me and I'll scram."

"Nah, count me out."

"You'll be pissed when I'm in the money and getting banged-up, mother-fucker."

Jaws looked away, then down, then turned back towards Pat. Humanity and reason could still find lodging in Jaw's world but sometimes were tossed out whenever opportunity walked in. Sure enough, they were about to get the boot.

"Someday, I know we'll burn in hell together," Jaws said.

"You can worry about that later, can't you?"

"You're a fuckin' screwball. You're gone. That's all I'm gonna say."

A week later the scene was set. Mrs. Gray appeared in the doorway right on schedule, and off she went. Pat and Jaws were camped out in a nearby alleyway. They watched her disappear around the corner. It was time to score. Then score again and get high.

Pat didn't waste a minute as he forced open a window at the rear of the house and slid his slim frame through it and onto the floor. He immediately zeroed in on his target, the desk in the living room. He bee-lined to it and discovered six hundred dollars in the top right drawer. He glanced at a picture on the nearby mantelpiece of his aunt with her sister-his deceased mom. He stopped and stared. Something stirred inside him. He didn't know what it was exactly. But then the realization hit him hard. The sensation was that of love. But to him "love" was a long time ago. These vague memories and feelings weren't welcomed in his world anymore.

He only welcomed regret.

He stuffed the money in his pocket.

He looked through a few other drawers but came up empty. As he was about to leave the house he got a coded text from Jaws. It was time to leave. Someone, possibly his aunt, was outside.

Pat's dad had dropped his aunt off and kept on driving. Jaws knew he had to stall Mrs. Gray. He walked across the street. "Hi Mrs. G.," he yelled, smiling like a politician looking for her vote. "Hey dear, how are you honey?"

"I'm good Mrs. G."

"Where's my Pat?"

"I'm about to meet him."

"What are you guys up to today?"

"We're going down the L, gonna lift some weights...take a sauna."

"Oh good for you boys. Stay out of trouble."

Jaws knew the only way Pat could leave without being

noticed was by climbing over a six-foot high stockade fence in the back yard. "How are you doing today?" Jaws said, knowing he needed to stall her a little longer. "Fine, but if my head wasn't screwed on, I'd probably forget it. Didn't bring any money with me. Lucky I ran into my brother-in-law."

Mrs. Gray started to walk up her front steps. Jaws looked at his phone. Pat still hadn't texted him that he was in the clear. It was cold outside but Jaws noticed that he was beginning to sweat. "Hey Mrs. G, you still making those flags and hats?" he blurted out. She turned and stopped on the steps. "Of course but you know I only make the Irish and American flag. You're not Irish are you?" she asked. "No…no…I'm Polish but I need something for the parade."

"Okay," she said, with a smile. "I'll make you an Irish knit hat. I plan to buy some new material today. Stop by next week."

"Thanks so much."

"It's my pleasure."

Mrs. Gray fidgeted with her house keys. Jaws' phone buzzed. He looked down at the text. Pat was out of the house, and clear. Confliction stared Jaws in the face. A false smile covered his mouth. "See you later," he said, as he began to walk away. She yelled after him, "It was nice talking with you."

"Same here," Jaws replied. "Good seein' you too."

"Don't forget to come by for the hat."

He found himself choking up.

His stomach was doing flip-flops.

He felt like throwing up.

But he didn't.

He simply waived without looking back and got out of there as fast as he could.

TWENTY-EIGHT

The Saint Patrick's Day weekend snuck up on us once again and we found ourselves celebrating at Calo's. Where else? The tables were filled with customers ready to fill their empty stomachs with Angela's great cooking and they didn't leave disappointed.

Angela had outdone herself once again and we let her know it. She smiled and walked back into the kitchen. We finished our meals and looked towards the TV as the buzzer sounded ending the first half of the Celtics-Lakers game. The TD Garden was rockin'. The Celts were up by twenty. Anxious to get down to Saturday night business, the guys were ready to catch a buzz.

"Hey, guys. We ate. It's halftime," Sully said. "I'm ready. It's time to pray."

'Praying' was Sully's code word for smoking weed. "Anyone coming?" he asked. TK replied, "I'm in."

"Yeah, certainly time to catch a buzz," Sal said. "Is it good shit?" TK asked. "What do you think? Does a bear shit in the woods?" Sully asked. TK shook his head back and forth. He said. "I know. It was a stupid question!" We all went outside the café to light up. They had their weed. I had my once-a-week cheap cigar. "Hey TK," Sully said. "An old friend of yours wants to talk to you."

"Where's the old friend?" TK asked, feigning ignorance.

"Right here," Sully said, as he pulled out a big, fat joint. "Nothin' but the best. Green crack."

"Green crack?" I said. "Ya shittin' me."

"Five hundred an ounce," Sully said. He handed TK the

joint. "Is it really worth that much?" TK asked. "Wait til you smoke then tell us," Sully said. "I got it especially for Saint Patrick's Day. Celebrating the green."

"About time you finally bought something you cheap bastard," Sal said. "Fuck you," Sully said. "Let's be nice tonight guys," I said. "Yeah...everyone's pals tonight," TK said, surprisingly. Sully looked at TK. He said, "Betcha eat again after smoking, get the munchies." TK said, "I'm not betting nothin'."

"Well, what ya waiting for..." Sal said. "Do the honors. Fire it up."

They passed the joint around. It smelled strong. "Johnny, want a hit?" Sully asked. "Nah," I said. "I'll pass. Smoked my share in college."

"Just thought you'd like to mellow out," Sully said.

"I'll stick with these cheap cigars."

"Thank God it's legal now," TK blurted out.

Even though marijuana was just legalized in the state, he knew they'd continue to debate the moral issues surrounding marijuana use. TK said, "I get a kick out of people. Okay to get fucked up on vodka but pot's a no-no. A gateway drug. Give me a break."

I said, "Some people have different opinions on the matter." TK continued on with his usual weed crusade speech. "People on weed don't get into fights and cause problems. Just want to mellow out and enjoy life."

"Well," I said. "The other day a guy in Colorado ate marijuana-laced candy and then shot his wife." TK said, "Never heard 'bout anyone overdosing on weed. Sure it wasn't that synthetic K2-Spice shit they got now?"

"Pretty sure it was the THC levels that fucked him up," I

said. "But you're right about the synthetic weed. Young kids in every community should know about this. I read a story about a High school senior in Iowa who smoked this crap with his pals, said he was 'going to hell' then went home and shot himself. Another victim dead before his time. Plenty of stories about people smoking this shit and ending up in the ER."

"They're allowed to sell that crap in a lot of states," Sal said. "That's crazy."

"The owner of a store on Dorchester Street was selling that spice shit-fake weed-but BPD told them to stop and they did," I said. "Shit's *really* dangerous!"

"I'm with you guys," TK said. "That shits sprayed with chemicals somewhere in China and sent over here. But I'm talking about *real* weed not that poison."

"What about the dabbing ?" I asked.

"Daba Daba do?" Sully responded, childishly. "Ya know there's a reason why the phrase 'I'd rather be dead than red in the head' came into existence," TK said. "Never heard that one before," Sully responded, sarcastically. "Don't you watch the news Sully?" Sal asked. "No."

"Figures," TK said.

"Fuck you guys," Sully said.

"That fad is coming from out West. Stoners are smoking super weed at home with THC levels ten times more concentrated with highs that pack a wallop beyond description," I said, "People are getting fucked up. It's no fun when you're freaking out. Rapid heartbeats. Blackouts. Pychosis. Paranoia. Hallucinations. That's getting high? I don't think so guys."

"Those people are spoiling it for us," TK responded. "Nothing wrong with smoking an old-fashioned joint. I don't need to 'dab' my shit using a butane-lighter and a bong. I want to appreciate a good buzz without passing out."

I didn't respond. All the new ways to smoke weed, how potent it can be, and the associated dangers have opened up a new array of questions yet to be answered. But there wasn't any sense of starting a debate concerning the good or bad about 'real' weed. I wasn't going to let the issue of marijuana legalization spoil my night.

The argument over weed being a gateway drug has been debated for years. Some say it is and some don't think it leads people down the dark alley of drug addiction. I mulled this argument over and over again and concluded that the first spark of a joint could lead to further abuse. 'Could' however would depend on the individual's will power. I wasn't sure if that premise allowed one to condemn marijuana use but to caution those who smoke it that it's a slippery slope not to be lightly dismissed as morally feasible or free from unforeseen complications. I smoked weed in college. After a while I didn't like the high at all. I'd get paranoid and become speechless. I eventually decided it wasn't worth it and realized I didn't need to 'spark it up' to appreciate life.

Yet my guys did and were busy getting stoned. Sully took the last hit. I took one more puff of my cigar, blew the smoke in the air, and then tossed it in the gutter. We went back inside and watched the remainder of the game. The Celtics were cruising along, hammering the Lakers. TK was ecstatic. He was passionate about the Celtics. When they won, he was happier than a kid at Christmas, but when they lost, he needed to be consoled. He especially loved beating the hated Lakers even though the rivalry had lost much of its luster.

The guys were on cruise control, laughing and joking, telling exaggerated stories about their athletic accomplishments and exploits of the heart. Then the munchies took over. TK ordered two slices of pizza. He would've lost that bet. Sal and Sully subsequently asked Angela for two meatballs apiece.

We drank more wine.

Then it was time to drink some beers.

A lot of beers.

After all, it was the Saint Patrick's Day weekend.

And like the Irish diddy says, "In Heaven there is no beer, that's why we drink it here."

TWENTY-NINE

After a few more refreshments we left the café and headed across the street. Looking through a window we could see the bar was jammed. We knew it would be. Always was the night before the parade. Luckily we knew the doorman, Kevin McCluskey, and as regulars, were given the high-sign to walk down to the side door. This wasn't appreciated by outsiders waiting in line hoping to capture a taste of Southie. But fuck them. McCluskey suggested if they were growing impatient they could imbibe at Mike's Bar and Grille or the Sea Edge up the street. After all, there are many bars in Southie, too many for some people, not enough for others.

We went inside and walked down to the end of the bar. Everyone was having a good time. Many were drinking green beer celebrating the Irish. We looked around and realized we didn't know half the people. One character did stand out, our boy Robbie Fallon, who was looking worse than usual. He was sitting at the bar drinking draft beer. "Hey Johnny. Hey boys. Happy Saint Patrick's Day," he yelled. "Same to you," I said. "Don't drink too many beers," TK said. "Never," he said. "You know me." He laughed, and his beer vanished in a second. Then he shouted, "Hey Johnny, any luck?" I waved him off and kept on walking. I hadn't gambled since the last time I spoke with Robbie and felt good about that. We grabbed a spot near the back wall in the corner. "What was that all about?" TK asked. "Nothin'," I replied.

Sal interrupted. "What do ya guys want to drink?" he said. "I'll buy since it's my day."

"Yeah right," Sully said.

The song 'Four Green Fields' resonated throughout the bar. It was my favorite song. TK said, "Jesus, Southie's becoming more and more yuppified every day." I said, "It's called gentrification."

"I don't care what they call it," Sal chimed in. "I ain't complaining. Look at all the girls. I love it."

"Think we can score?" Sully asked.

"You guys couldn't score with a fistful of fifties," TK said.

"Oh yeah, we'll see who scores and who goes home to jerk off," Sal added.

"Fuck the yuppies," TK shot back. "They're arrogant and don't even talk to us, never mind go home with us, or do anything else." I said, "They aren't that bad. They just need to stop once in a while and say hello to their neighbors. I don't think we'll bite each other. And they're good for the local economy. They're pumping money into local businesses."

"Yeah, the drug business too. One yuppie at the Blueberry Café asked me where to score some coke. I told him he had the wrong guy," Sal mentioned. TK said, "Should've told him to go to Hell. Fuckin' yuppies are only going to be here a few years before they get married and move to the suburbs. Then more of them, like pesky ants, will take their place." I said, "You don't know that." TK said, "Anyone wanna bet? Loser pays up in five years." Sully said, "That's a stupid bet."

Sal asked TK, "Do you like anybody?"

"I like my sister and my dad, I like you guys, sometimes, only kidding, love you guys, you know that."

Distancing myself from the conversation, I looked up at the television and started watching the Spurs-Warriors game. About an hour later, McCluskey opened the side door and in popped a familiar face.

It was Al.

He was back.

Reality slapped me on the back of the head. But it all made sense. After cleaning up significant numbers of drug riffraff, complacency entered the fray. Many fell into the same trap, thinking all was well in Southie and it was time to pull the plug on additional resources. Those involved in the rehabilitation programs, and many residents, were adamant about keeping up the pressure. They realized battles had been won yet the war still raging. But pleas for continued police presence fell on deaf ears at the steps of Boston City Hall and in Washington. The DEA pulled out of town and the additional BPD drug units were re-assigned to other parts of the city. Politicians only make believe they're listening when they want your vote. I had written an editorial response in the local paper that read, "City, state and federal agencies are wrong in dismissing the problem as 'manageable'. It's a smug conclusion based on wrong assumptions. Cutting back on manpower is a huge mistake. This drug problem must be continuously assaulted head on and the serpent's heads cut off. Otherwise, it will only result in more heartache and more innocent people will fall victim. More deaths will surely follow and tears will flow throughout the streets."

This warning wasn't warmly received by some for obvious reasons. Although the anti-drug pressure was effective, one could still witness the same old shit going on and transactions being made.

It didn't seem to be the right thing for authorities to do at that time.

179

So it hurt the effort to combat drugs.

And now there Al was.

All decked out and sporting a tan.

"You guys don't all look now, but our buddy's back in town," I said to them. Of course, they all looked at once. "I can't believe it, that piece of shit is back in Southie," TK said, glaring. "Heat's off and he comes strolling back like Caesar entering Rome with his Praetorian guards."

"Don't let him bother you," Sal said. He knew deep down inside his plea was falling on deaf ears. TK wasn't amused. "Don't tell me not to let him bother me. It *does* fuckin' bother me. He's got balls. Don't know about you guys, but seeing him back in town really blows. Seeing that scumbag again spoils Saint Patrick's Day."

Sully said, "Fuck him, let it go. Like you said before, what goes around comes around."

"Don't wanna hear it," TK said. "Sick of that cliché."

I wanted to believe Al wasn't coming back. But deep down I knew otherwise, knew he'd resurface like a water rat. The bad guy always does. Minutes later, Al's two muscle heads, Joey and Ryan Murphy, walked into the bar and joined him.

"I guess you can't keep a good drug dealer down for too long," Sal said. "Not in Southie anyway."

The bar was packed and noisy with nonsensical conversations. The crowd was getting louder and drunker as the night wore on, which usually happens throughout the Saint Patrick's Day weekend. TK squeezed by me and walked right over to Al. I knew whatever was going to happen next wasn't going to be good.

Although he didn't talk about it, I knew TK still blamed Al

for his uncle's death. When we got together, TK's moods were up and down. He was outward one moment, distracted another. He never mentioned Big Kane or how he and his dad were dealing with the loss but I knew he was hurting; especially his dad who TK was worried about. TK's dad, Thomas, and Big Kane, were twin brothers. They went to Southie High, were members of the Knights football team in their heyday, and upon graduation joined the Marines and fought in Vietnam. On the day Big Kane was ambushed, his brother was confined to his bed with serious flu-like symptoms. He never forgave himself for not being out on that particular patrol to protect his brother. After Nam, they both worked as postmen. In their fifties, they both had heart attacks although three months apart. After retiring, they played cards at each other's homes and always took walks, weather permitting, to Castle Island. They were much closer than ordinary brothers and had that psychic connection most twins enjoy. So TK feared what might happen next.

Recently during one of his smoke breaks outside of Calo's, I asked TK how he was doing. He deflected and said everything was great. He was working hard hoping to be promoted to a supervisor's position at the auto service center where he worked so he could afford a new car. He was excited about the thought of not having to drive around all day picking up car parts. When I tried to dig deeper to see how he was really doing, he started talking about the Celtics, Bruins, or the Patriots, nothing heavy. But TK didn't like the Red Sox. He always said he'd rather watch grass grow.

Then TK's voice brought me back to the moment. He was face-to-face with Al.

"Ya might wanna back off," Al said. TK stood his ground.

"Didn't know you were back in Southie. Thought you retired in Florida. Maybe you should go back," TK said. "Nice to see you too," Al said. "You always were a wise-ass. Guess some things never change."

"Yeah, like some people never fade away like they ought to."

Al smiled. "Careful TK."

I walked over. "C'mon TK, forget about it."

"Stay out of it Johnny Boy. I'm just starting to warm up."

Al was losing patience but just watched and listened. He'd let his boys do his talking for him for the moment.

"Back off," Joey said.

"Don't be disrespecting Al," Ryan blurted out.

"That's a good one," TK said.

"Shut up," Joey said.

"Don't tell me to shut up. I remember beating your brains out in the ring. You weren't that good. You were about as tough as toilet paper."

"Yeah whatever but you should still shut the fuck up," Ryan said. "Listen to my bro."

"You shut the fuck up…and fuck you both…you muscle heads."

Al continued watching in silence. He didn't show any emotion. The twins were unusually diplomatic. "No need for name calling," Joey said. "Just wanna have a few drinks."

"Fuck off," TK shot back. Ryan clenched his fists. TK inched closer to Al. Al calmly said, "Do yourself a favor and get outta my face."

"What the fuck you gonna do, sic your mongrels on me?"

When he said that, Joey took a few steps towards him. Surprisingly, Al stopped him. He wanted to show us who the boss was, who was in control. Al said, "It's okay, we're old pals."

"No, we're not," TK said. Al smiled. TK said, "How do ya sleep at night knowing you're fuckin' up people's lives and making money doin' it?"

Al should've gone to Hollywood instead of Florida. Without missing a beat he responded. "Don't really know what you're talking about. I'm an honest businessman trying to make a buck."

"People know what you really are. You're delusional."

"Some think I'm a gift from Heaven."

"Jesus. Really think so?"

"Don't think, I know."

Sensing a brawl about to break out any second, I said, "Come on let's ease up guys. We're supposed to be celebrating here. It's Saint Patrick's Day."

"Listen to your boy, he's always been the smart one out of all you guys," Al said. He took a few steps back and looked at TK. "No hard feelings."

I looked at TK. I could tell he was about to explode. Al smiled at me, feeling like he had won. "Hey Johnny, make sure 'Tough Kid' gets home alright. You never know what might happen right in your own neighborhood. It's just not safe these days." Al turned away to order another round at the bar and before I could stop him, TK yelled, "Oh really? Is that a threat? My uncle is dead because of you. One of these days I'll be standing over you laughing my ass off when you get what you deserve you fuckin' drug-dealing piece of fuckin' shit."

With that last outburst, Al glanced towards Joey. Joey cracked TK on the jaw. TK hit the floor. Sully grabbed Joey and they tumbled to the floor, rolling around exchanging body blows. Sal stared down Ryan and I was nose-to-nose with Al, when two

183

bouncers, ex-Boston College jocks, appeared out of nowhere, broke it up, and told us to leave. We left. Al and his crew walked out behind us. They stood across the street, staring.

TK was dazed.

He needed some fresh air.

"Are you okay?" I asked. I knew he wasn't. His ego was bruised.

"Yeah. Yeah. Leave me alone will ya."

He took a deep breath.

I took one too.

He was pissed.

"You sure you're okay?"

He didn't answer. He rubbed his chin. Blood slid down from his nostrils like ketchup. "Give me a minute. I'll be fine." I grabbed TK by the shoulder and told him that it was over. "You need to calm down. C'mon, time to go."

"Johnny. Stop it. I'm fine. Need a few minutes to gather my thoughts."

"Let's go. We'll walk you to your house. Enough bullshit for tonight."

"I'm all set, not gonna cause any more problems."

We started to walk down L Street. Sal and Sully were mumbling to each other. They weren't happy about missing out on all those girls. I was just glad it was over. It could've been uglier. I looked at TK. He finally appeared calm then suddenly yelled across the street to Al, "Hey asshole you're a fuckin' coward, c'mon over and let's finish this!"

Fuck.

Shit.

Guess I was wrong.

Not over.

It all happened so fast. Al motioned to Ryan and Joey to stay back. TK and Al stepped into the middle of the street and began fighting. A crowd formed outside. Others looked through the bar windows. Al swung but only found air. TK threw a right jab, hitting Al square on the nose. Al regained his composure, dragging TK down onto the sidewalk. They wrestled and exchanged facial and body blows drawing unsolicited "ooh's" and "aah's" from onlookers. They were both getting in some good hits. Their faces were red with blood. They got up, dazed. Like two bulls facing off, just looking at each other. TK was weak, it was written all over his face and body. He said in a resigned voice, "Someday you'll pay for everything you've done, everyone you've destroyed." He started to walk away, knowing this was a fight he couldn't win. Not tonight anyway. Emotion took over, unexpectedly. He looked back at Al. His voice cracked, "Remember after Tools died? The park. The Pact. We promised we'd stick together. It was you. It was you who said 'let's do it right and mean it.' You said, 'Never forget. It's our Pact forever.' I trusted you that night. But you forgot. You betrayed us. You betrayed yourself."

Al looked stung, but before we could see any more of his humanity, two officers arrived on the scene. Officer Frank Noto, a local kid, took the lead. "Hello boys. Friday night at the fights I see, huh. Who won? Let me guess. You both lost and now you can both leave. Go home. Don't want to see you two again tonight."

David Costello, the bar owner, emerged from the crowd. "Hey officer, can ya tell those two they're no longer welcomed in my bar."

"You heard the boss. You two are barred until further notice. Take your sorry asses elsewhere," Officer Noto said.

Costello took a second look and realized Al was one of the combatants. "Ah, Officer," he blurted out. "These two guys aren't that bad. They can come back in two weeks but need to avoid each other. No more fights. One more chance."

"Guess it's your lucky day you two knuckleheads. You heard 'em. He's givin' you guys a break. Get out of here and stop acting stupid."

At that moment, an unmarked car stopped right outside the door. Detectives McDevitt and Guiney stepped out. Guiney looked at the crowd. "Time to break it up," he said. "Either go back inside or go home." The crowd began to disperse. McDevitt spoke briefly with the officers to get the lowdown on what occurred. He knew everyone in Southie worth knowing. He shot Al and his boys a dirty look then turned his attention towards us. "Hey TK, come into my office." TK didn't know what to expect. McDevitt pulled him aside so no one else could hear. "Whatdafuck is wrong with you?"

"Hey, he's back in town walking around like Al Capone. He's a piece of shit and you know it."

"So what? You think you're some kind of vigilante or something?"

McDevitt put his hand on TK's left shoulder.

"Do me a favor. Avoid him. Only gonna cause problems. Can ya do that?"

"Guess I'll hafta."

"Guess you betta," Guiney said, as he walked towards TK and McDevitt.

"Go home. Sleep it off," McDevitt said. "Big day

186

tomorrow."

THIRTY

It was parade day. It's always on Sunday. Sunday Funday as they say. Every year on this day, Southie transforms into a madhouse. Electricity fills the air and drunks fill the streets. Saint Patrick's Day in Southie is unlike anywhere else in the world. While other cities in America merely wear green shirts and drink green beer in bars, Southie takes it to the next level. Everyone wears authentic Irish knit sweaters, sometimes brought down from generations. The men and boys wear scally caps. Mothers push their children around in old-fashioned Irish prams. Everyone has on Irish colors or Southie Pride shirts. Irish music blares from all angles throughout the neighborhood. It's truly a great day for the Irish.

Saint Patty's Day wasn't just a time for getting drunk. For me, it always signaled the end of the dreaded winter, the anticipation of spring and the approaching summer, a bridge from darkness to light. The weather on parade day is always a question mark dictating the size of the crowd and whether or not Irish eyes are smiling. One year, it can be twenty degrees and freezing, and the next, sixty degrees and summerlike. Today the sky was blue and clear, without a trace of clouds and the sun was shining brightly. It was only forty degrees so to keep warm I wore a South Boston Pop Warner Football League sweatshirt, with a leprechaun, the Fighting Irish emblem, displayed prominently on the front, and an Irish-knit tam my grandmother made.

I met my friends on Broadway adjacent to M Street Park to view the parade and do some girl-watching. As soon as I approached Sully, Sal and TK, I gave them the look that any conversation about last night's fight should be avoided. They got the message. We didn't want to get TK all riled up again.

The parade route was lined with people from start to finish. Luckily we found a spot on the sunny side of the street next to a group of older guys. "Can you believe the talent?" Sully said, with a wide smile surveying the female landscape. "It's incredible!" Sal blurted out. "Never seen so many beautiful girls in my life. Wish they had the parade every day."

"Are you crazy? We'd have nowhere to park. On a regular day it sucks and today it's ridiculous," TK said. "Hey, lighten-up and enjoy, you Irish-potato-heads," Sal said. "Yeah, like he said, embrace the day," Sully said. "Embrace this!" TK responded, grabbing his junk. He laughed out loud and threw Sully that go-fuck-yourself look.

Suddenly, I heard Jaws and Pat's voices. Jaws was with Kaleigh McDonough, they were still going strong, so it appeared. Pat was with Dee. Pat walked up behind me and covered my eyes with his hands. "Who loves ya baby?" he asked, in a poorly disguised voice. "Who else," I said. "Your boy, Pat," he said as he gave me a hug. "What are you guys queer?" Kaleigh asked, shaking her head. "Hey mind your own business," Jaws said. "I'll mind my own business next time ya wanna get down to business you punk ass fuck."

"Don't start," Jaws said. "I don't need your shit today. Ya hear me."

She didn't respond but her look could have scared a bear.

In the streets, men dressed in revolutionary war uniforms fired their muskets.

Adults jumped.

Babies cried.

"Tremendous day hey guys," Pat said. "Love Saint Patty's Day. Best day of the year in Southie as far as I'm concerned. How 'bout you Dee?"

"Always great when I'm with *you,*" she said, with sarcasm perched on her lips. "You betta believe it," Pat said. "You're lucky I'm lettin' you hang with me today."

"You're the lucky fuck," Dee said.

"Hey, can't you control your honey?" Jaws said, jokingly.

"Yeah just like you control Kaleigh," Dee responded. "Blow me."

"Wow, you and Kaleigh eat with those mouths?" Jaws said.

The boys laughed.

Dee curtsied.

Kaleigh looked away as Bitterness cast a shadow across her face.

Pat said, "C'mon enough bullshit. Let's go, gotta meet some people up the street. See you gents later."

"We're off to see the wizard," Jaws roared. "Enjoy the day you guys."

"Who's the wizard? Their dope man?" Sully asked, after they were out of earshot.

"Better them than me," TK said, looking around at the crowd with curiosity.

Better them than me kept playing in my mind. Their lives were a vicious cycle of making scores, buying drugs and getting high, making scores, buying drugs and getting high. But after a while, you just get numb to it. People will do what they want. It's uncontrollable. I took a swig of Pepsi and pushed it from my head. Like TK said, better them than me.

"Hey, what's Pam doing?" Sal asked.

"Oh, she's watching the parade with her cousins," I said. "House is on the parade route. Might come by the house later. Might not."

"Surprised you didn't strong arm her to watch it with you," TK said.

I didn't answer him.

We continued watching the parade.

And the girls.

Across the street, I saw Mrs. Gray walk out of a neighbor's house and start handing out small American Flags. As youngsters, Pat and I went to her house many times, taking out the garbage or shoveling her sidewalk. She'd give us hot chocolate or a cold drink afterwards, depending on the season, and put a few bucks in a small bag filled with candy. Although we pretended to protest she'd 'shush' us and stick the bag into our pockets.

Mrs. Gray noticed me so I crossed the street and gave her a big hug and a kiss. "I got something to show you," she said. She reached into her large bag and took out a beautifully crocheted American Flag blanket. "I know you love America. I made this for you."

Needless to say it was beautiful.

I smiled.

"You didn't have to do that."

"I'll give it to your mom. I see her all the time. She's always told me you loved this country and I love that story about how mad you got in high school once when a few of the students didn't want to say the Pledge of Allegiance. You almost got thrown out of school for that."

"I was young."

"You were right."

"Thanks for the gift. It will keep me warm at night."

"You're welcome."

I waited for a band from New Hampshire to pass by before I walked back to my friends. They were playing one of my favorite songs, 'The Star and Stripes Forever'; the magnum opus of composer John Phillip Souza. Appropriate I thought as chills enveloped me.

Fun and Laughter were in attendance as applause reverberated along the parade route. People were cheering, paying tribute to all the unselfish veterans and the service men and women. Local politicians also walked along the parade route, waiving to everybody and running to the sidelines to shake hands with friends as well as future voters. I always got a kick out of watching locals shaking hands with the local politicians to show onlookers how important they were. I could care less if I ever shook any politician's hand. They're all full of shit. Call their office a week later and they're unavailable. Behind them, Star Wars characters like Darth Vader and Princess Leia marched along, waiving to kids. Storm troopers stopped to take some pictures with fans. Along with our military heroes, Star Wars characters still inspire me. I can't lie about that.

Various cartoon characters like Pluto, Mickey Mouse, Buzz Lightyear and Woody tossed pieces of candy on the sidewalk as they paraded on. The kids eagerly picked the candy up and sometimes fought over the last few pieces. The kids had fun throwing pop rocks on the ground. Vendors rolled by selling cotton candy, soft pretzels, parade horns and hats. The Pillsbury Doughboy posed for selfies with pretty girls. Patriot cheerleaders with ruby red lips and pretty faces waived to every one as marching bands from New York to New Hampshire played

192

crowd-pleasing songs. The local South Boston Youth Hockey League Bantam team walked happily along with their state championship banner. Irish band trios and old timers on buses were playing jazz songs that got the crowd clapping their hands and stomping their feet. Guys and gals riding unicycles whizzed by, waiving to the crowd. Irish step dancers did jigs and reels in soft shoes on the pavement. Miss South Boston sat comfortably in a new convertible car looking beautiful, endlessly smiling and waving. The South Boston High School ROTC team stepped in unison, proudly displaying the American Flag. State-of-the-art police and fire vehicles drove by sounding their horns and sirens, as parents placed their hands on their infant's ears. A gay pride group that walked by received mixed reactions from the crowd. Boston Police lined the route, keeping a watchful eye on the crowd, shutting down underage drinking and telling out-of-control drunks to put a lid on it, leave, or be escorted to the police station on West Broadway.

The street cleaners signaled the end of the parade. Another parade was history. It had been entertaining. Tradition had been served. I invited the guys back to my parent's house. As we walked down the street, we talked about all the food we were going to eat. We had a ton of traditional Irish food at my house; corn beef and cabbage, boiled dinner, beef stew, Irish Bread, desserts, and of course, plenty to drink. Naturally, we added some Italian food on the menu, meatballs, pasta, and cold cuts to round it out. And as Sal often pointed out, 'Yeah, you need some Italian food on Saint Patrick's Day, cause' everyone knows Irish food sucks.'

THIRTY-ONE

We walked down M Street towards my house and noticed the aftermath of the parade. We saw a group of young teenage girls, about fourteen years old, in a circle. They were holding up one of their friends, dressed in green from head to toe who was intermittently throwing up then looking to them for sympathy. Her face was pasty-white and multicolored vomit was splattered over her clothes and her new UGG's. Like to know how she was going to explain that to her mom and dad.

We all laughed. Been there. Done that. I could sense we were all recounting our individual Saint Patrick's Day experiences when we were younger and drank too much. Even though you'd be surrounded by friends, you inevitably were all alone when you'd finally stumbled home, knocked on the door and faced your parents. Dread just about describes that situation. Once in your bed, dizziness and the threat of more vomiting was your companion before sleep finally gave you a reprieve from your own stupidity. You'd suffer the consequences, especially the next day, and put the experience in your back pocket for future reference.

As we kept walking we saw a group of yuppie girls in their twenties in a similar situation. TK shook his head in disgust. "Will ya look at that? Fucking yuppies. They're all over the place like ants. Southie has turned into Yuppiedom."

"Is that a word?" Sully asked.

"Yes it is you bean head," TK said.

"Just asking."

"At least those young kids have an excuse not bein' able to

hold their liquor," TK said. "As if we don't have enough problems, with people being drunk and high in Southie, the yuppies are worse! They act like they never drank before. Like they're in fucking college still. I swear they do the stupidest shit. One of 'em got drunk and walked into Uncle Kane's apartment last year, God rest his soul, fuck them scaring the piss out of people."

A few carefully drove past us since a lot of people were still walking on the street. TK's mind continued to race. His words flowed like a broken faucet. "I fuckin hate yuppies, dude. I'm tellin' ya."

We reached the corner of M and Fifth. We saw TK's sister stopped at the stop sign in her new car. She rolled down her window. "Happy St. Patrick's Day! See you losers later!"

"Yeah, yeah" we shouted in unison and she drove off but suddenly slammed on the breaks when a wise-ass yuppie on a ten-speed bike came barreling up the one-way street and was almost introduced to her front bumper. The yuppie kept riding but drunkenly looked back, "What the fuck lady?" TK exploded. "You're going the wrong way shithead! What do ya *want* her to hit you?" He picked up a half-empty beer can from the gutter and whipped it at him. He missed. The yuppie laughed, and slurred his words, 'So...so...so sue me. I'm...a crimma-ni-nal.' He rode off and gave everyone the finger. TK shouted, "You stupid fuck! Speak English. See what I mean guys. What a fuckin' asshole."

"I'm with you," Sully said. "But I still like the yuppie girls. I say we make a law that only yuppie girls can move in. The yuppie guys are outlawed."

We laughed.

TK didn't.

With all the excitement, it seemed like we had been walking forever. TK said he needed to stop by his house for a second before going to mine. As we turned the corner of M and Eighth, we saw two guys urinating on the side of TK's house. One was tall and heavy-set, muscular, and his pissing buddy was short and lean, and looked like he could use a good meal. We didn't know who they were, probably out-of-towners but definitely out-of-control. They were so drunk they kept on pissing, even though they knew we were watching.

They didn't give a fuck.

TK did.

"What the...stick those dicks in your pockets," TK yelled. This was the final straw for TK and we all knew it. "Get the fuck out of here," he screamed. I exchanged glances with Sal and Sully. This wasn't going to end well.

"We'll leave when we're finished," the taller guy yelled back.

"You're finished now."

"Fuck you."

"Fuck me? Fuck you! That's my house asshole."

TK grabbed him by the shoulder and whipped him onto the sidewalk. He tried to get up but TK slapped him hard on the face and pushed him down to the ground. "You like getting slapped like a little bitch? You betta stay down until I take care of your stupid partner."

The short drunk laughed. "What are you a Southie hoodlum?" he slurred, as he drunkenly laughed, putting his hands up to fight. "Get your dirty dick hands away from me." Without hesitation, TK hit him square in the face and blood gushed out. He fell to the ground. TK's other battered foe then sat up. "I wouldn't do anything foolish," Sal yelled to him. He slinked

196

down, trying to hide his humiliation. TK kept hitting the short guy, smashing his face into the concrete, over and over and over again. "That's enough!" I screamed. Parents walking by with their children crossed the street, covering their kid's eyes. A small crowd began to form. TK walked over to the bigger guy and kicked him in the gut one more time for good measure. I looked at the smaller guy. Blood covered his face. It made me sick. I looked around. His blood was all over the sidewalk. TK walked over, seeing all the blood, which enraged him. He struck the guy hard in the back. "You got blood on my fucking sidewalk? Blood and piss on MY FUCKING SIDEWALK."

We pulled TK off the guy. "What the fuck? You tryna kill someone today? Stop. That's enough!" I said. TK looked at the bigger guy. "Get the fuck up. You and your friend get the fuck outta here before I get really mad." I looked at the smaller guy, who was trying to see straight. He sure wasn't laughing now. The tall guy helped his pal stand up and they stumbled off. Good, I thought, he seemed like he'd be okay. They didn't look back.

TK then looked at the crowd. "What are you looking at? Show's over. Screw!" People mumbled. Everyone dispersed. TK looked away and then walked over and sat on his front steps. We let him stew for a few minutes before we joined him on the cold steps.

"You okay?" I asked.

"Yeah, everything's just great."

"C'mon, let's go to Johnny's. Forget all this. The food's getting cold," Sal said.

"I'm not hungry."

Without another word, he stood up, walked into his dad's house and slammed the door.

The following Wednesday evening I wanted to see how TK was doing so I stopped by the guy's apartment on K Street. What a combo. Sal was a neat freak, TK was a slob, and Sully was Sully. Actually Sully leaned more towards Sal when it came to cleaning up. Once and awhile Sully cleaned TK's mess in the TV room but TK never thanked him. That was TK being TK.

I sat down waiting for their TV reality show to end. The boys were snacking on peanuts, chips, pepperoni, crackers and cheese. They were eating healthy tonight. TK seemed to be in a good mood. Sal told me he'd been quiet the past few days. TK looked at me several times during the show but didn't say anything. He knew what I was thinking.

"Listen, I know I fucked up at the bar the other night. You guys know me. Shit happens. Sorry. I really do try to keep my mouth shut. Sometimes I lose control after a few beers. Don't get me wrong, Al sucks. That's not over yet but that wasn't the right time or place to settle with him. I'll settle that sooner rather than later, you can all count on that."

I didn't even want to ask what TK meant by that statement.

"What about Sunday's blood bath?" I asked.

"Well, that was a different story."

Anger and TK are the best of pals sometimes. We knew he reached a breaking point with Al at the bar and with the drunks the next day. His hatred of Al had a life of its own. And he had had enough with outsiders acting like dickheads, especially on Saint Patrick's Day. Couldn't blame him but we were concerned.

"Look either way, you gotta calm down. We don't want anything happening to you. You're probably my best friend if you can believe it."

Before I barely got the words out, Sal said, "What are we?

198

Fuckin' assholes?"

"I thought we were all best friends," Sully said.

We laughed.

"Sorry guys, you know what I mean. We're family. The Pact solidifies that. The Pact will always be with us."

"We're like the four musketeers," Sully said.

"It's the three musketeers you knucklehead," TK said.

"I know I was making a joke, you dick."

"Yeah, it was terrible," TK said.

Notwithstanding these foolish interruptions, I could tell TK appreciated what I said. He got the message. We had unconditional friendship, a rare commodity in today's world.

"When I see Al I see my dad's sad face and know he's still hurtin' about Big Kane. He's too proud to admit it. For Christ sake, he lost mom and then his brother. Never complained, never vented. Always hiding it inside but you can see the pain on his face and hear it in his voice."

Silence enveloped us. We weren't sure what to say next.

"Al's heartless. He's a fuckin' nigga," TK blurted out.

We all exchanged glances.

"Whoa, back up man. You know I hate that word."

"The word nigga is color blind. It doesn't matter if you're black, white, or fucking blue. I really don't care…if you're any kind of nigga you're a bad person."

"Can you stop saying *that* word? This shit is why everyone hates Southie and thinks we're racist fucks."

"Sometimes I say the 'n' word by mistake when I'm singing along to rap," Sully said.

We all looked at him as if to say shut the fuck up.

"Al's a nigga," TK said again, ostensibly irritated. "And he's ruining Southie. People are dying because Al's selling them poison. The heat's sorta off now and people think things are going okay. But it's not. Take a look around. Open your eyes. Junkies are still everywhere, selling shit, doing shit."

TK took a deep breath. "Al's killing his own people and on top of that, with each new condo built, we lose a little of the 'Old' Southie. That's also buggin' me. Fuck Al, fuck the yuppies, fuck the pols who sold us out, and the fuckin' developers who are making all the money while our fuckin' neighborhood identity disappears."

I didn't want to readily admit it yet I knew he was right. My thoughts wandered to what Southie would look like in a few years. I envisioned myself standing at Dorchester Heights, where you can look across the neighborhood in every direction possible. The once blue collar neighborhood dotted with family homes was now a monolithic condo reserve filled with faceless people. TK's words matched my thoughts. 'Fuckin' condos. Look like projects without the cockroaches.'

"Well, you can't stop change or hold back time," Sal blurted out. "Fuck off," TK said, as he uncharacteristically lit a cigarette, hoping the embrace of nicotine would settle his nerves. "Save that bullshit for somebody else. I don't want to hear it."

"It's called progress," Sully said. "I think."

"No," TK said. "Sometimes so-called progress is an illusion. Ya know what it's really called. What it really is. It's called the dismemberment of a neighborhood. The displacement of good, decent people by greed and profit. *It's the death of a neighborhood.*"

Again I thought it was tough to argue against that. Really didn't want to anyway.

It all happened so fast. Before you knew it, churches and

schools were closed and converted into condos so fat cat developers could get fatter. Nobody says anything about that in the papers. Families are dwindling along with our youth sports' teams. Everyone is moving out. They don't want to because they love Southie but they're forced to leave. They can't afford their own town anymore. Middle class families can't buy in Southie. Prices are too high. Ironically, the suburbs are more affordable now, a reversal of times past.

TK was all fired up. He kept on talking.

"Politicians talk about affordable housing. What a fuckin' joke. You'd have to be making a lot more than a middle class income to afford anything in Southie. And as soon as the yuppies with the puppies are sick of partying on Broadway and ready to raise a family, they'll flee to the burbs where they can get quality public education for their kids. It will be a vicious circle of yuppies moving in and out. Every time you see a funeral procession take the Castle Island route before heading to the cemetery you know another Southie old timer died, and when you hear about another young kid that OD's…its simple math guys. Pretty soon The Old Southie will be completely gone and that will be FUCKIN' sad."

"That's a pretty bleak picture you're painting," Sully said.

"It happened in the North End and Charlestown," Sal said. "It's happening in a lot of other places in Boston too."

"I don't care 'bout other places," TK said. *"I only care about Southie."*

"I gotta admit it does suck bigtime," Sal said. "Seeing this happen seemingly overnight bites it."

"Johnny, why don't you write an editorial piece about it in the paper?" TK asked. "You can entitle it 'The death of a neighborhood' like I said before, or 'The Yuppie Takeover' because that's exactly what it is."

"Now you know how the Indians felt," Sully said.

THIRTY-TWO

Pat uncharacteristically retreated into his bedroom. He didn't even say hi to Jaws as he walked past him in the parlor. He was sitting on their stolen leather couch watching a hoop game on their stolen, 50-inch HDTV. It seemed a bit weird that he didn't acknowledge him, but Jaws let it go. Moments later, he heard a big bang outside the front of the house. Jaws peered through the window down into the darkness and saw, what was once a TV, laying in smithereens on the sidewalk. It was right below Pat's bedroom. Neighbors came outside to see what happened. More timid ones peered from their front windows.

Jaws burst into his room.

"What the fuck did you do?" Pat didn't answer. He was in his own world. "And what the fuck's that smell?"

"What did you do?" Jaws repeated. He wasn't gonna get an answer from Pat. He looked around the room and found a pinner in an ashtray. Whenever Pat smoked weed, he always rolled a fattie so Jaws knew this wasn't weed. He smelled it. "Fuckin' angel dust!?" Pat laughed, "Just adding new things to my resume."

"That's really great. Do you know you just threw a TV out the window?"

Pat started laughing manically. Jaws snapped his fingers at him. "Hello?" Suddenly, Pat jumped up and started to tear his room apart violently like he was experiencing a major adrenaline rush. He threw clothes and sheets everywhere, slammed his lamp against the wall, smashed an empty beer bottle on the floor. All while spewing nonsense. He shielded his eyes from an invisible light, "Aw so bright" He kicked off an imaginary thing that was holding on to his leg. "He's chewing my foot! The motherfucker's chewing my foot!" Jaws reacted, "Jesus Christ" he tackled him and threw him on the bed face first. Jaws sat on Pat's back and held his hands down. "I'm not letting you up until you calm down you crazy bastard. Stick with the fun drugs, for Christ sakes."

Jaws sat on top of Pat. Pat struggled then looked up to the shadows on the wall. They were dancing. With the noise and constant movement of the city, the shadows were very much alive, as much as he was. He tried to close his eyes and rest but his brain was moving too fast. Aggressively fast, like it was assaulting itself. And if he wasn't careful, would implode. He looked over to the dresser where there was medication. Klonopin. He pointed towards the bottle without saying a word and Jaws obliged him. Jaws sat next to Pat on the bed, listening to his nonsense for the next forty five minutes, until he finally passed out.

The next morning Jaws was sitting in the living room when Pat walked out of his bedroom.

"Jesus, what da fuck happened last night," Pat said. "Room's a mess. Can't remember shit only shadows dancing in my head."

"You threw the TV out the fucking window you mental case! You said you *tossed it aside.*"

"I did? Fuck. Man. I was whacked out I guess."

"You guess? You thought you were being eaten by some imaginary creatures. Whacked ain't the word."

"Well, sorry I thought I was being eaten! Wow, I guess it was a good night."

"You need to get a grip Pat. You're losin' it."

"Hey don't need any lectures from you."

"Okay whatever you say."

"Worry about yourself. Not me. I'm in control."

"Seriously?"

"Still looking in the mirror every day and like what I see."

"You might have to get your eyes checked down at the local clinic."

Nothing Jaws said bothered Pat one iota. Pat made some coffee and sat down. "Wanna take a ride and score some percs," he asked. "Nah. Broker than a cheap toaster. You holdin' any cash?"

"No. Still know where we can score."

"How?"

"Fallon the other night was talking 'bout how he's on disability still, he must have a ton of pain meds in his house, percs, Oxy, who knows."

"I think I'll pass."

"C'mon."

"No."

"Why not?"

"Why not?"

"Yeah."

"Cuz I'm not fucking stealing from an old friend. That alright with you?"

"Oh forgot you were an angel. Didn't have a conscience when we stole thousands of dollars of booze last month at that winery in Worcester and beat the shit out of that security guard."

"You did most of the beating up you savage."

"You didn't stop me."

"Yeah that was business, but I'm not beating up someone I played hoop with down the Boys Club. I do have morals, ya know?"

"Oh sorry." He blessed himself. "Father forgive me for I have sinned."

Jaws pushed him. "Fuck you."

"One last chance."

"Call the Junk Man and leave me out of it. He'd steal from his own mother."

Jack "The Junk Man" Jenkins was a D Street project rat. He had a tough upbringing and shot up more heroin (junk) than anyone else in Southie. And it showed. He was so far gone in his addiction that he had no moral tissue left. Jaws sensed Pat was heading in that direction and he didn't want to be a part of it.

A few hours later, Robbie Fallon heard a knock on his apartment door. He opened it and in walked two of his old drinking buddies. "Hey guys, what's goin' on?" Fallon asked, as he put on the Sports Channel.

"Just thought we'd drop by. Say hello," Pat said.

"C'mon, grab a seat. You guys want a beer?"

"Of course we do," the Junk Man said. "Think we just wanna look at your ugly puss?"

Robbie came back with three Bud Lights. "How you been? What's up?" he asked.

"Just wondering if you're holdin,'" the Junk Man said.

"Usually are, aren't you," Pat budded in.

Right then, Fallon knew he shouldn't have opened up his drunken jaws the other night at the bar.

"We were wondering if you could spare a few percs," Pat

said. "We'll pay for them." Pat didn't have any intention of paying for anything. Fallon knew it. He twitched unexpectedly, signaling he was nervous. "I need 'em. Sorry."

"C'mon man," the Junk Man pleaded.

"Only got a few left. Need them for myself. My back is killing me dudes."

Pat and the Junk Man glanced at each other. They looked around the room. Opportunity was painted on their faces. Fallon's stomach did a flip. Pat said, "We need a few to ease the pain too. What do ya say? Help out a few old friends?"

"Next week, I can refill my prescription. I'll hook you guys up I swear."

As soon as those words hit the air, the Junk Man got up and punched Fallon in the face. He fell down to the floor holding his nose as blood gushed out, covering his hand. "You broke my fuckin' nose!" Fallon yelled. "I'll break your face if you don't tell me where the percs are," the Junk Man said, as he struck him again. Fallon collapsed to the floor and he retreated into the fetal position. "They're in the second drawer in my bedroom dresser."

The Junk Man and Pat went to Fallon's bedroom, got the drugs, and headed to the front door. "Hold on one second," the Junk Man said. "C'mon dude let's go," Pat said. The Junk Man walked over to Fallon, who was still on the floor. He kicked him hard in the gut. "See you next week for our refill."

THIRTY-THREE

The First Resort Restaurant, owned by the O'Callaghan family since it first opened in 1953, was one of the busiest and well-known places in Southie. Former presidents toasted residents there. Actors partied there. Pols and gangsters broke bread there. Locals punched well-known, drunken sportscasters there. I looked around the room. The place was jammed. My parents took me here when I was a kid. I'd always have a hot turkey sandwich with French Fries. Afterwards I'd eat a big piece of apple pie with vanilla ice cream on top.

"Their scallops are good here," Pam said.

"Yeah, I like everything on their menu," I said.

Our waitress came over with our drinks, some bread, and took our order. In the far corner of the restaurant a man was playing the piano and a group of older men at the bar were singing, pretending they knew the words to the songs.

"Thanks for calling," Pam said.

"Figured you'd like to get out and grab a bite."

"You figured right."

"Good...I'm glad."

"Where are the boys?" Pam asked.

"Busy watching that new crime fighter's show," I said.

"Must see TV huh?"

"Must see TV alright..."

"TK training for his next fight?" Pam asked.

"Yeah in between eating junk food and lying on the couch, he's going all out."

I drank some water. Pam buttered her bread and took a bite.

"So how are you doing in school?" I asked.

"Fine. Just taking two courses this semester. Should be finished next year."

"Still nursing right," I asked.

"Yeah, lookin' forward to saving the world. But seriously I'm looking forward to it."

"How about you? How's teaching?" Pam asked, as she began eating.

"I'm good…and my job is great.…kids never fail to surprise me one way or the other."

"What else is going on?" Pam asked.

"I'm working at the new rehab center."

"Oh, I didn't know that."

"Just two nights a week as a volunteer. No big deal."

"Sure it is. It's nice. Helping others for the donut."

"Yeah thanks. It's going good…but a learning curve for me. Got to make sure I say the right thing without lecturing. Without offending anyone. Talked Robbie Fallon into attending some counseling sessions on Mondays and Thursdays. He's doing better. Looks better after getting beat up."

"Really, that's great. Not that he got beat up but that he's doing better."

"Got my fingers crossed as the old timers say," I said.

"Whatever happened with him and his wife?"

"He's hoping she'll come back if he stops drinking and abusing his painkillers. He's got legitimate pain issues but is taking too many pills. Has to buy more on the street when his prescription runs out early. We're hoping he can do that, wean off them a bit…and he's progressing."

"Good for him. I always liked Robbie."

The waitress brought over our meals. "Do you want some more bread," she asked. "Yes. And could we have more water please?" She returned a few minutes later with the bread and filled our glasses. "Thanks," I said.

We ate, talked, laughed and had dessert. We were about to leave when Al walked up to our table. He was with a woman in her early twenties who we didn't know. "Hey Johnny. Hi Pam," he said. "Guess I had the same idea." I said hello but Pam just looked. "Say hello to Christina," he said. "She's from Farragut Road. Little younger but that's how I like 'em."

"Nice to meet you Christina," I said. "Always a pleasure Al. Enjoy your meal."

It was unbelievable that we ran into him. Ton of restaurants in Southie and he comes strolling in. Talk about giving someone indigestion.

On the way home, Pam was seemingly frozen in thought. Then she spoke. "Al's really a piece of work. He's a snake. Just doesn't get it. He thinks people like him. He's so self-absorbed. It's no wonder he doesn't consume himself. We were having a great time and he shows up. When I see him I think of Pete. I see Pete."

It felt like she was going to cry but didn't. She fought it and it passed.

We arrived at her house.

She caught me off guard as she kissed me on the lips and said goodnight.

THIRTY-FOUR

It was morning and Dee Modica heard a knock in her door. She opened it and saw her mom standing there with two cups of coffee and a paper bag. Dee looked terrible, hung over, strung out.

"I'm afraid to ask. Can I come in?"

"Sure. Why not," Dee said, as she rubbed her head.

"Here's your butts," Mrs. Modica said.

Dee took them.

"You're welcome," Mrs. Modica said.

"Oh…ya…right."

"You're a beaut," Mrs. Modica said, shaking her head in resignation.

"Yeah…whatever Ma."

"Here. Thought you'd like some coffee from the Java House."

"Love their coffee."

Mrs. Modica passed Dee the coffee. She took a few Motrin out of her pocket and washed it down with the coffee.

"Got a couple of Danishes too."

"Great, just what I need." Dee laughed. "C'mon, we'll sit in the kitchen."

The kitchen was simple and ordinary. Tiny. The sink was full with dirty dishes. The counter littered with junk mail. Dee removed some magazines from one of the chairs and told her mom to sit down. "Sorry about the mess," Dee said, as she removed a few coffee mugs from the table and added them to her dish pile. "Why sorry…your place is always a mess. I just don't understand it. I've always kept a clean house but you're terrible."

Just then the bathroom door opened and Kaleigh walked into the kitchen singing an old love song. She abruptly stopped. "Oh hi Mrs. Modica. How you doin'?"

"Doin' great how 'bout you."

"Fine as green grass."

"Original," Mrs. Modica said. "I like that."

"Try to be."

"Yeah, that's great," Dee said. "Do you want some of my coffee?"

"Nah, I'm good. Thanks anyway."

"Half a Danish?"

"No you need it more than me."

"Very funny," Dee said. "Sorry, didn't know you'd be here," Mrs. Modica said, looking at Kaleigh. "Not to worry," Kaleigh said. "I gotta go anyway. Getting my hair and nails done. Gotta look good ya know what I mean."

"Look good for Jaws?" Dee asked. Kaleigh only paused. "You got that conniving look all over you stupid face," Dee said.

Kaleigh said, "Hey nothing wrong with a girl branching out. Guys do it all the time but nobody says shit. I ain't got no ring on my finger."

"You don't have to talk jive because you're gonna cheat on your guy," Dee said. "Have fun, you cheatin' whore."

"I always do."

They laughed like schoolgirls.

Mrs. Modica stood there listening in disbelief at the conversation she just heard. She thought she was watching a soap opera on TV. Wanted to give them both a piece of her mind, but figured it was a waste of time and energy.

"Call you later, Dee. See ya Mrs. Modica."

Kaleigh left and then Dee's phone went off. She looked at it. "Who's that?" Mrs. Modica asked. "Just Pat, being a bug. Asking me to order him a pizza later on. Imagine that, like he's thinkin' about pizza already. Someday he's gonna turn into one and probably eat himself the animal."

Mrs. Modica wasn't amused. She disliked Pat and blamed him for Dee's drug problem. Dee could read her mind. It was obvious.

"I know Ma...you don't like Pat...but he's not as bad as you think he is...seriously."

She ignored Dee's statement.

Dee didn't blame Pat. It happened before she hooked up with him. She drifted back again to that dreadful night in the hotel with Al that started her journey into hell. Every time this pain of recollection grew stronger not weaker and was undeterred by time. She would have exchanged this regrettable experience for anything yet knew she couldn't change the past.

On many an occasion, she dreamt about Al and how he took advantage of her. She'd wake up sweating and overwrought with anguish. Dee wanted to tell her mom that Al was the real villain, not Pat, but inexplicably couldn't summon enough courage to do so. Or perhaps she just didn't want to listen to her mom's response if she did. Either way Dee felt this nightmare would never end, couldn't end, because life wouldn't allow it to fade away.

"I think you need to slow down," Mrs. Modica said, awakening Dee from her thoughts.

"Slow down with what?" she asked defensively.

213

Mrs. Modica's eyebrows almost hit the ceiling. "You know. Drugs! Booze! You name it!"

"What's this? A fuckin' one person intervention? I thought family and friends got together and like ganged up on someone. Just you? My mom. The Lone Ranger to the rescue!"

"The other day when I saw you…you looked like shit. You still do. When was the last time you showered?"

"Fuck showers. I like a layer of filth on me. So do the French."

"Are you listening to yourself?" she asked.

"I'm fine… under control."

"C'mon, can't shit a shitter."

"Honestly, wouldn't lie to you."

Mrs. Modica looked at her daughter. Last time someone promised her "I wouldn't lie to you," he ended up dead. It was her nephew Michael who overdosed on downers.

"I'm here for you. You know that right?"

"Of course."

"You gonna try to…?"

"Yes," Dee interrupted. "Girl Scouts honor?"

"You were never a girl scout," Mrs. Modica said. "What am I gonna do with you."

Mrs. Modica took a big bite of her pastry. She drank some coffee and looked at Dee. I wish she'd reach inside herself for the willpower to do what was right, Mrs. Modica thought. It's her life and if she doesn't change, she'll regret it. Then she remembered. "Oh, I got somethin' for you. I walked along the beach today. It was beautiful, deserted. I love it when nobody's around. Gives me time to think, reflect on things. I found some things that made me think of you." Mrs Modica said, as she dropped heart rocks on the table. They clinked on the table, about a dozen, all different sizes but all unequivocally shaped like hearts. Dee didn't like to cry in front of people, especially her mother. She never liked to look weak but couldn't help it; the visual was all too much. *Please don't give up on yourself. Remember God is watching you.* She thought about how she felt when she was younger, having those heart rocks. Feeling contented with her perfect potential. Her young self would be so disappointed in who she has become. What she has done.

At that moment she wanted to change. She knew she'd do anything she could. But she also knew she was weak and a liar. The thought of being sober forever frightened her, the same way the idea of infinity frightened her as a child. "What do you mean it goes on forever?" she'd ask. The answer was it never ends. Right when you think its ending it's beginning again. That's what being sober felt like. An endless hell with no release. A harsh reality where hope was sucked from you into the hole you kept digging and digging. And yet there were the heart rocks looking at her. *God is watching you.*

The moment was filled with sadness, a sadness that took over the whole room and traveled through her veins and weighed her down. Dee let out a cry again, a mix of hope and doubt as to her future. She remembered a saying from one of her self-help books. 'You could drive from coast to coast, take a long drive at night and you can get there safely even if your lights only shine a few feet in front of you at a time.' Dee could see a few feet in front of her and was hoping her unspoken promise to change would prove to be true in the end.

Mrs. Modica's message seemingly hit home but she felt it was time to lighten the mood.

"Baby's sleeping huh?"

"No, he's reading the paper."

They both laughed.

"C'mon, I want to see him," Mrs. Modica said. "He always puts a smile on our faces."

THIRTY-FIVE

The day drifted into night and so did Kaleigh McDonough. She had been in four bars already along East Broadway and had a nice buzzing going. Next up was the Brass Hat. Recently renovated by new ownership, the bar was built in 1956 and was originally called the Beer Stop. Some of the old customers-and characters-still drank there and Kaleigh knew it.

"I'd like something different," she said, to the young bartender. "Surprise me please."

The bartender put on his thinking cap, started working his magic, and poured her a drink. "You'll like this. Trust me."

She tasted it and nodded approval.

"Thanks."

"You're welcome."

"Ya know you're kinda cute," she said. He smiled, simply said thanks and told the bar-back he needed a bottle of Bailey's Irish Cream. Then he walked away to serve another customer.

Kaleigh sipped on her drink and looked down the end of the bar. She saw Mark "Devil-Dog" Bailey sitting with several friends. Bingo. She smiled inside. She stood up and walked down to him. She put her arms around him and planted a big kiss on his lips.

"That's for being such a good guy," she said. He laughed. "You're only saying that because it's true."

"I'll be right back. Gotta go to the ladies' room."

Mark was surprised. He went to high school with Kaleigh. They weren't exactly total strangers. He hadn't seen her in about a year. When she returned, Mark's friends were gone. "What did I

217

scare them off?" she asked. "No. They had to leave. Already drank too much. They're getting old and boring." Kaleigh sat down. "Well. Are you getting old and boring too?" He put his left hand on her right thigh and said, "Never."

"Good then let's get out of here," she said. They walked outside and got in Mark's car that was parked in the back lot. "You holdin' anything?" she asked. "Got some Oxy 80's," he said. He took a small bottle out of his front pocket. Kaleigh took the pill. "C'mon," she said. "It's party time. Let's go down to the Hub Bar. Have a few drinks. Then I'll show you how grateful I can be."

"Okay. Why not," he replied. "It's still early."

Minutes later they walked into the Hub Bar, sat down and ordered drinks. They had several more drinks and were buzzed out of their brains. She was all over Mark, rubbing his leg and whispering in his ear. The door opened and Jaws walked in. She didn't see him until the damage was done. He walked up right behind them.

"What the fuck," he said. "What are you doin?"

"What?"

"What your ass."

"Hey Jaws…don't want to…"

"Shut up. I'm not talkin' to you."

"Hey. Nobody said we were exclusive," Kaleigh said.

"I thought…"

"You thought wrong."

"Ya know you're a fuckin' bitch. Get the fuck out of my bar."

"I haven't finished my drink yet."

Jaws visualized punching them in the mouth, one by one,

knocking both out cold on the floor, but opted to leave before regret paid him an unwelcome visit, regret accompanied by the police.

"And stay the fuck out of my life," he yelled, as he opened the door to leave.

THIRTY-SIX

Jaws hadn't seen Pat for over a month. They had parted ways as roommates. He was trying to get his life in order and was off the shit but suffering from withdrawals. He wasn't sure why he wanted to find Pat...to save him too? Or because he knew he could get drugs with him? He was battling inside himself and wanted to see his best friend. He did a loop around Southie, a "Southie 500" as he liked to call it and finally spotted Pat at the entrance of the West Fifth Street Park. He was about to get out and talk to Pat, but something stopped him. He sat in his car and just watched for a few minutes. Nobody noticed him sitting there. He found himself deep in thought, trying to figure out what he was going to say to Pat.

Local kids were playing hoop while others were sitting on benches sweet-talking the girls. Pat walked into the park and hugged the Junk Man. Suddenly, a car filled with young, suburban-type guys pulled up to the entrance to the park. Pat walked over to them and took the lead.

"Hey gents, what's up?" Pat asked.

The kid sitting in the passenger seat said, "Just lookin' for Jaws."

"Why are you looking for this Jaws guy?"

"He said he could hook us up with some white powder and good weed."

"Don't know anyone named Jaws," Pat said.

Jaws heard this and it affected him more than he'd like. The Junk Man came over and stood beside Pat.

"We met him a few months ago on East Broadway near the

Writer's Bar," said the driver. "Said this was one of his hangouts if we ever needed to hookup."

"Maybe I can help you guys out. Where you from?"

"We go to UMass, Boston."

"Yeah, but where you from?"

"Hingham," said the driver. "I'm Eric and these guys are from all over. We heard there's good shit here."

Pat looked at them and smiled. "Hi guys from all over. If you got the cash I'll supply the stash." That's pretty good Pat thought, proud of his clever rhyme. "I'll pay now," said a guy in the back seat. "And you guys can pony up later." He handed Pat $200. "Here's half for weed and the other for coke."

"Okay we'll be right back."

"Where are you going?" one of them said, clearly nervous they were about to get screwed over. "Relax. Got you covered. Gotta make a phone call."

Pat and the Junk Man walked down the sidewalk a bit and made a call on their cell. A few moments later, a car drove by and dropped something off to them. They handed over the goods to the guys. Simple as that.

"Thanks dude."

"Pleasure doing business with ya. Don't do too much of the white stuff. It's pure. Gets you where you want to be."

The guys drove off and as soon as they turned the corner, Pat and the Junk Man burst into hysterics. Naïve suburbanites. Eager to score, they fell into a trap. Pat and the Junk Man bunked them, gave them fake drugs. They laughed and laughed and laughed until Pat chimed in "C'mon, let's get the fuck out of here."

As they started to walk away, a car screeched up behind

them and the young guys jumped out of the car. It was the first time they saw them outside the car and they were bigger than they seemed sitting down. They looked like athletes. Pat and the Junk Man momentarily froze. Eric had the bag of white powder in his hand. He tasted it in front of them. "Are you guys fucking serious? This is baking soda."

"And the weeds shit. Smells like crap," another guy said.

A group of teenagers playing hoop didn't miss a beat and walked over towards the commotion. One kid lagging behind with his head down suddenly looked up and whipped his basketball at one of the outsiders. Blood covered his face as he hit the ground. The brawl had begun. The local teenagers joined Pat and the Junk Man as they attacked the guys. Pat kicked another one in the groin. He fell and hugged the ground, moaning. The Junk Man took out a knife and waved it in the air. "Should get goin' while the goin's good," he yelled.

"C'mon guys, let's go." Eric said. "Let's get the fuck out of here."

"Right. Get the fuck out of Southie," the Junk Man yelled.

Pat and the Junk Man roared with delight.

Others followed their lead.

"Thanks for the money," Pat bellowed.

"We'll spend it wisely. See you next week," the Junk Man sarcastically yelled.

"Tell Jaws we said hi!" Pat roared, as he and the Junk Man fell into hysterics.

Watching this drama unfold nauseated Jaws.

He had seen enough.

And heard too much.

He drove off not looking back.

THIRTY-SEVEN

Dee Modica couldn't escape the demons which invaded her being. They were not willing to give up such a willing host. Her insides screamed for help but nobody was listening. Dee called Pam and asked her to stop by the apartment and talk. Pam didn't hesitate and agreed to come over that night. She thought Dee was reaching out for help. Dee opened the door. To her surprise I was standing beside Pam. Dee stood speechless. Moments passed. "Are you gonna let us in," Pam asked, abruptly. "Of course…c'mon in…good to see *both* of you."

"How you doin'?" Pam asked, as she walked inside the apartment.

"Good, just needed a little company. Just wasn't expecting Johnny," she said to herself.

"He's my bodyguard" Pam said, reading Dee's mind.

"Somebody has to protect her," I interjected. Pam gave me a slight nudge.

"I thought Sully was the comedian," Dee said.

"Good to see you too," I said.

"Johnny you know you're always welcome."

"Well thanks," I said.

We walked into the living room and sat down. The room was small with one dark green couch and two plain chairs filling up most of the space. Two pictures hung on the rear wall, old castles pictured in the Irish countryside. Beautiful. Empty book shelves and a large mirror, which made the room look larger than it really was, occupied the side wall. Dee picked up a few cups and glasses off of the coffee table and walked towards the kitchen.

"Does anyone want a drink? Wine? Beer?

"No Thanks," I said, speaking for the both of us.

"I got vodka?"

"You got water?" Pam asked.

"Yeah."

"Water would be great," I said.

Dee grabbed two bottles of spring water out of the refrigerator and then poured herself a straight shot of vodka.

"Cheers," she said, as she gulped it down.

Neither Pam nor I were amused.

Dee looked dirty.

Pale white.

"You should slow down. It's only Tuesday," I said.

"Just one to take the edge off."

"Haven't heard from you lately?" Pam said.

"Just taking care of Patrick."

"How is the little guy?" I asked.

"He's doin' great the little bugger. He's napping. C'mon."

Dee got up and motioned for us to follow her into the nearby bedroom. Little Pat's room was sky blue with pictures of him, Dee, Pat, and Dee's mom hanging on the walls. Toy cars and trains were on the floor and a big teddy bear sat in the corner beside the baby's crib. More baby toys were huddled in another corner next to the diaper table.

"This room's great," Pam said. "I love the pictures especially your mom holding the baby."

"Ya. She's been terrific too. Comes over a lot and helps me out...babysits ya know."

"That's what grandmas do," Pam said. "You're lucky she's

224

there for you."

"I wish I could be as good a mom as she's been."

"You are," said Pam, as she walked over to the crib. "He's beautiful. He looks like an angel from a book. I can't tell who he looks like."

I couldn't tell either so I stood there listening, silent.

"Definitely Pat," Dee said. "I can't wait for a little baby girl who'll look like me that's all."

"Looking ahead, that's good," I said.

"How's Pat with the baby?" Pam asked.

"He's a good dad *sometimes*. He loves little Pat. Brings him toys but doesn't spend much time with us. Not as much as I'd like for sure."

"He'll change…be patient," I said.

"He aint ever gonna change trust me."

"Why not?" Pam asked.

"Pat likes his freedom. He's not someone who likes staying home and watching TV. He won't admit it but he gets high off of the action even before he gets high. Stealin' and all that shit. Being the man. Once in a great while he pretends otherwise but don't like let him fool ya."

"Can't do anything about it?" Pam asked. "Nothin,' Dee said. "I might have his baby but I'm not expecting him to change his ways. It would take a miracle."

Pam said, "Ya never know. People do change. Just gotta have a little faith that's all."

"I'm not that optimistic just saying it as I see it." Pam knew she was irritating Dee, so she changed the subject. "Does the baby sleep through the night?"

"Yeah, he's good like that. Just taking a late nap today. I

225

expect him to wake up soon."

"We can wait...not in a hurry. I'd like to hold him before we go," Pam said. Dee looked down at her baby. She tucked the blanket in around him. We left the room and sat down. Pam said, out of the blue. "Maybe someday you guys will get married. Settle down. Grow old together." Dee turned sullen. "What's the matter?" Pam asked. "Pat and I had a big fight. He left and we haven't talked since then."

"I'm sorry to hear that," I said.

Teary-eyed she mumbled with false bravado, "Hey life goes on."

"Little Pat will keep you busy," Pam said.

"Wanna watch a little TV?" Dee asked.

"Why don't we just talk," Pam said.

"Sure. Let me show you guys some more baby pictures."

Dee went through some pictures on her phone. Her face lit up with every photo. Little Pat with baby cereal all over his face, smiling. Little Pat playing with the neighbor's dog. Little Pat at Grandma's house trying to crawl up the stairs and then falling. She showed Pam Little Pat dressed up as a jack-o'-lantern. "We took this one at Castle Island when they have their annual Halloween party. Love going there."

Happiness seemed to make a brief appearance as she showed us more and more photos. Then Dee stood up. She walked over to a nearby table and grabbed the bottle of vodka and poured herself a double. And then another. Pam was pissed. I was amazed she could down so much vodka so fast. I let Pam take the lead.

"I thought you were only havin' one?"

"Hold that thought," Dee said. "Be right back. Mother

Nature's calling." She went into the bathroom for what seemed to be a long time, came back out and sat down again. We knew right away that Dee was high. And it wasn't just vodka.

"You called me over so you can get banged up?" Pam said, angrily.

"No...No...I'm fine."

"No you're not. You're getting drunk... just got high and your baby's in the next room," Pam said.

"You don't understand."

"Seriously?" I said.

"Yeah."

"Wrong. We do understand. You're the one who doesn't understand what you're doing to yourself," Pam said.

"I'm tryin' to be a good mom. Really am."

"Not tryin' hard enough and you've got a lot to lose if you don't wake up," Pam said.

I couldn't imagine how hard it must be for Dee but booze and drugs weren't the answer.

"You're a tough Southie girl," I said. "Look to the future."

Dee didn't answer.

"I could call the Center and get the names of a couple of rehab places that take in moms and their kids together," I said. "Give you some time to get yourself together and feel better. What do you say?"

"They'll let me take Patrick. They won't take him away from me?"

"Yeah...and no. Patrick can stay with you. They won't take him away. Don't worry about that," I said.

"Can ya give me some time to think about it?"

"Only so many beds at these rehab centers."

Then Dee turned the TV on and we sat there in silence. Suddenly she started nodding off. Then she stood up and fell on the floor. We knew. Our insides screamed for help. Pam shook Dee but she didn't respond. She wasn't breathing. Her lips were turning blue. Pam started giving her CPR. I looked around the room and saw Narcan nasal spray near the back of one of the empty shelves next to the huge wall mirror. I grabbed it and sprayed both nostrils. Two minutes passed by. Nothing happened. "Do it again," Pam screeched. I sprayed her nostrils again. It seemed like a lifetime to us. "C'mon…c'mon…." Pam kept saying, barely audible. Finally, Dee awoke.

Pam took her phone and started dialing 911. "You need to get checked out by EMS."

Dee grabbed the phone from Pam. "No they'll take my baby. Please don't. I'm okay. Really I am."

We waited around and Dee regained her composure. She drank some coffee and seemed to be okay. But Dee still needed help. We needed to persuade her to take the first step. She needed to persuade herself to take the first step. Otherwise it would be a fruitless endeavor.

"Do you want me to make that call?" I asked.

"I'll think about it….seriously."

"Might not be anyone here the next time you OD," Pam said. "Think about that."

Dee avoided answering Pam. "I've gotta get Pat's food ready…he'll be waking up soon. Hope you guys don't mind."

That was our cue to leave so Pam hugged Dee and we left. As we walked towards the car I hoped Dee would *seriously* consider getting help.

Back in her apartment, Dee sat on the couch.

She laughed and simultaneously mumbled incoherently.

She laughed again and grabbed the bottle of vodka and drank what remained.

THIRTY-EIGHT

Jaws was standing outside of Calo's Café. The sky was black. Foreboding. Lifeless. It started drizzling. In his younger days, he loved standing in the warm rain. Those feelings surfaced once again. He felt invigorated. Life was good back then. But only when he stepped out of the house and left the misery behind.

Jaws was a prime example of how one can become a product of his environment. His parents pathetically paved the way for his current trajectory in life. His dad was in prison more than he was out. He was a small-time drug dealer and introduced his wife to the pleasures of OxyContin. She was always fucked up. When we saw her she looked like she was sleeping even though her eyes were open. Jaws didn't have anyone at home to love or guide him when he needed it the most. In cases like these, unless a kid's extremely independent, self-motivated, and confident, he too will plummet into the void.

Suddenly he was jolted back to the present.

Life wasn't the same.

He was trying to change.

Pat had reached out. Wanted to meet him and talk about some stuff. About what? Jaws wasn't sure. Maybe Pat wanted to get clean. It was day 37 for Jaws, and things were starting to get a little easier. Suddenly Pat emerged from a car parked at the nearby red light. The Junk Man waved from the driver's seat.

"How ya hittin' em Junk Man?" Jaws asked, masking his apprehension.

"Everything's good."

"Great, glad to hear it."

"Hey how you doin' these days?"

"Doin' okay."

"I loved it when we'd get together up Sully's and chow down on those hot dogs."

"Yeah, the good ole' days," Jaws said.

The Junk Man laughed. Then he said, "See you guys later."

Jaws waved goodbye and then turned to Pat. "How you been?"

"Staying with the Junk Man. Dee and I are finished. She's crazy. Fucked in the head. Doesn't want anything to do with me. Told me to jump off a cliff. Imagine that fuckin' whore bitch thinks she's betta than me. Said I can't see the baby."

Like most accounts, always three sides to a story and the truth is usually found wrapped around all three.

Jaws heard all about it but feigned ignorance. He merely said, "That sucks."

"Sure does. The bitch wants me out of her life. Nothin' I can do about it. She was close to getting her wish in reverse. She almost bought the farm last week. Heard she OD'd. Pam and Johnny were there…her guardian angels."

"She was lucky," Jaws said.

"Lucky ain't the word. Narcan is. It saved her ass again," Pat said.

Pat paused then said, "Other than that I'm doin' great." He was on edge. It was time to get to why he wanted to see Jaws in the first place. "Hey, can ya lend me a couple of bucks 'til next week."

"Next week? Next week hasn't come for you for years. You shittin' me or what."

"Come on."

"I'm broke."

Pat said, "Well, I'm hurtin' man. Ya got anything?'"

"No I'm clean."

"How about your secret stash?"

"No more stash."

"Seriously? What the fuck." Pat started to sweat.

"Sorry."

"Shit. I need to score."

"Go steal some shit downtown and sell it at the bar. Those booze-bags will buy anything."

"I can't do that now. I look like a homeless dude. They'll throw me out before I go in."

"Ask your friend, the Junk Man."

"He's broke too."

"I'm sorry I can't help you pal. I gotta go."

Jaws turned and started to walk away. "Don't like my company anymore, huh?" Pat yelled after him. "I move out of the apartment and I'm not your friend anymore." Jaws stopped, turned, and walked back towards Pat. "Your choice to move out," Jaws said. "And your choice to turn your back on me and hang out with the Junk Man."

"I asked you a question," Pat said. And then repeated, "Don't you like my company anymore?" Jaws sneered at Pat. "I think the feelin's are mutual," he said. "Don't ya think?"

Pat looked around. The intersection was lifeless. He needed money. He needed a fix. Without warning, he took out a knife and charged toward Jaws, who was momentarily shocked, but acted quickly and knocked the knife out of his hand. Pat punched him in the face. Jaws fell to the sidewalk and his head bounced off the cement. It sounded like a firecracker exploding. Blood painted the sidewalk. He screamed in agony. Pain blinded him. Pat stared at his fallen friend. He looked through his pal's pockets and took out his wallet but came up with a fistful of nothing. Frustrated, he kicked Jaws several times in the face and knocked him unconscious. "Motha-fucka," he yelled, as he ran down the street and disappeared from sight.

Thunder and lightning rocked the Heavens as the sky opened up as if in defiance of his unprovoked misdeed.

It started to rain buckets.

Martin O'Malley heard a knock of his front door. He pulled the pure white lace curtain aside and saw his son on the steps. He could smell him through the door. He was standing in the rain and wearing dirty clothes which were soaking wet. He was unshaven and had ugly red spots all over his face. He reluctantly opened the door and stuck his head out. Stunned by his son's ragged appearance, he paused before he spoke. He didn't think there could be any more surprises. Any more heartache. But seeing him standing there he knew. He was wrong.

"What are ya doin' here?" he asked.

"Got no place to go."

"You're not welcome here. You know that."

"Dad, c'mon please."

Pat's father started to close the door. Pat desperately grabbed the door, holding it open.

"Dad I promise. I'll change."

"Change? Really? You promised your mother too! Countless times and every time she wanted to believe you and every time you screwed up."

Martin looked across the floor to a safe he had installed. That's where the family put all their valuables, money, jewelry, IPads, IPhones, anything worth stealing, whenever Pat was around. He thought to himself 'that's normal for us now but it's really not normal.'

Pat's parents gave him everything, including a lot of second chances. They were patriotic, God-fearing, church-going people who were well-known in the neighborhood for their strong work ethic. They owned one of the last mom and pop corner stores in Southie on K and Sixth. When he was younger Pat was surrounded by people who loved him, but people he would, over time, alienate, and eventually emotionally destroy.

"I'm hungry, dad."

"Can't help."

"I'm in trouble. Please."

He'd been in trouble since he was sixteen years old. It was like he hadn't changed since he started getting high. He was told he needed to stop getting high so he could let his brain heal a little bit and grow up. How many times did his mom tell him to go to rehab? 'Please get help,' she'd say on many occasions and he said he would but never did. 'Please get help.'

Martin grabbed a hold of the door. Panic started to sink in with Pat. "You can't do this to me. I'm your son."

"You were my son. Goodbye."

He closed the door in his face. Pat knocked again several times but Martin ignored it. He went to the window and watched Pat as he sat down on the rain-soaked steps. He was hunched over with his hands burying his face. Martin wanted to go outside and help him. Wanted to bring him in, give him another chance, but he knew deep down that he couldn't relent. Some say it only takes one bad turn. *One bad turn* to ruin your life and he felt his son made that life-altering decision a long time ago. But was he right? Could his son be saved or was it really too late?

His daughter's sweet voice brought him a moment of relief. "Hey dad, who was at the door?" Erin yelled, from the kitchen. "Some guy looking for the Assante family. Told him he had the wrong house." Erin put down her book and looked out the kitchen window at the bad weather. "Tough day for someone to get lost."

"Yeah…sure is."

Martin wanted to say more but couldn't.

He started choking up.

He walked into the bathroom concealing the tears that streamed down his face.

THIRTY-NINE

I was taking a short nap. My cellphone rang and my dream vanished along with my slumber.

"Hey Johnny, wanna take a ride with me?" Sal asked.

"What's up?"

"Gotta go see Jaws at the hospital. Got banged-out two nights ago right in front of the café. Hurt pretty bad."

"Come by and pick me up. We'll grab some coffee on the way."

We walked into his room at the Boston Medical Center. Room 505. Maybe I'll play it in the lottery. Jaws was sleeping. Sal sat down. I hate hospitals so I walked over and looked out the window. We remained quiet. After a few minutes, Jaws' eyes slowly opened, and a faint smile arose. It was hard to tell though because his face was so swollen.

"Jesus. You look like you got hit by a truck," Sal said. Jaws gently caressed his face, silently informing us it hurt too much to talk. We nodded. He reached for a pad of paper next to his bed and wrote. *"They had to wire my jaw, it hurts like a whore."*

I just looked at Sal but didn't say anything. "What the fuck happened?" Sal asked. Jaws started writing again and handed me the pad. Sal looked over my shoulder. He wrote, *"It was Pat."* We couldn't believe our eyes. A nurse came in asked us to step aside. She had to take some blood. It only took a few minutes but it seemed like eternity. Sal, Jaws, and I kept exchanging glances. I accidentally caught a glance of the blood and the needle and quickly looked away. Once the nurse was finished, Jaws waved his hands signaling us to give him back the pad. He scribbled, his hand shaking uncontrollably, his mind overwrought with agony. *"Help him,"* he wrote. Jaws tried to stay strong. Several tears attempted to escape from their prison but he caught himself. We said goodbye and found ourselves on Albany Street. Four young guys walked past us. Four more zombies walking the streets. One of them turned around and stuck his Dunkin Donuts coffee cup out. "Got any change?" he asked. I thought Sal was going to explode. "Get a fuckin' job," Sal shot back, uncharacteristically.

Moments after we left, Kaleigh walked through the automatic doors of the Boston Medical Center. She immediately got a pit in her stomach. Just a few months ago she was here and in a world of hell. Every detail, every word spoken, every feeling of remorse was still deeply etched within her being. It was the day she lost the child she didn't even know she had. What's worse was she felt relief about her miscarriage, but in a weird way, that death was like a new beginning for her.

A nurse outside Jaws' room told her to wait outside until the other nurse inside was finished. Kaleigh sat down on a nearby chair and *drifted back in time*. She was back in the waiting-room at the Boston Medical Center. It was crowded. She had walked in all hunched over and zigzagging. Slightly disoriented, she looked around and realized she was all alone. She had plenty of friends when it was time to get banged out but none to be found right now. She wobbled towards the nearest chair and almost fell. Luckily, as soon as the nurse saw her struggling she came right over to her. "Come with me," said a pleasant-looking, gray-haired nurse in a reassuring voice. The nurse grabbed a nearby wheelchair and took her inside the ER. She helped her onto a bed. "I need to check your vitals." The nurse took her temperature and vitals and jotted them down. Her temperature was 101.

"What are your symptoms?" the nurse said.

"Something's not right. I don't know I'm having a period from hell...never felt like this before." Without warning, she threw up. The nurse put some gloves on and helped clean up.

"The doctor will be in soon," the nurse said, as she was leaving the area.

Kaleigh sat there, trying to take deep breaths. Her back and stomach were killing her. She felt like she was being knifed to death. She was burning up. She looked down and saw blood oozing down her leg. There was just so much blood. Everywhere. It was out of control. She started screaming in pain. It was too much to handle. The last thing she remembered was getting an IV. And then there was just darkness. She woke up a few hours later to see a doctor over her hospital bed.

"I'm Doctor Solomon. How are you feeling?" She was in a daze. "What happened?" was all she could muster. Dr. Solomon never liked this part of her job. "Ms. McDonough, I'm sorry to tell you that you've suffered a miscarriage." The doctor noticed her surprise. "Were you aware you were pregnant?"

"No."

"You were about seven weeks."

"Shit," she thought to herself. "Fuckin' menstrual period was never regular anyway."

"Have you been using any illegal drugs?" the doctor asked in a matter-of-fact manner. Kaleigh averted her eyes. Of course. She knew it was obvious she was a user.

"I'm going to have an addiction specialist come in and go over some treatment options you might want to consider. I'm

238

sorry for your loss. Good luck." The doctor closed her medical folder and left the room.

Motherhood sat on the edge of her bed, cloaked in black clothing. Kaleigh looked away. She didn't even know who the father was. She had been sleeping around Southie, hopping in and out of bed with whoever was willing to get her high. She tried to appear or even feel ashamed but she came up empty. She couldn't feel anything except the urge to tear off her hospital gown and get fucked up again. She would have even done the doctor if she'd hook her up with some prescriptions.

Kaleigh's brush with parenthood was over before it began. Sadness now called out to her. Then guilt engulfed her entire being. She closed her eyes and her soul cried. How could it come to this? How had she become so heartless, so uncaring about a loss that happened within her?

Realizing her own indifference scared her, and in a way brought her back to life. Although alone in her hospital bed, never before did she feel so vulnerable, so naked in front of the world. Only an awakening like this could bring about a new beginning. She didn't want to feel this way again. She wanted to feel the joy of life within her. She wanted to live and be happy. Have a normal life and not end up dead in some dive all alone. She prayed that she could soon feel good about herself and desperately clung to the hope that people can change if they really wanted to.

Kaleigh was brought back to the present, a shrill voice interrupting her thoughts. "You can go inside now," said the nurse, as she came out of the room. Kaleigh walked in, bent over and gave Jaws a big kiss on the cheek. "Just wanted to stop by and see how you were doin'." He was surprised to see her. She said, "I like you better when you can't talk." He smiled slightly, as much as he could since his jaw was wired shut. Kaleigh laughed but then got quiet. Jaws reached for his pad of paper. *"Great to see you, bitch. You look good,"* he wrote. She slapped him on the shoulder. "I heard you've been doing good," she said. Everyone in Southie knows that 'I heard you've been doing good' is code word for getting sober, doing the right thing, etc. Jaws wrote down *"37 days."* Kaleigh smiled when she saw the number. "I'm at 45. I always beat you at everything." Kaleigh nervously chuckled and they found themselves awkwardly looking at each other.

What was interesting was Kaleigh and Jaws had had countless conversations, but this was probably the first real one they ever had when they weren't boozing or doing drugs. In a hospital, sober, and one of them with their jaw wired shut. You never know what circumstances you might find yourself in when reality finally settles in. Amazing things can happen when you're at a low point in your life. Some people surprise you – they're there for you. Sometimes, the people you least suspect step up and are there for you. For Jaws, it was Kaleigh. She asked him for his pad of paper. She wrote something down and handed it back to him. He read the note and cupped it in his hand. She grabbed his other hand and held it until he fell asleep.

FORTY

Pat's betrayal spread like wildfire. It was the main topic of conversation at the café. Everything eventually comes out in Southie.

"Anyone see that dirtball around?" TK asked. "No," Calo said.

TK turned to Sal and I. "What did Jaws say? What's he gonna do?"

"Nothin'," Sal said.

"Nothin'?" TK said.

"He didn't want to *talk* about it," Sal said, as he exchanged glances with me. "Just wants to recover that all," I said. "That's it?" TK asked. "He's fine with Pat fuckin' him up?"

"Jaws asked us to help Pat," I said.

"What? He's a betta man than me. I'd kick his ass from L to P Street then spit on him."

"Maybe he skipped town," Sully said. "He has a sister living in New Hampshire."

"Nah," he's around. He can't have any money," Calo said. "I gotta find him, gotta talk to him," I said. "Why don't you go down to Buddie's Place? The last dive in Southie," Calo budded in. "Last place anyone would look."

"Wow, forgot about that dump," I said. "Hard to believe it's still open."

Buddie's Place, located on Old Colony Avenue, the last of the old holdouts, hadn't succumbed to the new beginnings in Southie. When we were underage we all drank there. I drank my first hard drink there, a screwdriver. I still remember that night. I was told the bartenders never asked for ID's but this bartender did. "You're too young to drink," he said, waiting for me to produce my ID. I sat speechless, motionless, sweating inside, until he grabbed a glass and a bottle of vodka and started pouring. The bartender messed with me and I fell for it.

As I walked in, the same dust and the same flies seemed to remain as a reminder of days past. Lefty Loftus was behind the bar. Amazingly he was still working there and presumably still telling his Korean War stories. We used to listen to them with mixed emotions. He always told them verbatim and never omitted any gruesome details of the war. He was a tough son-of-a bitch in his day; and kind of scary yet harmless.

Pat was sitting slumped over in a chair at the end of the bar. I snuck up behind him. I was going to hug him but didn't. Smell and appearance will do that to you. I sat down beside him. He didn't say anything and Pat kept looking straight ahead as if I was invisible. Finally, I spoke. "What's up?" I asked. "Gonna buy me a beer ya cheap prick?"

"Doubt it," Pat said. "Lefty already lent me twenty bucks and gave me two on the house. I think I've maxed out my credit line with him."

"We'll have two Bud Lights down here," I said to Lefty. "Long time no see."

"Same here. It's John, right?" Lefty asked. "Yup, it's me."

"Where you been hiding?"

"With the boys. We've been around. Taking it easy." Lefty nodded, and shook my hand.

"Good to see you," he said. "Same here," I said. "You never change."

"Try not to," he said. "Gotta keep on ticking like that Eveready Bunny."

Lefty cleaned off the bar area in from of us. He gave us our beers, shuffled down to the other end of the bar, and started fidgeting with the television. "Damn new TVs are a pain in the ass," he mumbled to himself.

I looked on the wall to my right where a picture of Lefty in his army uniform had collected years of dust. "What a picture," I said to Pat. "His war stories were great but gave me nightmares."

"Yeah, that's wonderful," Pat said. "Listen, it would be best you left me alone."

Pat lifted up his shirt sleeve and showed one of his tattoos that read, 'Fuck off.' I couldn't help but laugh, "That's a terrible tattoo, Pat." Pat didn't respond but swigged his beer. "Saw Jaws the other day," I said. "Yeah? How's he doin'?" Pat abruptly asked.

"His jaw is wired shut."

"Jaw's jaw is wired shut? Funny hey?" He tried to laugh but couldn't muster it. "He's gonna be okay," I said.

"Did he say anything about me?"

"He asked me and Sal to help you."

"Yeah right."

"Nope, swear to God."

"You're lying."

"Here's the note he wrote." I threw it on the bar. Pat read the crumbled-up note. His eyes moistened. "I fucked my own friend and he asks *you* guys to help *me*. Jesus Christ." He banged his fist on the top of the bar.

"You weren't thinkin' straight."

"I haven't been thinkin' straight for a while. I was jonesin'.

243

Freakin' lost it."

"We all make mistakes."

"Mistakes? Breakin' his jaw is more than just a fuckin' mistake. No excuse for that, even for a guy like me."

"You can't change the past. You can only start where you are now."

"Ya know I wish I never met Jaws. We both would've been betta off. I wish. I just wish it could've been different. Wish it could be different right now."

I wasn't sure what else to say. So I just sat there for a minute.

"Do ya know what else I wish? I wish we were still playing Little League at the park. After the games I loved swinging on that big tree next to the playground. Can still feel that cool ocean breeze on my face."

"Can still be that way. Plenty of good times left for us. Time to start a new chapter in your life."

"Too late for that. Too late to ever feel like I did before. Too late for anything. I fucked over everyone I cared about. I can't blame them for hating my guts." Pat shook his head. He pulled up his left shirt sleeve and revealed another tattoo. It was the face of a man in ostensible agony with the words 'No More Pain' underneath the chin. "That's me all over. I'm done," he said. "Don't talk nonsense," I said.

"No. No. No. For once in my fucked-up life I'm talking sense. I've poisoned everyone against me. I'd steal your eyeballs if you weren't looking."

"C'mon."

"I'm done."

"No you're not. You got plenty of fastballs still left in you."

"Wow, baseball analogies to cheer me up, that's good."

Pat shrugged his shoulders and scratched his scarred, dirty face. I asked Lefty if there were any sports on TV. Lefty started changing channels but could only get the local news. I could feel Pat slipping back into the abyss.

"I don't wanna talk about it anymore. Just want to sit here and drink," Pat said.

I looked at Pat. Inside he was searching for answers. The uncertainly in what I should say or not say next overwhelmed me but I continued. "Anything's possible if you want it bad enough."

"Listen, can ya do me a favor and cut the shit?"

"Sure, course. Give me a knife."

"I'm fuckin' lost. I'm sitting here with you but might as well be in Siberia."

"Siberia?"

"Yeah. Siberia. I don't belong here anymore."

"That's funny for a kid who hates the winter."

"I can connect with nature," Pat said, as a grin snuck out from the corners of his mouth.

"So, what ya gonna do about it?"

He didn't answer me. I felt that deep down inside he was trying to escape from the Hellhole he had dug himself into, hoping to garner enough strength to reach the top and see the stars once again. But was it too late or not? I wasn't going to give up on my friend. He could be saved. I felt it.

Pat was looking straight ahead but didn't say a single word. I waited for him to speak first. It seemed like a long time. I made believe I was watching the TV. "I know what I'm gonna do," Pat finally said. "Gotta get out of Southie. If I don't I'll never change. I've got to forget this place and start over ya' know? New life. New friends. New clothes. Sick of being a loser."

245

"Then if you need to do it," I said. "Make the move. Get outta town."

"It's my only move," Pat said. "I can't do the detox dance again. Not here anyway. Only way out for me is out of Southie. It's too tempting here to fall back." I said, "Leaving Southie will help but it's not the answer to everything. Remember wherever you go, there you are." Pat started laughing. "Jesus, I got a philosopher hitting me with corny phrases. Give me a break will ya. Talk English."

I nodded.

He smiled. "I can go down south and get a construction job."

"You always wanted to work with your hands. Certainly used your hands to steal shit."

"Very funny."

We laughed together.

"I'm serious as shit," Pat said. "A new beginning. Leaving everyone and everything behind."

"Good idea."

"I'm thinking Florida. Always wanted to sit on the beach after a tough day of work, soak up the sun, and check out the babes."

"That wouldn't be hard to take."

"I'll get my shit together, do some reading... maybe even go back to school."

"That's all good," I said.

"Then I can come back and someday be with Little Pat. Be there when he plays t-ball and puts on his first pair of skates."

With each passing word, Pat seemed to be reinventing himself, visualizing a new version of what his life could evolve into if he really wanted to change. Pat's enthusiasm was contagious.

"You can start workin' out again," I said. "Gotta put on a few pounds."

He raised his arms then looked at his shrunken waistline but his smile only widened.

"No problem," he said. "After what I've been through it will be a piece of cake."

"Gonna have to look good for the women," I said.

Pat took another gulp of beer. Lefty looked towards us but I waived him off. No more beers for us.

"So where have you been staying?"

"Sometimes at the Pine Street Inn."

"Okay."

"But mostly I've just been a hobo."

"Did you just say 'hobo'?" I asked, laughing.

"It's a funny word huh? Ho-bo."

"C'mon, let's go get somethin' to eat on West Broadway. I'll treat. We'll talk some more about you getting out of town. Starting over. Getting your shit together."

Pat stood up and to my surprise hugged me.

"People care about you Pat. They do. Myself included."

"You're a good shit ya know that don't you? And you're right, tomorrow is another day."

"Now you're talking," I said. Suddenly I was smiling from ear to ear. It felt good.

"I'll get you some fresh clothes from my house before we eat. Time to throw those rags away."

"What? You don't like my clothes?"

"Love the clothes. It's the smell I can't take."

247

We laughed, said goodbye to Lefty, and walked out of the bar.

FORTY-ONE

It was time to say goodbye and see Pat start his life anew in different surroundings minus the daily temptation. I had five hundred dollars I was going to give him to help with his new journey down south.

"I'm here to pick up Pat O'Malley," I said to the burly man sitting at the front desk inside the front lobby of the Pine Street Inn.

"Only a few clients left upstairs," he said. "Don't think your guys one of them."

"Do you know him?" I asked.

"Not really sure if I do. How old is he?"

"He's 30."

"Only older men left. The younger guys leave early in the morning. Sorry."

I got back into my car. "Where's Pat?" Sal asked.

"Don't know. He's not there."

I drove through the Andrew Square intersection and was driving around the rotary near Saint Monica's Church. Lights flashed and horns startled me as an EMS cruiser and a BMC medical examiner's car sped past us. I don't know why but I followed the emergency vehicles along Old Colony Avenue. Across the way in Moakley Park blue lights were flashing. Several police cars were parked near the playground next to the Little League fields. "Let's see what's going on," I said. I parked and then we walked over to the park. Officer Noto was talking to his sergeant. Other officers were interviewing bystanders and taking notes. We walked up to Officer Noto. "What's going on?" Sal asked, apprehensively. Officer Noto took off his hat and nervously ran his fingers through his thick, black hair. "It's O'Malley. He hung himself on that tree. Maybe last night or early this morning. Coroner can decide the timeline betta' than me."

I didn't believe it. I couldn't. I looked at the tree and saw a small piece of rope still hung up, swinging back and forth in the wind. Officer Noto pointed to Pat's body covered up in black on a stretcher about twenty feet away. Suddenly, his arm fell and hung on the side of the stretcher. For a second I thought he may still be alive but knew he wasn't. Regret consumed me. I had tried to help but now it didn't matter. Pat O'Malley's pain was no more.

"They're ready to take his body to the morgue and detectives are on their way to his house to notify his family."

"Thanks Officer," Sal said.

I put my hands in my pockets. In the left pocket I could feel the crisp, new one hundred dollar bills. Funny I thought how important people think money is, but to the dead, it didn't mean shit. It was worthless.

I couldn't talk. I walked over to the tree that held so many memories. Sal stood silently beside me. I bent over and yanked a few pieces of grass from under the tree. One, two, three, four pieces of grass and I blew them to the wind. Pat loved doing that. He said it brought him good luck, something his mom told him. My eyes shot upward and the mighty tree's majestic appearance stood in stark contrast to what I was greeted with. The tree was sturdy and strong and the leaves dancing about to and fro in one gigantic motion which signified solidarity and liveliness. It withstood thunderous rains, relentless winds, the scorching sun, and surly snowstorms, but persevered. Every elemental adversary was brushed aside and dismissed. The tree truly personified life. But this moment also reeked of death. Against the backdrop of the endless sky the irony of this moment dug deep into my soul and would remain within forever.

My eyes filled with tears. The blue sky darkened in agreement and the tree faded into the blurry background as I imagined Pat sitting there in his Little League uniform full of life, full of anticipation, joy, and hope. What a waste I thought. Things could've been different. Then I imagined another Pat, the Pat that got out of town and started over, that cleaned up, got that construction job. He was happy. Maybe he even had a girlfriend. He was relieved he didn't give up. He was grateful that he was steered in the right direction. That he did the right thing. He had a five year NA coin and worked hard to fill a void in little Patrick's life. I thought about this Pat for a while until it made me too sad. That was an alternate universe, wishful thinking at best. The Pat I knew was gone and now hopefully at peace.

The emptiness I felt made me sick to my stomach. Why did he give up? What made him end it all when he had so much more to experience in life? I would like one more chance to talk to him JUST one more time. I would tell him that it was foolish to consider surrendering. Foolish to throw it all away when so much more awaited him. I just wish that I had done more. Said that.

But it was too late for him and too late for me to change anything now.

It was too late.

FORTY-TWO

Seeing Pat lying dead on the stretcher broke my heart. I told Sal I was going home but bee-lined it to the nearest Keno parlor. The five hundred dollars I was going to give to Pat soon became a gift to the lottery. I won a few games and was up three hundred yet it didn't take long for me to give it all back plus the five hundred. Then I called my bookie and started betting sports games on TV. I won a few games and kept on playing. I finally left when the store manager told me they were closing.

I repeated the same routine the next two evenings and proved to be consistent. I'd win some, lose some, win, lose, and then leave a loser. I knew deep within my heart that I wouldn't change these bad habits unless I changed what I did on a daily basis. They say doing the same thing over and over again with the same negative results is insanity. I didn't consider myself insane and ready to be put in a straightjacket, but I realized I was merely fooling myself into thinking the outcome would be any different than it has been untold times before. I understood I needed to embrace change.

While driving home these thoughts kept resurfacing and my mind drifted back to simpler days. I took a left onto H Street. Ten, twenty, thirty miles an hour I drove down the street still angry with myself. Confused about my future. Who I really was and didn't want to become. Then I found myself on Columbia Road. Forty, fifty, sixty miles an hour I sped along the boulevard, past M Street Beach, the yacht clubs, and the Lagoon towards Castle Island. I heard police sirens in the distance but that didn't deter me. I kept on speeding along the strip as my thoughts sped with me.

I finally reached the Island and parked my car on the right side of the parking lot overlooking the water. It was a dark night. Moonless and starless. Appropriate I thought for the occasion, for the mood I was in. I looked at myself in the rear view mirror and didn't know who I was.

I sat there looking and looking and searching for answers. The only obvious answer for my behavior was that I was running away from reality. Didn't want to believe Pat was dead. Another friend gone. Another life snuffed out way before it should've been. But was this the answer to my fears? Would this heal anything? Resolve anything? The obvious answer to that question was it only worsened the situation. What good was that?

I sat motionless, still thinking about Pat's death and my folly until I leaned back and fell asleep.

I was only awakened by the brilliance of the morning sky and the voices of the runners from the L Street Runner's Club as they jogged by my car.

FORTY-THREE

"911. What's your emergency?" the operator asked.

"Hi. I'm Maria Santiago. Um I just got to work and...Mr. Al...he's in bed. He's not moving. Something's wrong."

"What's the address?"

"Ah. 17 East Third Street. The first floor."

"Is this a business address?"

"No. I clean for Mr. Al. It's a house."

"Okay. Everything will be alright. Stay calm. Boston Police and EMS will be there in just a few minutes. Just wait at the front door. Okay?"

"Okay."

Moments later, Boston Police and EMS arrived. Maria was standing in the doorway. She was shaking. One of the EMT's put a blanket over her shoulders. The other two EMT's went directly into the living room. Officer Frank Noto asked Maria to sit down in a chair located in the interior hallway of the apartment.

"Hi, I'm Officer Frank Noto. This is my partner, Officer Joseph Finn. What's your name?"

"Maria."

"And what do you do here?"

"I clean his house."

"What's his name?"

"Mr. Al. I don't know his last name."

"That's okay. How long have you been cleaning this house?"

"Once a week for a year I think."

"Please tell us what you saw?"

"I walked into the room and saw him on the floor. He

254

wasn't moving. I shook him. He didn't wake up. He was on his back. I saw a cut on his head."

"What did you do then?"

"I called the police."

"Good," Officer Finn said. "You did the right thing."

"He looked dead," Maria said, her voice housed in apprehension.

"Miss, don't..."

"Oh my God," she cried out, interrupting Officer Noto. She did the sign of the cross several times and kissed the Jesus necklace hanging loosely around her neck. "Do you think he's -?"

Officer Noto wouldn't let her say that word again. "Don't worry," he interrupted. "EMS is taking care of everything from here."

"I'll pray for him." She kissed her necklace one more time.

"Maria, listen to me," Officer Noto said. "Did you notice anything different or out of place today? Anything missing? Anything at all unusual?"

"No...everything looks okay."

"Let's walk around real quick and check out the rest of the apartment. We're gonna have to go back into the living room for a real quick look. You okay with that?"

"Yes."

"I'll be right beside you. Just don't touch anything."

"Okay," she said.

She looked around the room and flinched when her eyes met Al's body again.

"Anything out of place?"

"I don't think so."

Officer Noto then took her into the kitchen, the other

bedroom and bathrooms. Al even had a workout room. She shook her head and Noto understood that nothing looked out of place to her. "Okay. Maria, thank you. Officer Finn will be outside in a minute to ask you a few more questions." He nodded to the other EMT who led Maria outside. Officer Noto turned to his partner. "Hey can ya take down her information. I'll stay inside. Gotta take a closer look. See what the hell went down here."

Ten minutes later, Officer Noto appeared at the front door. "Get the yellow tape," he called out to his partner. Detectives Guiney and McDevitt arrived and soon afterwards the place was swarming with police. Taking pictures. Sweeping for prints. Examining the body.

It didn't take long for a couple of reporters, Billy Jameson from the Boston Globe, and Peter Hynes from the Boston Herald, who were obviously listening to the police scanner, to arrive at the house. Hynes didn't waste any time trying to dig up some dirt. He walked over to a few of the local teenagers who were standing around.

"Hey guys can ya tell me who lives in that apartment?"

They looked at him as if he had two heads. "Don't bother us," yelled one of the teenagers. "We don't like reporters." The teenager flipped his lit cigarette to the ground in front of Hynes' feet. They walked away and then a middle-aged man walked up to him. He offered Hynes a cigarette which he graciously refused. "His name is Al Sawyer," said the man, in a hushed tone. "He's lived there for a few years. Don't say much. Keeps to himself but plenty of traffic in and out especially on the weekends."

"Really?" Hynes responded. "What do you think goes on?"

"I don't know," the man said. "Why don't you use your

imagination?"

An hour later, Guiney and McDevitt came out of the house. As they were walking to their car, Hynes and Jameson approached them. "Detectives, could you tell us what happened here?" Jameson asked. "It's an ongoing investigation right now," Detective McDevitt replied. "When we find out something, you'll know about it."

"Who's the victim?" Hynes asked. "No comment," said Detective McDevitt. "Is it Al Sawyer?" he asked. "Is he dead?" The detectives ignored his questions. "Was he a drug-dealer?" Hynes asked. "He had a lot of visitors I've been told." Again, their inquiries were met with silence. Taking his lead from Hynes, Jameson piped in, "Drug Deal gone south?"

"Like we said, it's ongoing," Detective McDevitt said. "C'mon, ya gotta give us something?" Jameson blurted out. "Could you tell us if there was foul play?"

"Don't you understand English," Detective Guiney shot back "Ya get nothin' until we know more. Jesus."

"Give us something. Anything," Hynes repeated, not giving up the chase. "We've got a job to do just like you guys. Any comment at all?"

"Yeah," Detective McDevitt replied, anger slowly creeping across his face. "Don't ask us any more questions."

FORTY-FOUR

Pat's dad had him privately cremated. No obits. No wake. No prayers. No funeral. Just the family. No one else. Pat, even if he didn't realize it, had broken his mom's heart and his father didn't want to see his daughters suffer. The pain would end without notice, but only on the surface. Then there was the Al saga. Al's demise spread throughout Southie quicker than lightning. I was the only one of my crew who went to his wake. I'm not even sure why I went but I found myself there. There's certainly nothing worse than parents feeling hopeless against the forces of life itself. And then when Death is victorious all seems lost.

I doubted Al deserved pity. He thought he was the "Man" but what did it get him except an early trip to the grave. His parents hugged me and thanked me for stopping by the funeral parlor. The sitting room next to the casket was filled with young and old alike. Al's mom introduced me to several relatives who had flown in from Virginia. It appeared as if most of the people were family members save a few young guys sitting in the corner of the room. I knew them from the neighborhood. They weren't junkies but not exactly law-abiding citizens. I waved and they waved back. Ryan and Joey Murphy sat in the corner talking to each other. Father Joe walked into the front room and began reading the customary Catholic prayers. The room was eerily silent. Al's mom sat down and her husband stood beside her. Their pain could be read all over their faces. Words can't describe how they must have felt. They were suffering, searching for answers. I couldn't imagine the pain my parents would have suffered as the priest prayed for me.

Father Joe then spoke briefly with Al's parents, speaking softly with his usual reverence. After he left I walked over to the casket again, and kneeled down. I started silently talking to Al as if he was looking straight at me with undivided attention. I asked him why he forgot about the Pact. Why he didn't think about the consequences of his actions and how they'd impact his parents. I asked him if it was all worth it. Was it worth an early exit from life? Worth his parent's agony and grief they'd live with for their remaining days? And was it worth being indirectly responsible for the death of others?

When I finished I told him he better be ready for whatever awaits him on the other side. I stood up, and counted the number of flower arrangements near the casket. One, two, three, four in back of the casket. Five to the right of it…another three to the left. It seemed ironic that such beauty surrounded the ugliness which Al embodied.

I conveyed my condolences once again to his parents and started towards the door. "He was our *gift from Heaven*," I heard his mom say to a nearby mourner. "Oh my God," I thought as the door closed behind me, "those were Al's exact words at the bar."

While I was driving down the street I realized the finality of death was devastating especially if one's afterlife philosophy was filled with so many uncertainties. So I was relieved that it was Al and not me lying in that casket, motionless and lifeless. I wasn't ready to meet my maker if indeed there was one to meet.

Several days later, on a Saturday, I met the boys at L Street for a quick workout and a steam-bath. TK was in the adjacent room punching the shit out of the heavy-bag. Afterwards we headed to the café for lunch. Sully told some stupid jokes. We shared stories. We laughed. Then, we laughed some more, told more stories and told more jokes. We bought bottles of wine and the boys "prayed." Like the haddock, they were baked. Angela brought more bread over to our table, and using my corny Italian accent, I said, "You da best cook in da whole wide world." She laughed and said, "Mangia! Mangia!" and went back into the kitchen.

"Good job," Sal said. "Hold on while I get your application to the Italian-American Club."

"Hey, I think Sal just told a joke," Sully said.

"Ya great," TK said. "You can watch him on TV next week."

"Man, I'm starving," Sully said. Sal rolled up a piece of bread and threw it at Sully. "Here's some more bread."

The door of the café opened and Mitch Duncan from the mayor's office walked in. Born and raised in Southie he was the newly-appointed neighborhood liaison officer. "Hi guys," he said. "How you guys doin'?"

"Great," TK said. "How much is this gonna cost us?"

"I'm here in an unofficial capacity. We're trying to raise some money for Mrs. Cavanaugh. Her son James, eighteen years old, overdosed last week. Her husband left town a few years ago. She can't even afford to bury her son. Here's an email address if anyone is interested in making a donation."

"Hey take this." I gave him a fifty dollar bill.

"Thanks Johnny."

"We'll spread the word," Sal said, passing Mitch a twenty.

Mitch paid his bill and left.

"I wouldn't give any money for that," TK said. "And fuck spending taxpayer's dollars on rehab. Never works."

"You're a heartless bastard sometimes," I said. "People need help and rehab does work. I see it at the rehab center. People doing great working helping other people."

"What are you gonna save the world with all your words and worrying?"

"I'd like to save someone. Save someone instead of going to funerals." I thought about Pat hanging from that tree in Moakley Park; lifeless.

"When are you ever gonna learn," TK said. "People will do what they want and when they want. Can't change shit."

"Can't change 'shit' if you don't try."

"So how's that been working out for ya?"

How could I argue that point? Pat was dead. I hadn't saved anyone. I felt stuck in an endless cycle of becoming without really being the person I thought I could be but wasn't? Would I travel through life only dreaming about a future that I would never realize? But I truly felt I was making a difference at the rehabilitation center; trying to make an impact on the lives of others.

"I think by working at the center I'm helping out, hoping to change others. Give them hope," I said.

"Right," TK said, with a wry smile. "You keep on believing that."

The door of the café opened and in walked the Junk Man. He walked over and stood near our table. He looked like he had just shot up. TK was pissed. "Hey, what's up?" Sal asked. "The sky, that's what's up?" the Junk Man replied. He looked ragged, disheveled to the max.

"Hey, you okay," Sal asked. "You look like shit."

"Geez thanks."

"Hey Johnny," TK interjected. "Why don't you give the Junk Man your card and set up an appointment for him for some counseling sessions at the rehab center? He's got that look. He could use your help. He's a perfect specimen for rehabilitation that would make you famous if you ever saved him from himself."

The Junk Man wasn't amused. "Thanks but no thanks. I'm fine."

TK grunted.

He was still pissed.

"What's your fuckin' problem?" the Junk Man asked.

"Ya know ya never gonna have gray hair. Never get senior citizen discounts."

"What are you talking about?"

TK shook his head. "You're on death's door. You're lucky if you see next week." The Junk Man looked at TK as if to say "I don't give a fuck." That's the nature of a junkie. That's their lives in five simple words; 'they didn't give a fuck.'

TK looked at him. His anger growing. "I haven't seen you for a while so I couldn't tell you to stay the fuck away from Robbie Fallon."

The Junk Man was surprised but not concerned.

"He told us what happened. He's a good guy. Don't bother nobody. So don't bother him."

"Won't happen again," the Junk Man said. "My bad."

Of course he wasn't going to bother Fallon again-not right now anyway. He knew Fallon was on the bright so he was of no use to the Junk Man.

262

"Bet your ass it won't," TK said. "I don't care if I know your sisters. I'll beat the shit out of you."

The Junk Man wasn't fazed by the threat. He was in so many brawls he felt immune to TK's words. Sal wanted to lighten the moment. "Looks like you've been busy," he said. "Yeah. Just left the Brass Hat. Sold a few items. Had a few drinks. Lunch. Ready to make a few more bucks."

"What's today's special?" Sully asked, as he drank some beer.

"Got some nice dress shirts. A hundred bucks each. I'll take thirty. Top of the shelf."

"Sold by the bottom shelf," TK said.

The Junk Man smiled, impertinently. TK didn't notice as he looked down at his watch. Calo rummaged through the pile and bought three shirts. Everyone else passed. The Junk Man asked Angela for a slice of pepperoni pizza then put his 'hot' shirts back in the bag and left. As soon as the door closed, TK started. "The Junk Man's a piece of shit. He should've been hanging from that tree not Pat."

Wow, never expected that but the Junk Man was a tough character to defend. I said, "He's a lost soul who needs help."

"Jesus Johnny," TK said. "That rehab center is really rubbing off on you. Thinkin' everyone's salvageable?"

Sully looked to Sal. "Yeah. SALvageable. Get it!" As always, only Sully laughed at his own joke.

"What makes you think he's got a chance? He's too far gone dude. Brain dead," TK said.

I looked at TK. I didn't have an answer. Everyone was thinking it but fearful to mention Pat. I thought Pat was going to turn his life around. Wasn't even close and now I was implying the Junk Man could change if he was helped. I guess I just don't want to give up hope.

"Speaking of the Homeboy Network, where the fuck has Jaws been anyway?" Sully asked. "I think he doin' the right thing that's why you don't see him that much," Sal said. Jaws had enough shit going on in his life and after his hospital visit he was scarce. "He's another fuckin' piece of crap," TK said. I looked at TK but was speechless. He knew what I was thinking. I understood his anger, didn't totally agree, but wondered if he'd ever change.

Time flew and day turned into night as dark gray skies surrounded the moon. Finally, the topic turned to *him*. "I told you he'd meet his maker. Pay for his sins!" TK roared, basking in the moment. Then he slugged down a half-bottle of beer in a few seconds and smiled at everyone.

"Ya think God forgave Al for what he did?" Sully asked. "I hope not. He sucked," TK responded. "You know how the saying goes - never speak ill of the dead," Calo interjected, as he brought over more food. TK answered, with a devilish grin. "Yeah, whatever." Calo shot back. "Whatever, your ass." He walked back into the kitchen.

"It's in God's hands now," Sal blurted out. "He'll take care of everything. Out of our hands. So like Calo said, leave the dead with the dead and their God."

"Sorry. Forgot our altar boy was here," TK said. "You need to grow up," Sal said. "Don't be disrespecting something you don't know shit about."

"Excuse me," TK replied. "Is it okay if I propose a toast to the one who sent Al packing?"

Nobody answered. But that was the key question. Who sent Al on his way? We wanted more information on Al so I went outside the café and called Okie. The phone rang. No answer. I hung up. I stood there for several minutes and called again. This time Okie answered. "Sorry" he said. "Can't make it to the gym tomorrow. See you soon." And he hung up. Obviously code because we never shared dumbbells at the gym. He was more of an Oreo cookies and milk type of guy.

I walked back inside the café and sat down. "Do you believe that shit," I told the guys. "Okie basically just gave me the 'I don't know anything rap.'"

"That's certainly different," Sal said.

"Do you think they issued a gag order," I asked.

Calo laughed. "Gag order? What gag order? Guiney and McDevitt are working day and night attempting to piece together what really happened. They didn't find any money or drugs in the house, only a lock box with a Remington .45 caliber pistol and GLOCK 27 inside it. But word is they're not happy with the lack of any substantial evidence to help their case."

"Wow, good source, hey Calo," Sully said. "The best," Calo responded. "Not like your guy who just came up empty."

TK couldn't resist. "In between eating jelly donuts they'll have to interview every other person in Southie. It's gonna be a long list."

"Yeah, long list," Sully repeated.

"Hey maybe it was you," TK said. "Did you kill him?"

"Fuck you," Sully blurted out. "Don't be saying that shit."

Sal said, "Hey TK, don't forget about that fight you had with Al. Remember. Cops came."

TK just laughed, blew it off.

"Everything's a big fuckin' joke to you," Sal said. "What are ya taking Sully's place? You could be the Laughing Leprechaun on stage."

"There you go again with that Irish shit," TK said.

"Yeah well, ya know what? It's payback," Sal said.

"Didn't Christ say turn the other cheek?" TK asked.

Sully said, "Speaking of Christ. When was the last time you walked into a church?"

"Get off my dick," TK said. "I believe in God. I just don't go to church anymore. All they care about is money. Too many scandals so why should I trust the church? Look at the churches and schools they've closed in Southie to pay for their depraved priests' legal fees. And now they're condos. I feel sorry for those people who dedicated their lives to the church and all they get is a slap in the face."

Sal, not amused with the direction of the conversation, spoke loudly. "You need to stop talking bad about the church. Godless societies mean Godless leaders and that's not good for anybody."

"I'm with Sal on that one," Calo said, as he dipped a piece of bread into some olive oil. "TK, watch it or you might get struck by lightning."

Trying to lighten the mood, Sully chimed in. "Hey guys, do you know the recipe for Holy Water?"

"What are you talking about?" TK asked. "There's no such thing."

"Yes there is. Take a pot of water, put it on the stove and burn the Hell out of it."

Again, as usual, nobody laughed at his joke. But he wouldn't give up. "How 'bout this knock-knock joke I stole off the internet."

"'Course ya stole it," TK said. "You never told an original

joke in your life. They should put you in jail for being an imposter...civil disobedience...breach of the peace...somethin' for Jesus' sake."

Sully didn't listen to a word TK said. He was determined to tell his joke. "A police officer knocked on a drug-dealer's door. He replied, 'Who is it.' They said 'the police.' Drug dealer asked them what they wanted and they said 'to talk.' He said, 'how many are you?' The cops said 'two' and he said 'talk to each other.'"

"Hilarious. Keep the jokes on the internet where they belong," Sal said.

The 'Al conversation' continued.

"Maybe the Murphy boys were sick of being his henchmen and figured they could run the business themselves," Sal said. "Our boy's been watching Law and Order again," TK interrupted. Then looking directly at me, he said, "Who'd *you* think did it? Who masterminded this wondrous deed? Break it down for us."

"I'm not breaking anything down," I said. "C'mon, you're the smartest one here. Tell us your theory. Ya know what? Fuck Al, anyway," TK said. "He was a sleazebag, a bloodsucker without any remorse. He poisoned people with that shit. Deserved what he got. My uncle was killed by one of his scumbag-junkies. Fuck them all. They get what they deserve. They can all burn in Hell as far as I am concerned."

The guys kept talking and I heard them but it was like I wasn't there. I thought I was trapped inside a television watching *them* but not listening. I continued to *run the engines in my brain to full capacity.* Who killed Al? Was it revenge? Was it an accident or murder? Was it a junkie or a fellow drug dealer knocking off the competition? Or was it a plain old robbery which took a bad turn? Would the perpetrator be lionized or made out to be a villain?"

My thoughts returned to the present when interrupted by Sal's loud voice. "Johnny, you okay?" He put his hand on my left shoulder. "You okay, brother?"

"I'm fine. Just thinkin.'"

Calo brought over more wine, opened it, and told us to let it breathe for a few minutes. Sully downed yet another piece of bread. Sal said, "Hey Sully? Ya know what? For an Irishman, you've got a good appetite."

As I was eating, I couldn't erase Al's image in the casket. I couldn't believe another person in the Pact was dead. Someone as evil as Al was dead. Like flowers in the fall, people die. Their power fades. We didn't see it coming and neither did Al. I recalled words of wisdom from my parents. They said everything happens for a reason. Everything was meant to be.

I shivered with fear because I felt guilty.

Guilty because I never thought I'd be relieved that he was dead.

FORTY-FIVE

The boys had just finished praying outside when Steve the bookie walked into the café. He walked right over to our table. TK stood up and gave him a big hug.

"Jesus, haven't seen you for long time," TK said. "How you doin' these days?"

"Everything's fine. Got diabetes so off the sweets…and it's killing me. Love desserts. But you gotta do what you gotta do to survive in this world."

He knew I was ducking him. I should have known better. You can't hide from these guys. They'll always track you down sooner or later. And that's not a cliché but reality.

"Hey Johnny, need to speak with you outside for a bit."

Everyone's eyes widened as if they were watching a TV mystery.

"Sure…be right back guys."

We walked outside and Steve lit up a cigarette. "At least I can still smoke."

"Been meaning to call you," I said. "Just a lot has happened lately and…"

"Not to worry Johnny. I know all about Pat. I know you're good for it but it has been a few weeks now."

Stupid as it sounds I wasn't positive about how much I owed him. Those three days were a blur.

"Everything was crazy. I'm not even sure how much I owe you."

"You owe me twenty grand. Had a tough few days."

He considers losing 20k 'tough.' What did I do? Bet on every game on TV.

"Tough's not the word. Did I win any bets?"

"You covered the spread a few times but overall you...you..."

"I get it," I interjected. "Like my dad would say I shit the bed bigtime."

"I tried to get you to slow down...but you kept on repeating... 'I got this. I got this. I'll start winning...you wait and see.'"

"You should have strangled me through the telephone," I said. "Maybe that would have brought me back to my senses."

What the fuck was I thinking?

"You can always bounce back but not until you pay that off."

"Okay...can you give me *just* a little time?"

"Sure...but only a little."

He left and I walked back inside the café.

"What the fuck was that all about," TK asked.

"Nothing."

"Nothing my ass...guys a bookie for Christ sake..."

TK wouldn't let up.

"C'mon...fess up...what's going on?"

"I owed him a few bucks. I took care of it."

"A few bucks," Sal said. "How much is a few bucks?"

I took a deep breath. My heart was pounding. I thought it was going to explode.

"Twenty grand."

They shook their heads simultaneously in disbelief. TK almost swallowed his tongue.

"Geez...twenty thousand dollars," Sully said. "That's a lot of pizzas."

TK shot Sully a dirty look. "Jesus," TK interjected. "Since when the fuck did you start gambling?"

"In New York," I said. "Kept me preoccupied."

I could read it on their faces. They were surprised I was so good at keeping this a secret.

"Where the fuck are you going to get that money?" Sully asked.

"Maybe we can help him," Sal said. "Pitch in."

"No...I'm all set...just going to divert money I have saved. But thanks anyways."

I was going to divert money alright. Money I was saving for a down payment on a house. What a dick. I was embarrassed...exposed as weak, and as a sneak perhaps not to be trusted by my friends.

TK asked, "You sure?"

"I'll figure it out. I'll survive."

I wanted to crawl in the corner and be invisible. I drifted away. How in the world did I manage to gamble away 20k? I guess it was easier than I thought possible. Three nights of pure stupidity. But now I needed to pay the piper.

I wanted to shout to the Heavens.

Scream.

Cry.

Swear.

Yet all I could do was hang my head in disgust.

I sat motionless and it seemed like an eternity. I could feel my friend's gazes searching for a further explanation.

I was alone yet in the midst of others. Lonely, immersed in my weaknesses like so many other people who are unable to gather the necessary strength to overcome them. Lonely to the edge of despair unable to see clearly and to answer questions that needed to be answered. Solve problems that needed resolution.

"Johnny, are you okay?" Sal asked.

They looked in my direction waiting for my answer.

"Not really," I finally murmured. "Can't believe I did this."

"Think of it as a second chance in life," Sal said, hoping to ease my obvious pain. "We all make mistakes...sometimes they're big...sometimes they're small. Just need to learn from them. That's all we can do."

I left and walked home. I was still kidding myself. I had money saved but not enough to cover the entire gambling debt. But more importantly I needed to be honest with my parents. Honest because it was the right thing to do. Honest because I needed their financial help. As I inched closer to my house, anxiety overtook me. I didn't know how they'd react. I was afraid I'd break their hearts with my foolhardy behavior. I was afraid I had let them down.

It was the lowest point of my life and something I never wanted to experience again.

I walked into the TV room.

Disappointment escorted me in.

Shame snickered at me.

My dad was reading and my mom crocheting. I sat down across from them unable to speak. My mom instinctively knew something was wrong but didn't say anything.

I just stared at them as tears blinded my eyes.

Finally I spoke.

"Ma...dad...I've got something to tell you."

FORTY-SIX

A week later I walked down the stairs into the basement of a local church in Dorchester. It was the closest Gambler's Anonymous Meeting I could find on the internet. Robbie Fallon was with me. I talked to him about it and he agreed it might be beneficial to his overall rehabilitation. After all, he was a Keno fanatic who wasted his money like so many others, including myself.

Sitting around a few tables was a dozen or so people. The meeting was already in progress. We sat down.

"Hi," said a middle-aged woman, sitting across from me. "I'm Joanne...the secretary. "And I'm Sally, the treasurer of this group. Welcome," said the elderly woman, sitting next to her.

"Thanks for coming to our meeting," Joanne said.

"Thank you for having us," I said. "My name is John."

'Hi John' the group responded in unison.

"My name is Robbie."

'Hi Robbie' the group replied together.

"Okay," Joanne said. "On with the meeting. Who wants to share?"

After a moment, a man at the end of the table spoke up. "Hi, my name is Peter." Again, in unison the group responded, 'Hi Peter.'

"I haven't been to a meetin' in about two months," he said. "That's because I've been too busy gambling. I started gambling about five years ago, off and on, but want more out of life. I know I can do betta. I feel that I need to change from within...inside for this to work for me. I know this is affecting

273

me physically and I can't continue doing this to myself. I want to feel worthy. I want to feel free from this." He paused and looked down. "Thanks for listening to me."

Everyone clapped a supportive clap.

"Anyone else want to share?" Joanne asked.

A well-dressed man in his thirties started talking.

"Hi, my name is Thomas."

'Hi Thomas' the group responded as one.

"I feel good about myself. Haven't watched a sporting event in 70 days and haven't gambled either. Planning on seeing my wife and boy after this meeting but I'm kinda scared because I'm not sure how her mom is gonna respond. She might hit me over the head with a fryin' pan. But I guess I'll take the chance. If you don't see me next week you might want to check a few of the local hospitals."

Everyone laughed.

"I'm seeing a therapist too," he continued. "And going to as many meetings as possible so I won't have a relapse. I feel good about myself and started going back to the gym. Ya know mind and body. Feel healthy…eating betta. So…every day is a challenge but I'm ready. I'm happier now and I know why. I'm not gambling. Not deceiving myself or others. So…I'm hoping God will give me the strength to stay strong and do the right thing. So far so good. Thanks for listening."

Everyone clapped.

"Anyone else want to share?" Joanne asked.

Nobody spoke.

She looked at me.

"Would you like to share with us today, John?" Joanne asked.

I was hesitant, unsure what to say.

"I. I'm glad I came today. I realize now that I'm not alone. Not alone with this burden. I don't even know why I gamble. I'm not even lucky. I work hard for my money and I throw it away like fake money. It's stupid....wasteful. But I'm here to change my life. Rid myself of the unnecessary stress I create every time I gamble. I feel good and I thank you for listening."

Everyone clapped.

"Anyone else?" Joanne asked.

Robbie raised his hand and stood up like a schoolboy.

Joanne motioned that he could sit down while speaking.

"I just wanted to say that this is a good thing. People helping people cope. Help put their lives back together so they can be happy and lead productive lives. I like to play Keno when I'm drinking a few beers but I'm on the wagon and realize that nobody really ever wins when they gamble. I can't afford to lose the money so it's totally stupid. I may win one day but the next day I lose. It's like a rollercoaster ride but when it ends the money's gone. So is the phony rush of elusive euphoria we seem to be chasing along the way. I know this because I've been there. Hopefully I've taken my last rollercoaster ride. I'm sick of the emptiness that it brings to my life. Sick of everything associated with it. Thanks for letting me speak to you guys."

Everyone stood up and clapped for Robbie.

"Well!" Joanne said, smiling. "Anyone else?"

Nobody responded.

"Last call?" Sally said.

Again, only silence.

"Okay, see you guys-and gals-next week," Joanne said.

"Have a great week," Sally said.

Joanne slid some GA literature and contact information across the table towards us.

"Hope to see you guys again," she said. "We're here to help. To share and listen."

When we were back outside in the church parking lot I looked at Robbie.

I smiled.

"Ya know what?" I said. "You should be counseling me not me counseling you."

FORTY-SEVEN

One of the local burnouts walked into the café and made a joke about Pat. I almost tore his head off. He may have been a junkie but he was 'our' junkie and someone who may have been saved under the right circumstances.

Losing Pat was an aching episode that only my friend, Time, could ease. As I was reflecting upon his death another drama was unfolding. I guess you could say there's never a dull moment in Southie. TK was dragged down to the police station on West Broadway for questioning. They knew he and Al fought outside the Hub Bar during the Saint Patrick's Day weekend. They made him wait an hour in a small interrogation room before Detectives McDevitt and Guiney came in to question him. TK couldn't resist a wise-ass comment.

"Geez. Good to see you guys. For a minute I was waiting so long I thought I was in my doctor's office."

"Very funny," Guiney said.

"You need a drink?" McDevitt asked.

"How bout a Bud Light?"

They passed him a bottle of Poland Spring's water and began their questioning.

"What was your relationship with Al Sawyer," McDevitt asked.

"I wasn't related to him."

They didn't appreciate the humor.

"We know you didn't like Al," said Guiney. "You're a person of interest."

"I'm a suspect? That's hilarious! You're funny."

277

"*Did* you kill Al?" Guiney asked.

"Are you serious?"

"Well, did you?" Guiney asked.

TK didn't like that question. Things were getting serious much too fast. "Aren't you guys supposed to read me my rights?"

McDevitt turned to Guiney who in turn read TK his Miranda Rights. "Are ya happy now?" Guiney asked.

"I'm thrilled. Maybe I'll lawyer up, but not just yet. I've got nothin' to hide."

"C'mon. We want to help you. You cooperate and we'll let the prosecutor know. They'll go easy on you," McDevitt said.

"You hated him right?" Guiney asked.

"Yeah. He was a drug-dealin' scumbag and got what he deserved. *But I didn't kill him.*"

"You and Al have a heated past," McDevitt said. "You recently fought outside the bar."

"Yeah, a fight. It was a fight, nothing more. I've been in plenty of fights and didn't kill the guys afterwards. I took your advice. Stayed away from him."

"Your only uncle and your dad's best friend was murdered by one of Al's junkies," Guiney shouted, hoping TK's anger would betray him. "You blamed him for your uncle's death didn't you?"

"Fuckin' right I blamed him for my uncle's death. He supplied those punks with that shit. He might as well have been the one who beat him up. *But I didn't kill him.*"

The detectives didn't react, their poker faces hiding their thoughts.

"There's an old saying that when you start planning for revenge, make sure you're ready to dig two graves," Guiney said.

"Whoa. Quoting Confucius? I'm impressed," TK said. Guiney sat on the corner of the small table and leaned forward close to TK's face. He was relentless. "So you lost it and decided someone had to rid Southie of this scumbag and it was gonna be you. You admit you hated him. A strong word. Hate. Hate makes people do vicious things they usually regret and can't change. So you went to his apartment with the intent of being a hero and took care of business."

"Are you fuckin kiddin' me? I'm not that stupid. Like I said, I hated the prick. So did a shitload of people in Southie. You got a long list to check. Good luck with that."

Guiney jotted down a few lines in his notebook.

"Better go order some more notebooks, fellas, you're gonna get writer's cramp before this crime is solved if it ever is."

TK could see he was getting to them. He decided he was going to play detective. "Yeah I had motive, but as far as opportunity, there was none. The word is it happened inside his apartment during the day and there wasn't any apparent break-in. Why would Al just let me in his apartment? What the fuck would I being doin' knocking on his door?"

"We'll ask the questions if you don't mind," Guiney shot back.

"Where were you between 8 a.m. and 12noon on that day?" McDevitt asked.

"I was working."

"You pick up parts from dealers," McDevitt said. "You're out of the office and on the road most of the time. Am I right?"

"I'm impressed. You guys have been doin' your job. You must be mad you had to work and missed the daily donut run."

"Answer the question and stop fuckin' with us," Guiney

said.

"I drove to Dedham that morning and then to Chelsea for Christ's sake. Check with my boss. I start work at 8 a.m. and have to punch in and out."

"In between pick-ups you could have made a quick stop back in Southie," Guiney said.

"I could have done a lot of things but didn't sneak into Southie to kill *anybody*. Call Pete's Diner in Chelsea and ask the owner if I was there for lunch. I had a roast beef sandwich, chips and a Pepsi, no, a diet Pepsi to be exact. I was there around 11:30."

McDevitt said, "We will what's his name?"

"It's Billy. Billy Esposito."

"What street is it on?" he inquired. "Hey I gave you the owner's name. The name of the place. Not gonna do your job. You're the detectives so you figure that one out if you can."

"Don't be a fresh prick," Guiney blurted out.

"I'm just trying to fit in."

"After lunch, what did you do?" McDevitt asked. "I had to go to about five places in Chelsea which took up the rest of the day. Check with my bosses they can give you the list. Didn't get back to Dorchester until 6 p.m. Southie about 7."

Guiney paused and took a deep breath but continued with his interrogation. "You waited for the opportune time to stop by his house during the day so he wouldn't be suspicious. You knock on his door and he lets you in. And then you killed him. All that anger and hate dissolved when you saw him lying there. You were free from the pain."

"The only pain I feel is listening to you guys and these far-fetched plots."

McDevitt took over. "You're about the same size as Al and easily could have hit him with an object when he wasn't expecting it. He knows you. You drop by his house to talk. You tell him you want to mend broken fences putting him at ease. Now he's not on the defensive and the last thing he's thinking is you're there to finally get revenge for your uncle. Murder never crossed his mind. He considered you a big mouth but harmless. You were like a bug he could step on at any time…nothing more."

Guiney jumped in on cue, being repetitive, continuing to grill TK, hoping to trick him into saying something of an incriminating nature. His voice grew louder as he inched closer to TK. "And so there you were, finally an opportunity to make amends for those you lost. You smashed him over the head, he fell and you left him for dead. It felt great. Now you and Southie were free of him."

"You need to get the fuck out of my face and stop talking stupid. I didn't smash him with anything. I wasn't there. You aren't going to freak me out into confessing. I've got nothin' to confess."

They looked at him for a few moments without saying anything then TK started laughing.

"What's so fuckin' funny?" Guiney asked.

"So, this is your entire case? Really? Is this your first one? You've been watching too many cop stories. I know earlier I said you guys were funny, *but this is really funny*. Are you jerking my chain? I thought you were experienced dicks for Christ's sake! Opportunity! I was working. I wasn't in Southie that day. Check my GPS. Tough to kill someone when enjoying the sights in Chelsea all day. Motive! I wanted revenge? Yeah I wanted revenge but murder is definitely out of my wheelhouse. By the

281

way, everyone in Southie had motive except his mom and dad. Means! Anyone would have had the means to take him out, but it wasn't me."

McDevitt sat down and offered TK another drink but he declined. Guiney stood against the wall. TK asked for a cigarette but already knew what the answer was; no smoking in public buildings.

"We want to go easy on you," McDevitt said. "Like I said earlier, if you cooperate we can cut a deal with the DA's office."

"Are you serious, don't tell me you're serious? Listen you know me better than that."

"Take the offer. Save yourself a lot of trouble," McDevitt said.

TK looked at McDevitt. "I can't believe you're pitching the company line," he said. Guiney interrupted. "You're guilty, why not admit it?" TK shot back. "You don't have any concrete evidence. Do you know why? Because I didn't fuckin' do it! The fact that I hated Al don't mean shit. Fighting him don't mean shit. Everyone knew he was a scumbag and you guys know it."

"You got all the answers don't ya' boy," Guiney said. TK looked at McDevitt. "I've cooperated enough out of respect only for you but I'm done. So charge me or let me go." They didn't answer right away so TK added, "C'mon. I'm getting hungry. Might even have a roast beef sandwich, it's my favorite."

"You're free to leave," McDevitt said. "We'll be in touch," Guiney said, trying to intimidate him. TK had to have the last words. He turned to Guiney. "Yeah 'We'll be in touch.' You couldn't find a hooker in a whorehouse. You're a fuckin' clown and you know it." TK got up and walked towards the door and left without looking back. Guiney looked at McDevitt. "Did you

282

notice he was limping?" McDevitt nodded yes.

TK walked down West Broadway towards City Point. He discreetly lit up a joint and took a few puffs.

He wasn't worried.

After all, he was innocent.

FORTY-EIGHT

I spoke with a few clients earlier at the rehab center and now was jotting down a few notes before leaving when Robbie appeared in the doorway. Behind him stood his wife, Anna, and their daughter, Cailyn.

"C'mon in," I said. "Long time no see, Anna. How have you been?"

Anna smiled. "I've been good. And you?"

"All's well."

"You know my daughter, Cailyn."

"Yes, but haven't seen her for a few years. Hi. My name is John."

She shook my hand. She was pretty with long blonde hair and blue eyes.

"How old are you?"

"I'm thirteen."

"That's a good age. Where do you go to school?"

"I'm in the eighth grade at the O'Hara Charter School in East Boston."

"I've heard that's a good school."

"I guess. But next year I might be going to the South Boston Charter School. That's what I want to do."

"That would be great."

"Yes it would."

"What do you want to do when you grow up?" I asked.

"I want to be a veterinarian because I love animals."

"And that would be great too," I said.

She briefly smiled then turned unusually serious for such a

young girl. "I want to thank you for helping my dad. We left because my dad was drinking and taking pills. But we're together again and happy. That's because of you my mom told me."

Tears streamed down her face.

"No...you don't have to thank me...it's your dad who did it...who's changed."

"My mom said that without your help he'd be the same and I still wouldn't see him that much."

She hugged me and murmured, "Thanks."

I looked at Anna and Robbie and they too were teary eyed.

"Anna...he's doing great," I said.

Robbie actually went cold turkey on the pills. He was taking Motrin now for the back pain and is going to AA meetings and counseling sessions that we set up for him. He'd be fine. I knew it deep within he would be good moving forward.

"He never stops talking about you and *his* Cailyn."

I fought to control my emotions. I counted to ten. I didn't think a mentor should cry. They left. I closed the door. I sat back down looking at the blank, white wall. I thought to myself I needed to bring a few paintings in from the house to spruce up this drab office. Then I cried.

I guess people can change. For now Robbie was whole again and hopefully he'd stay that way. If he could change why couldn't I? Everything happens for a reason has reverberated in my mind throughout the years, and once more surfaced to remind me that everything *does* happen for a reason. I believed that deep within my heart.

I left the Center and drove to the Brass Hat. I walked in and sat down beside my bookmaker, Steve. "Hi Johnny. How you hittin' em?"

285

I nodded and ordered two beers. I took a sip and slid an envelope next to Steve's left arm.

"Here's what I owe you. Everything's there…the whole 20k."

"Thanks."

"Thanks for the extra time to get it to you."

"Big games coming up the next few weeks," Steve said.

"Nah, I'm done. Do me a favor and delete my number from your phone. I just deleted yours on my way here."

I realized I needed to get on with my life and gambling wasn't a part of what I saw in my future. The foolishness was going to stop and I was going to enjoy life. No more regret. No more craziness. I no longer was going to appease anger or satiate stress by gambling my troubles away. I'd face adversity straight on, overlook obstacles and sneer at perceived setbacks by dismissing them all as inconsequential roadblocks in life and move on to better days.

"Yes sir," I said. "My gambling days are history."

"Well, it's not like you're good at it anyway."

We laughed.

I suddenly experienced a euphoria I had never felt before in my entire life. It was if a thousand pounds of bricks were removed from my chest and I could breathe again without effort. I could see Happiness dancing in the distance and I was ready to join in on the festivities. Peace of mind had finally found me.

"Hey," Steve said, awakening me from my innermost exhilaration. "If you ever get itchy…give me a call…I'll look forward to hearing from you."

Of course he'd be looking forward to that. An easy mark and easy money from a gambling fool. But that was yesterday. The only thing I was looking forward to now was attending another gambler's anonymous meeting.

And befriending change on a daily basis.

"Don't hold your breath, my man," I said, as I was leaving. "I'm all done with that bullshit."

FORTY-NINE

"At first I didn't take them seriously," said Chad Bailey, a newcomer to Southie.

"They were drunk. Slurring their words. But people talk like idiots when they've drank their body weight."

"Did you catch their names?" asked Detective Guiney.

"Well, I've been there more than once and saw those guys before. I'm a pretty good eavesdropper."

Guiney and McDevitt exchanged glances.

Bailey said, "They were so drunk they didn't even notice me sitting right next to them. One was named Sully. Other guy had a funny name, a nickname I can only assume. They called him TK."

"Think back and start from the beginning," McDevitt said. "Tell us everything. Everything they said." Bailey took a deep breathe. "They were talking about this guy named Al. Hated him. Cursed him. Especially that guy, TK. I sorta took it for granted that they were just blowing off steam. Drunk talk. The other guy, Sully agreed with everything TK said. TK wanted to 'finish' this once and for all. Sully asked TK when and where. TK mentioned something about taking care of business within a few days. 'We'll piss on his grave,' they said."

"Who said that?" Guiney asked.

"Not sure. I think TK."

"Did they say they were gonna kill Al?" Guiney asked. Bailey said, "This TK guy said Al was going to be history. Was gonna take him down. Make him pay. He had 'waited long enough.' Wanted to 'rid Southie of this cancer' once and for all."

"Did either one of them come right out and say they were gonna *kill Al?*" McDevitt asked.

"Not in those exact words," Bailey said. "But when I heard in the news that a guy named Al, this guy Al, was dead then I just put two and two together."

"Then what," McDevitt asked.

"They left the bar together. That guy, TK, was so drunk he almost fell as he was walking out of the bar. His friend had to help him up."

"Anything else?" McDevitt asked.

"No."

"Okay. Before you leave the station, we're gonna have you write this up and then sign it. They'll be an officer right outside at the front desk. When you're finished ask him to get a hold of us."

"Will do."

"Thanks for coming in. Much appreciated."

"Hey, almost forgot. You should talk to the bartender. The big guy. He overheard a lot."

It was early afternoon and Joey Westfield was working the bar. The bar stools were empty except for one old-timer who was reading the newspaper. The front door opened and in walked Guiney and McDevitt. Westfield poured a glass of draft beer for his only customer.

"Hey Joey. Need a few words you," said Guiney.

"Be right with ya."

Joey brought the beer over to the old-timer and threw in a bag of peanuts. They sat down at the end of the bar.

"You guys want anythin' to drink?"

"Nah, we'll wait until we're off-duty but thanks anyway,"

289

McDevitt responded.

"Sure. So what's up guys?" Joey asked, nervously.

"The night before Al died, TK and Sully were drinking here right," McDevitt asked.

"Yeah, I think so. Not totally sure. They drink here a lot. They're good guys."

"Yeah. Yeah, great guys," Guiney said.

"Tell us about that night," said McDevitt. "Anything unusual?"

"Nah. Nothin' Same old shit."

"Really," Guiney said. "You're positive about that?"

"Yup."

"Do you remember a short, skinny guy sitting beside them that night?" McDevitt asked.

Joey scratched his head. He grimaced. "No, not really, busy that night."

"Busy on a Tuesday night?" McDevitt asked.

"It's Southie. It's busy every night."

"Too busy to hear TK and Sully talking about Al?" Guiney asked.

"I forgot about that. You know those guys. They were drunk. Talkin' shit that's all."

"Joey. That was the night before Al died," McDevitt said.

"Hey. Didn't think much about it. All I heard TK say was that he was gonna piss on Al something like that."

"Oh. Somethin' like that," Guiney said, irritated.

"Anything else?" McDevitt asked.

"TK was angry and talkin' about gettin' even."

"And?" Guiney asked.

"And nothin'. They gulped down their last drinks. Left

suddenly. Left around 11. That's about it."

"You didn't think that was important?" Guiney asked.

"Guess I do now."

"Any idea where they went?" McDevitt asked.

"Nah. Not really."

"Not really? You either do or you don't," Guiney said.

"I don't know where they went."

"We'll be in touch. You can count on that," Guiney said.

They left.

Joey walked behind the bar and grabbed a bottle of whiskey.

He poured himself a shot.

Then another.

FIFTY

Mrs. Modica had witnessed a lifetime of despair during the past five years of her daughter's addiction. Not a day passed by or an occasion present itself without a reminder of her desperate existence. Now, even with a baby, she didn't think her daughter would ever put her life back on course again. Pat's recent suicide which Dee couldn't-wouldn't acknowledge-only exacerbated Dee's predicament. She was lost in a sea of denial but didn't see it. Her drug obsession worsened and was driving her to destruction.

Deep down inside the recesses of her soul, Mrs. Modica was sadly preparing for this eventuality. This day she thought would be like so many others. More lies followed by promises meant to be broken. She conditioned herself to dismiss her daughter's disingenuous declarations and played the sympathetic mother. Battling her drunken husband throughout her younger days had hardened her to the realization that happiness had deserted her many years ago. Such was her story lost beneath more pressing matters.

It was 11:45 a.m. and her cellphone rang. Her daughter was usually punctual when it came to her daily phone call, but this time she was late. Mrs. Modica was already on the bus and on her way to her daughter's apartment to see how messed up she was on this particular day. She saw her daughter's number flash across the screen but ignored the call. Several minutes later she arrived at her dreaded destination.

"Hi mom got my cigarettes?"

"Your smokes, yeah, bought with my money. Maybe one of

these years you'll shock me and buy mine."

"Sure you know I'll pay you back when I get a job."

She shook her head. It was the same song being played over and over again. More denial. More bullshit. Her daughter never had a real job. Her welfare card was her best friend.

"Never mind you. Let me see the baby."

They walked into the baby's room. Snuggled in his blanket he was fast asleep. He looked content. Happy. Secure.

"Patrick's so beautiful," she said. "I bought some new outfits I'll bring over next time. I was gonna bring them today but forgot. Getting old I guess."

"Let's not wake him up," Dee said. She sighed. "I wish I never named him Patrick. I hope he's not cursed."

Sadness enveloped Dee's face. Pat was dead. Al was dead. She thought she loved Pat. She knew she hated Al and sadly her recurring nightmares cruelly reminded her of this reality. Maybe Pat will meet Al in hell and beat him up she thought. Or maybe they'll end up being BDP's-Best Damn Pals down there. After all you could never expect which Pat would wake up in the morning.

Mrs. Modica didn't dare bring up Pat. Her daughter knew how she felt. Although they had their ups and downs she knew her daughter cared for the poor misguided soul, a classic hate-love relationship seen much too often. After all, Dee, herself misguided, had her own substance abuse problems she refused to readily acknowledge.

"Shhhish. Don't say that," her mother said. She kissed her grandson. Aggravated, she repeated to herself. "Don't say that."

They left the room.

"Ma if you don't mind I'm gonna' take a quick shower and then we can watch TV."

"Okay. I'll keep an ear out for the baby."

She plunked herself on the couch and started reading her Boston Herald. When Dee returned she lit up a smoke and sat down. The look was all too familiar. Her mother was bullshit. "You can't stop," her mom said. "You have little Patrick to care of. Ever think of that if you're not around."

"No mom. I'm just tired. You know how tired I get."

Tired and high is too different things. Mrs. Modica wasn't a fool. "You must think I'm stupid."

"Ma. I didn't."

"Even after what happened to Pat? You can't control yourself and take responsibility."

Dee fiddled with some magazines on the coffee table hoping the storm would dissipate.

"I gotta go. Had enough of you for one day. For one lifetime."

"Please mom. Don't go. You just got here. Watch a little TV."

"We should talk," her mom said.

"About what?"

"About you. Not being in control of your life. Before it was just you. Now you have Patrick. When are you ever gonna stop?"

"Mom?"

"Mom? You're *his* mom. Need to act like one."

"I will. Promise. Everything's gonna' be great."

"Gonna' be great. You gotta be kiddin' me. Look at you. You're a Goddamn mess!"

She ignored her mom's protestations and stared blindly at the TV. It didn't take her long to start nodding off.

"Wake up! Wake up!" Dee opened her eyes. "What ma?

294

What's the matta?"

For Dee it was an endless cycle of drug abuse, from prescription drugs to heroin then to methadone and Klonopins. For Mrs. Modica it was a vicious cycle of pain and disappointment. She wondered why her daughter didn't understand that she could be the next to die? When would she realize that? When it was too late and her body sent to the morgue.

"What's the matter? Ya think you'd learn ya lesson seein' ya friends OD and die. Patrick die. But ya don't. It's only getting worse, not betta. What am I missin' here?"

Dee hardly heard half her words and started to nod off again. "Wake up for the last time or I'm leaving."

"I'm *only* resting my eyes."

Minutes later, her head dropped. Mrs. Modica looked over at her. Concern engulfed her. "Dee Wake Up!!!" She wasn't breathing. She shook her violently, hoping to wake her up. Her lips were turning blue and her face cloud white. Her mom knew the drill. She looked on a nearby table then remembered she had some Narcan spray in her purse. She took the Narcan and looked at her daughter slumped on the couch. She paused. She held the Narcan in her hand very tight. She stood frozen in time. She was torn between reality and emotion, guilt and resolve, the present versus the future. She weakly dropped the Narcan to the floor. She was in full retreat searching for shelter from an invisible, devastating foe she couldn't defeat unless she chose not to act.

What else could she do?

Her imprisoned soul sensed salvation, yet would inaction really free her? She didn't care anymore. She'd suffer the consequences inwardly and keep her secret locked-up for eternity. Her fate had been sealed by her daughter's seemingly endless transgressions.

She made the decision.

She sat down on the floor Indian style and watched her daughter's last moments. Moments in which she could have been revived. She watched her slipping away into the night. Sitting there, slumped without breathing. There was no hope for her. It was better this way. It was as if the past five years of the addiction flashed in front of her eyes. So much pain, finally ending. Years of pain culminating in one brief moment of despair.

Her grandchild started crying. It seemed to signal her need to be strong for one while looking away from another. She picked up the Narcan and threw it against the wall. She had had enough. No more overdosing. No more bringing her junkie daughter back from the dead. She'd raise and take care of him. She'd live with the guilt but knew deep down inside that a part of her life was dead forever.

Mrs. Modica never thought she'd have to do what she did. Her decision placed a devastating burden upon her sense of responsibility. Her heart was sobbing, her mind racing back and forth. Sometimes catastrophes can't be avoided. She went into the room. The baby was in the crib. She bent over, took the child's hand and kissed it gently. She wiped away his tears. He looked like a little angel but sadness seemed to be hovering above him. Then she sat down and stared into nothingness.

Most drug addicts will say they didn't decide. They didn't choose to become addicted. They say they can't cope. That the addiction is overpowering. More powerful than reason. More powerful than the love for a child. Dee was living proof and she rationalized she didn't choose to become an addict.

To be fair Dee was right to a degree. She didn't start this nightmare. Al did. But she wouldn't let it end and begin anew. The ugly truth was that it wasn't anyone else's choice for her to remain an addict.

Only Dee's.

Her responsibility.

Her decision alone.

That was as apparent as the sun in a cloudless sky.

FIFTY-ONE

We didn't even have time to think about Dee's death when the detectives contacted TK and Sully and asked them to come down to the station house. Sully sat twitching nervously in one room while TK sat confidently in another. Guiney was interviewing Sully. McDevitt opted for TK.

"Thanks for coming back in," McDevitt said. "Have a few follow-up questions."

TK sat down. "Yup. Always cooperative. You know that. Fire away."

"Had a few drinks with your pal, Sully, the night before Al's death? Could ya tell me what you were discussing?"

TK sunk in his chair.

"Discuss? We don't discuss. We just talk and argue."

"Okay, so what were you talking-arguing-about?"

"Just talking sports, ya know the regular stuff."

"Really?"

"Yeah."

"What else were you talking about?"

"I don't know exactly. Had a good buzz."

McDevitt stood up and walked around the room. He turned and said, "Listen, you trust me don't you?"

"Ah, guess so."

"Well. Ya need to put that thinkin' cap on. Dig deep. Tell me what you and Sully were *discussing*."

"I don't know what you want me to say. I was probably talking shit about Al, which I always do."

TK was testing McDevitt's patience. McDevitt leaned

298

towards TK, placing his both hands on the table and his face within inches of TK's. McDevitt left his good guy suit at home. "We have witnesses. They'll testify that you and Sully were talkin' about Al. That you were gonna kill him then piss on his grave."

TK's arrogance disappeared. His world was spinning into the unknown.

"Yeah, I remember now."

McDevitt vacated TK's space. "That's good. So tell me what else you said."

"I said I had had enough of it and wanted to rid Southie of him. Something like that. Can't remember the exact words. But they're *just* words, nothing more."

McDevitt had more surprises for him. "I went back to Al's apartment. Usually do in these cases. Guess what I found? Small drops of blood on the back porch-hardly detectable but there they were. Got a sample ready to be sent for DNA testing. TK's brain was in overdrive. "What the fuck," he thought to himself.

"Any idea whose blood it might be?" McDevitt asked.

"No not really."

"We're gonna need to get a blood sample from you. See if your DNA is on that porch."

TK flinched.

"What's wrong, TK, you look nervous?"

The events of that night suddenly became crystal clear. TK's eyes went wide in panic. He knew he couldn't hide it anymore. "Listen, when we came out of the bar, we saw Al ride by with his boys. He beeped his horn and smiled that shit eatin' smile. He sped by. I could feel them laughing at us. Pissed me off."

"Okay, keep talkin.'"

"So I talked Sully into going to Al's apartment. Figured the coast was clear. Was planning on breakin' into his apartment and stealin' his stash. But when we got there, I was so drunk I slipped on the porch stairs. Fuckin' small nail was stickin' out on the step. Ripped my leg to shit. I started bleedin' pretty bad. Thought I was gonna puke. Told Sully we needed to screw."

"Bleeding bad but not much blood on the steps?" McDevitt said.

"Yeah, there were some old newspapers on the porch in a pile so Sully cleaned it up and threw the papers into a barrel we saw in the back yard. He stuffed the papers into the bottom of it."

"Last time you left the station we noticed you limping," McDevitt said.

"Yes I was," TK said, in a barely audible voice.

"From that injury you sustained that night on Al's porch?"

"Yes."

"Ya know how this looks. Don't you?"

TK took a deep breathe. "Hated Al but would never kill him."

His cockiness was on the run. It wasn't fun anymore. He didn't know what to expect next.

"One more thing," McDevitt said, after a pause. "The day Al died. You said you weren't in Southie until after work. But you didn't work that day. You called in sick. Found out after I double-checked with your supervisor. There was a clerical error, a mix-up with the payroll."

TK's response was delayed.

Then he remembered.

Then he realized.

"Oh shit. Must have fucked up the dates."

300

"Must have fucked up the dates. Well, that's a pretty big fuck up. Could you tell me what you did that day? Where you were?"

"Hung over really bad. Never left the apartment."

"Anyone home?"

TK paused. He had to zoom back in time to remember. It took him a few moments to collect his thoughts. "No. Sal and Sully worked all day. They didn't come home until after dark."

"No one to corroborate your story," McDevitt said. "You talk shit the night before Al dies. You try to break into his apartment that same night and then the next day when he's found dead you call in sick. Jesus, TK. That's not good."

"But I didn't do it."

"Just wait here. I'll be back."

McDevitt went into the other interrogation room. He pulled Guiney aside. "Anything?" he asked. "No, kid thinks he's on a comedy show. Keeps telling lame jokes." McDevitt turned to Sully. "Okay you can go. We'll get TK for you but you both need to stay put in Southie. This ain't over."

FIFTY-TWO

I found myself drumming on the table. Another nervous habit. I looked around. It wasn't what I expected. The room was small with dingy blue-painted walls without character. Two chairs and a table were in the middle of the floor. The air was stale. The room smelled. I thought there'd be a large rectangular mirror like on the TV shows, but I was wrong. I imagined one right in the center of the wall. I imagined the detectives standing on the other side analyzing information. What would they think of me? And my drumming?

I counted up to one hundred hoping to find clarity of thought in an unclear atmosphere. Within minutes, McDevitt and Guiney walked in. McDevitt looked tired and needed a shave. Guiney was disheveled. By now, I was standing, nervously pacing the room.

"Needed to ask you a few questions," McDevitt said.

I sat down again. I could feel my heart pounding as loudly as a base drummer in a marching band. McDevitt noticed my uneasiness. "Are you okay? Do you need a drink of water or something?"

I wasn't accustomed to being in a police station. First time actually. No, second time I realized. I was eighteen and hanging on the corner. Around 1 a.m. TK was plastered. I hadn't even been drinking, just got caught up in the crossfire. The cops lugged us to the police station and held us in protective custody until morning. We were never charged. The uniforms were doing TK a favor. Keeping him safe. I should have thanked them for him. He slept well, and I wanted to crack him the next day when

302

he laughed his ass off at me for being sober and at the wrong place at the wrong time, but I didn't. I caught hell when I went home.

"Since you're friends with TK and the boys, we need to ask you where you were the day Al was found dead?" Guiney said.

"I teach up at the Heights and start at 7 a.m. then went to the Long Rehab Center right afterwards where I volunteer."

"We'll check that out," McDevitt said.

"The night before did you talk with TK or Sully?" Guiney asked.

"No...went to the movies in Braintree with Pam."

"We'll check that out too," Guiney said.

"Is there anything you can tell us about Al's death," McDevitt asked.

I drew a momentary blank.

McDevitt sat down, finished his coffee, crushed the cup, and threw it in the trash can in the far corner as if he was auditioning for the Celtics. 'Swish' McDevitt was thinking to himself.

"I can tell you this about Al's death," I said. "I can tell you my friends aren't responsible for Al being in a casket. Couldn't do it in a thousand years. They like to talk stupid and they've done that quite a bit in their lives. Along with the booze their empty words relieve their stress."

"What are you their psychiatrist?" Guiney asked.

"They're not capable of doing anything like that."

"Why are you so sure?" McDevitt asked.

"Because I've known them since day one. They just wouldn't. They couldn't kill an afternoon and you know it."

"Since you're so sure your two friends aren't guilty, any rumors floating around town as to who might have been in Al's apartment that day?" Guiney asked.

"We'll never tell who the source is," McDevitt said.

"I wish I could help. Haven't heard anything about anyone. You can understand that not too many people care who took Al down. It's like a cancer has been removed and everyone's moving forward with their lives."

"Simple as that, hey Johnny?" Guiney responded.

"I don't mean to seem heartless. I went to Al's wake. I feel really bad for his parents. But I'm just telling you like it is."

"Then we're done," McDevitt said.

"That's it?"

"That's it for now. Unless you got something else to tell us," Guiney said.

"I'm good."

"We'll see who's good when we piece together those lab reports," Guiney mumbled as I left the room.

FIFTY-THREE

I just woke up from a late nap, took a shower, dressed and walked up to the café. The café was empty except for the guys. And Pam. I walked up back and sat down. The door opened and three young women walked in.

"Sorry ladies," Calo said. "The kitchen's closed." Calo got up, locked the door behind them and sat back down.

Several weeks had passed by and we were hoping no news was good news but it still didn't diminish the stress of uncertainty.

"How's everyone doing?" I asked, still shaken by the dream I just had. In this dream which seemed so real I was sitting uncomfortably in the courtroom waiting for the trial to begin. Every seat was taken. The room packed. Although the room was brightly lit the dreary gray walls could've used a fresh coat of paint and the highly perched paintings a good dusting. The room was buzzing. Some people appeared anxious, others excited as they awaited the arrival of the judge. Lawyers were busy jotting down last-minute notes and perusing legal briefs. The court officers were walking around telling media types and others to turn off their cellphones and remain silent. The judge entered the courtroom, everyone stood, the judge sat down, and then the Assistant District Attorney loudly declared, "Your Honor, the prosecution is seeking murder in the first degree and murder in the first degree joint venture in the death of Alfred Sawyer. The defendants are... The defendants are..." Then I woke up, soaking wet with fear!

"Just swell!" TK said, jolting me back to the present.

"Couldn't be betta!"

Sully didn't answer. He didn't have any one-liners to lighten the moment. Several minutes later we heard several taps on the glass door. Calo unlocked the door and in walked Guiney and McDevitt. They walked up to our table. We didn't know what to think. Was this the beginning of our Southie nightmare or the end of it?

"Ah here's the crew. Glad we got you altogether," Guiney said. I thought Sully was going to piss his pants because I sure felt like I was.

"Good, you're closed, so we can talk," McDevitt said. "If that's okay with you Calo?"

"Sure. We're family here."

Guiney and McDevitt sat down.

We didn't know what to expect.

Shit.

Here we go.

"Got something *really* important to tell everyone," McDevitt said.

"We finally have all the reports, all our findings, including the Medical Examiner's report," Guiney said.

"Yeah, unfortunately had some delays getting the medical results," McDevitt said.

They had our attention.

"Al had marijuana and alcohol in his blood," Guiney said.

"He might have been partying with someone," McDevitt said.

They looked around at us. We looked uneasily at each other.

"We found him lying on his back on the floor," Guiney said. "He had a bump on the right side of his head." Dread surfaced in

306

our minds. What would he say next? "He hit his head on the coffee table when he fell. We found his blood there."

"As it turned out he suffocated on his own vomit," McDevitt said." He paused. We gulped simultaneously. Sweat poured down TK's face.

McDevitt continued.

"Even though we had our suspicions we don't have any concrete evidence to suggest that it wasn't anything else but an accidental death. You're all off the hook. The case is closed."

Guiney couldn't resist. "I sorta liked the way this ended," he said. "With one less drug-dealer in Southie. Nobody charged. It's a win-win wouldn't you say?"

"This isn't our usual M.O. but we felt you needed to hear this from us away from the station," McDevitt said. Guiney mumbled. "His idea not mine."

"Ya know," TK said, still unnerved. "You guys gotta work on your delivery."

Nobody laughed.

Guiney smiled.

McDevitt nodded.

They got up and walked out of the café.

"Holy shit," TK shouted.

"What the fuck?" I mumbled.

Pam felt like crying. She had kept it a secret about overhearing Al in his apartment talk about spiking his heroin with fentanyl. She did tell Pete before he died what Al was up to but that didn't stop him from buying Al's shit. When her family was informed that Pete's death wasn't the result of any fentanyl misuse, Pam felt it best to let this matter die with Al. She was satisfied that Al had paid for his betrayal. Enough said about this

307

scoundrel and his scheming, too much time and thoughts wasted on such evil.

Everyone was shaking their heads in disbelief. Al died an accidental death. Rather an undramatic ending for him we all thought inwardly. Everyone's minds were racing all over. I could see it on my friends' faces. We were excited and relieved at the same time. Never thought it would end like this. But was glad it did.

"Guess we were worrying about nothin'," Sully said.

"And I guess we're not going home right away," Calo said, with a smile. "Wine's on me. Good night to celebrate."

"Bout time," TK responded.

"You feelin' okay Calo?" Sully said, jokingly.

We laughed. Calo filled our wine glasses. "We need to toast," I said. "It's time to toast lost friends… Tools, Pete, Pat, and Dee…everyone else caught up in this drug scourge."

"Here's to the future," Sal said. "May God show the way forward."

"You got that right," Sully said.

"Salute," Calo chirped in.

"What he said," Sully piped in.

"What he said," I said, mimicking my pal, Sully.

Sully, busy fidgeting with his coat, said, 'Huh? What? What did Johnny say?"

"It's no wonder people say you're not so bright," TK said.

"What people?"

"You know. People."

"Fuck you TK. I'm as smart as your dumb ass. People say that too."

I guess things were getting back to normal.

I got up, grabbed a Pepsi out of the nearby freezer and sat back down, but before I did, I walked over to the clock and straightened it out. "That's better," I thought to myself as I shot a quick glance towards Calo, who simply smiled. "I've been meaning to do that," he said.

"Hey, one more thing," I said, as I approached the table. I pointed my finger towards TK and Sully and then placed it momentarily on my lips. "Do yourselves a favor will ya? The next time you two knuckleheads get drunk in a bar don't go runnin' your mouths about killing someone. Ain't a smart idea. Don't forget that old sayin' that the walls have ears."

Sully nodded.

Sal grinned.

TK gave me the finger as if we were still in high school. I just laughed. Some people never change. Or do they? Uncharacteristically, TK subsequently leaned over, not in my direction, but towards Pam, and kissed her on the cheek. "That's from Pete," he said. "From his seat in Heaven he told me to do that. Told me to tell you he's okay."

FIFTY-FOUR

We'd never realize it but it was Dee who was in Al's apartment the day he died. Dee had her niece babysit little Patrick and she called Al that morning and said she wanted to see him. She was going to make him pay for what he did to *her*...to Pete... to her Pat, everyone else he sold that stuff to in Southie. She didn't have a plan. Things just happened. They were smoking weed and Al was knocking down the beers. She knew Al thought he was going to get in her pants. Wouldn't be the first time. She was high from the weed but he was buzzed, starting to slur his words. He hadn't even eaten breakfast. With outstretched hands he walked towards her saying, "Time to make the donuts". She read his mind. She pushed him. He fell and hit his head hard on the wooden coffee table. While he was on the floor unconscious she searched his room and found two duffle bags under his bed, one filled with drugs and the other filled with money. She left and drove to Castle Island. She grabbed the bag with the dope and walked over near the Korean War Memorial. She was shivering from anxiety. Then she slowly walked over to the edge of the island. It was high tide, unusually high after a recent storm. She dumped the entire drug stash into the dark, green ocean water and watched it disappear. She put some nearby rocks inside the duffle bag and threw it into the water. It sank to the bottom. She walked away. Kids were playing in the nearby tot lot. People were jogging by, and elderly men, sitting on benches a distance away near the sailing program, were smoking cigars and chatting about the past, she imagined. They were all too busy to notice her.

Dee didn't know what to do with the money. She needed a

safe place to go - to think - where there weren't any people. So she took a ride to Savin Hill. She parked her car next to the basketball courts and walked up to the top of the woods with the duffle bag filled with drug money. To her it felt like it weighed a thousand pounds. Nobody was there when she arrived. When she looked down she saw kids hanging around near the tennis courts. Four guys were now playing basketball but suddenly a man appeared. It scared her at first, but she realized he was just walking his chocolate Lab. He smiled and disappeared beyond the tree line. She sat down on the rocks overlooking the city. She could see the gas tank and traffic backed up on the expressway. Everything looked small and far away. Everything looked in place, except for her. She sat for a few minutes. At first she was going to burn it but thought that was stupid. Then she realized what to do with the money.

She left the woods and drove to Hyde Park. She dropped the money off at the Kirby Rehabilitation House. She knew it was on Hyde Park Avenue because her cousin Sean spent two weeks in rehab there. She kept her sunglasses on when she went inside. The receptionist was talking to a middle-aged man with raggedly red hair, heavy-set with a belly testing the limits of his belt buckle. Dee didn't know if he was a client or a worker, maybe both. She walked up to the counter and put the duffle-bag down. She walked away without saying a word. The receptionist yelled, "Miss?" "Miss?" but Dee left without looking back. She could only imagine the look of their faces when they opened it.

She went home. She felt like she was going to cry, but didn't. She fought it and it passed. She didn't know what to expect next. What she should do next? What Al would do to her? When she found out Al was dead, relief danced in front of her, and she decided she'd take this secret to the grave.

FIFTY-FIVE

It seemed like a new chapter in our lives was unfolding, a new beginning for everyone. I suddenly drifted away. I could hear everyone still talking about the detective's announcement but wasn't listening. I had to tune everyone out. I felt at ease with life and the universe. I believed in the goodness of Man. I was in another world walking along with my thoughts. My friends have always busted my chops when it came to my views about the existence of God. They've called me a non-believer, but I do believe. I do believe in God. I just have a different idea of who He is. I see God in every blade of grass and within every leaf on every tree. I see His implant in every animal and insect. I see Him entrenched in rocks and mountain ranges. I see Him floating around patchy blue skies and peeking out from the wondrous clouds. I see Him wandering endlessly around the continents and swimming in the depths of the oceans. I see Him on the face of every person on this planet. I see Him traveling throughout the universe spreading His word and creating new marvels. I see all life complementarily sustaining each other within His grand design. His footprint is everywhere. He's ever-present and all-knowing, but lets us determine our own paths. I believe He exists inside us and flows outwardly as we speak and act. We are the key which opens the door. Or leaves it locked. If we as individuals behaved in a Godly manner towards others, then it could be wonderful. But this isn't reality; just my own ideas, my dream for a better world.

As usual, TK patted me on the shoulder, awakening me from my thoughts. "Earth to Johnny, come in," he said. "Come back to us."

"All I can say is this," I said, discarding the Pepsi and now gulping down half a glass of cold Heineken beer. "Tough times don't last, but tough people do."

I stepped outside the café to catch a breath of fresh air. It was a beautiful day. I was glad to be alive. Happy. The intersection was busy with people going about their daily routines. Mrs. Modica approached with her grandchild. Sorrow walked beside her. She was clutching baby Patrick tightly, as if protecting him from the outside world, from the dealers, perhaps from Southie itself. She stopped briefly and said hello. Sadness rippled across her face. "He's a handsome little devil," I said. "He looks just like Pat." She held him even tighter if that was humanly possible. "Don't ever mention him ever again," she abruptly said, then shrank back a bit. "Sorry. I didn't mean that. I gotta go." She hurried away and never looked back. I thought I understood Mrs. Modica's pain, how she felt, but that was impossible.

Then I saw two guys do a deal across the street. A bag and a twenty, exchanged so fast, the unfamiliar eye wouldn't have noticed. Would this dealer be the new Al in Southie, filling the void? Only time would tell who would be the next in line. Who would step up to make fast money and be the destroyer of lives. Would drugs continue to haunt us and take away our loved ones before their time? With human behavior what it is; is it inevitable? Isn't everything in life reflected by the choices one makes? And if one wants different results, different choices must be made. It's simple logic but not simply followed.

One way we can battle this madness, slow it down, is to knock drug dealers out of business. So seeing Al meet his Maker could be considered a good thing. Then we reach out to those in

314

need and try to talk some sense into them. Help them. Be there for them. Educate people to the dangers, the temptation that surrounds all of us like an ungodly beast of prey ready to pounce on willing victims and devour them whole. Give people a purpose in life. Tell them life is good and getting high is destructive. Then rely on faith and hope to accompany us on our individual journeys.

I continued on, wrapped inside my thoughts. I drifted into the past, the present, and the future. I understood that sometimes there aren't second chances in life. One fatal mistake and there's no turning back the clock, no saying "take it back." How do family members cope with a loss of a loved one due to drugs? Every day for years – perhaps for the rest of their lives - those left to suffer wake up with the memory of loved ones, lost forever by their own recklessness. The memories pop up, reminding them of what might have been, reminding them that perhaps they didn't do enough, didn't listen enough, weren't there enough times to steer them in a different path. The living search for closure yet can't find it. Sometimes they blame themselves but shouldn't because their pleas and assistance weren't appreciated; simply dismissed. They unfairly torture themselves for their perceived shortcomings. They are collateral damage left to carry on with sorrow in their hearts. Collateral damage dogged by regret. They can only find solace if they ultimately come to the heartfelt conclusion that those who lost their way failed to do the right thing. Yet this realization doesn't have to diminish the love which will forever live in their hearts for their lost ones; it will only help in the healing process and hopefully bring closure.

I knew now that my feelings in New York about being

ashamed of my hometown were unwarranted, and deservedly short-lived. Living there was like a dream, but it was over. The friends I made faded into history. I was back in Southie for good. Southie had changed. Inescapable I guess as the winds of time. And more changes were coming. Perhaps TK was right and Southie was lost. Yet I sensed there was still plenty of the good old Southie left, plenty to embrace and that was good enough for me. I knew life didn't guarantee anything. That life was hard and demanding. But I was ready and confident. The yuppies would come and go but the essence of what Southie stood for, family, faith, and friends, would forever survive the test of time. I never doubted that.

A cab beeped and startled me as the driver flew through the intersection. Another cab stopped at the red light and out popped Jaws and Kaleigh. They were laughing and holding hands. Smiles consumed their faces. They were outwardly happy and seemingly at peace with the world. I guess her message that day in the hospital hit home, a game-changer. They said hello and went inside the café.

I was happy for them. And I felt good about myself. I was glad I realized truth catches up to us no matter how hard we try to hide it. With truth we can have hope. Hope so that life will be better. I'd retaken control of my life. I'd finally realized how self-destructive and nonsensical my actions were. I didn't need to repeat those episodes where I lost hard-earned money for some kind of elusive rush to win big. I was stupid. Foolhardy. Wasteful. When I gambled I'd tell myself it was the last time, always the last time but the last time was never the last time. Repetition was king and dominated me but now I was in charge not the Demon within. Going to the meetings made me realize that. They opened my eyes to reality, to a better way to cope.

I felt that helping others fight their devils would help me quell my own demons if they popped their heads to the surface. It would serve as a reminder that I always needed to be prepared to fend off what was harmful. I was ready to move forward putting those chapters in my life way behind me, never to be duplicated or experienced again. I knew I was on the right track. That's what I wanted, that's what I needed to do to live better. That's what any person with any addiction has to realize and accomplish. Put aside the past, dismiss mistakes and errors in judgment, enjoy the present, and look forward to the future.

Pam walked out of the café and lit up a cigarette.

And she was a major reason why I was going to be fine.

She stood next to me, silent. She knew I was drifting. She poked me on my right arm. I looked at her soaking in her beauty. My only response was sorta lame. "Hey. I can't wait to eat," I said. "Yeah me too I guess. Angela said it would be ready in a few minutes."

"I'm starving."

"Guys are always starving."

"That's how we roll."

She took two more puffs and snuffed out her cigarette. "That's my last smoke. I'm quitting as of right now."

"Really?"

"Don't wanna make the kids smoke a pack someday and turn green."

'The kids' I thought sounded good. Really good.

"Great," I said.

"And I'm buying dinner."

"About time."

She tilted her head and gave me that look. I loved that look.

"Only joking," I said. "Hey we're going to a new club in Revere after we eat. Ya wanna come with us?" I asked.

"Wow. Always thought it was impossible to pry a kid out of Southie."

"Not true, would go anywhere with you."

I caught Pam off guard.

She smiled.

I smiled back.

Then I opened the door for her and we stepped back inside the café.

The End

About the Author

Kevin Devlin grew up in Savin Hill, a tight-knit Irish Catholic community in Boston. He attended South Boston High School and subsequently received a Bachelor of Science degree (cum laude) and a Master of Arts degree in modern European history from Boston State College.

Although his Savin Hill roots remain strong, he eventually married a Southie girl and moved there in 1981.

For the past four decades, he's officiated local basketball games, and he was a public servant for the City of Boston for thirty-eight years, working for the Boston Housing Authority, Boston School Police, and the Boston Public Health Commission.

He has four children, Alanna, Deirdre, Kevin, Sean, and a grandson, Kevin. He currently resides in Milton, MA with his wife, Mary.

Made in the USA
Middletown, DE
09 November 2017